Meg O'Brien has written four ot...
Jessica 'Jesse' James: *Salmon in th...*
Hare Today, Gone Tomorrow and ...
by The Women's Press. A Jesse short story appears in the
anthology, *Reader, I Murdered Him, Too* (The Women's Press,
1995). She lives in the California countryside, and has a
passion for flowers, herbs, music, deer and birds. She is a
student of herbal healing, and practises hatha yoga and Qi-
Gong, a Chinese healing exercise. While bringing up five
children, Meg worked at a multitude of jobs from secretarial
to housecleaning, to freelance editing, before becoming a full-
time author.

Also by Meg O'Brien from The Women's Press:

Salmon in the Soup (1993)
The Daphne Decisions (1993)
Hare Today, Gone Tomorrow (1993)
Eagles Die Too (1993)

MEG O'BRIEN
A BRIGHT FLAMINGO SHROUD

First published by The Women's Press Ltd, 1996
A member of the Namara Group
34 Great Sutton Street, London EC1V 0DX

British Library Cataloguing-in-Publication Data
A catalogue record for this book is available from the British Library

ISBN 0 7043 4463 7

Typeset in Galliard by Contour Typesetters, Southall, London
Printed and bound in Great Britain by BPC Paperbacks Ltd

With gratitude . . .

Readers and interviewers have asked where the idea for a hardboiled yet soft-as-marshmallow-underneath character like Jesse came from. The only answer I can ever come up with is that she just popped into being one day as I sat in the hills of Paradise, California, at an old 1927 Underwood typewriter I'd purchased at a church rummage sale in the hope I might one day become a published author. One night, after I'd been 'practising' a few months – unsure as to whether the awkward words I'd put on paper even vaguely resembled a published book – Jesse was born. I'd been up all night; I sat on a kitchen chair in an old robe, a cup of coffee growing cold beside me as snow fell outside. I can't say I was unaccustomed to poverty, having raised five children more or less alone. Still, Christmas was upon us, and my youngest wanted a pair of skates. I was broke and desperate. I began to pray to all my lost saints – 'St Joseph, St Anthony, St Therese, please help. Get me out of this.' And just to cover all bets – 'Angels, guides, Universe . . . *hey, is anyone out there listening*?' The snow continued to fall; my coffee grew ever more cold.

Then Jesse began to speak. My fingers, after the first startled moment, went along with the game. When I'd finished a chapter of Jesse's brash, outspoken thoughts and dialogue, I read it over and laughed – though still with a touch of desperation. 'This isn't at all like other mysteries I've read,' I thought. 'It'll be a miracle if it ever gets published.' The rest, to coin an old cliché, is history. Jesse popped into my life just as hardboiled, smart-talking female protagonists were on the rise. She was a gift – nothing I ever planned, nothing I ever even dreamed of, but an answer to a prayer.

So, first of all . . . God, angels, saints, guides, Universe . . . thanks for the miracle. *A Bright Flamingo Shroud* is Jesse's fifth adventure in five years. Over these years she's mellowed on some issues; looked ever more askance at others. To me she's an alive, vibrant human being – a part of me, but also part of everyone I've ever known and everywhere I ever lived. She's been described by reviewers as 'tough and smart-talking', but I most like the following: 'Vulnerable, gawky, impulsive'. That gives her room to grow.

With that in mind, I would also like to thank Jesse's many wonderful readers and fans, for both sticking with her and asking for more. And to my children: Katherine, Kevin, Greg, Robin – and Amy, who I'm listing alone so she doesn't always feel like the middle child. Much love and gratitude for standing by me through the craziness.

Finally, I would like to thank everyone at The Women's Press, along with a very special thanks to Helen Windrath, and to my editor, Kathy Gale, who brought Jesse to the UK and has helped her along so beautifully all the way.

Chapter 1

'Call me a relic, a thing of the past, or any damn thing you please . . .'

'Relic', D.R. Lunsford

There was a monster blizzard going on outside. I had no heat in my apartment, no furniture; the wind was howling through a plastic-covered broken window and the sleeping bag had lumps. I hadn't slept all night, my back hurt, my throat was sore, and I was getting arthritis at the age of thirty-three. Further, I hadn't seen my sometime lover in months.

And if you think *that's* bad, let me tell you what happened next.

First of all, my name is Jesse (Jessica) James. Unlike my namesake, I'm not an outlaw, though I've been compared to one – the first time by a probation officer, at fourteen, when I got arrested for lifting a classic Sterling with my pals, the Boyz in Rochester's Hood. I cleaned up my act later, at least from my point of view, and became a reporter. There are some who would say I'm living an illusion and haven't cleaned up at all.

I say, screw it – we do the best we can with what we've got to work with on any given day.

My guru/shrink, Samved, is the one who taught me that. Samved's an old fraud, and the only reason I stick with him is because he tells me what I like to hear, and he's got a quote for everything. Plus, he keeps me sober. A while back I struck a bargain with Samved: if he'd come back to being New Age (which I'd formerly scorned – until he turned fundamentalist, proving yet again that things can always get worse), I would at least consider not falling off the wagon into a sweet, sweet vat of Genesee Screws.

'I don't know why you care what I do,' Samved had said, stroking his flimsy white beard. 'You don't like religion in *any* shape or form.'

'I'm just getting bored with your answer machine. All that 'Praise the Lord! stuff – and that 800 number for donations? It's so trite. Also, I liked it better when you trilled on and on about meditating in your garden in the light of the full moon, and all the while you were sitting on your prayer rug watching *Jeopardy*. It's a better visual image.'

'Only an author would think of a person's Life Purpose as a visual image.'

'I'm not an author. I'm a hack freelance reporter.'

'Nonsense. You had that short story printed in *Cosmo* last month.'

'A *love* story.' I made a face. 'Can you believe they actually let *me* write a love story? Me, the loser-at-love of all time?'

'You didn't lose it, you threw it away.'

'If you're referring to those two marriage proposals last spring, I couldn't just go and say yes. It wouldn't be in character.' I ran fingers through my tangled brown hair.

'Why are you talking this way lately? Visual images . . . character . . . hack? And the other day you said something about hoping for a deal – as in capital DEAL.'

'It's Hollywood lingo, Sammy-o. I'm working on a screen-play.'

'A screenplay?' Samved raised his bushy white eyebrows. 'You don't say! About what?'

'About a woman who throws love away, what else? By the way, do you think I look just the least bit like Debra Winger?'

(Now, look, I know what you're saying. You're saying that all this has nothing to do with a mystery. But just hang in, okay? It's what they call a 'set-up' in the movies. You set the story up in the first ten minutes, then hit the audience with a shockeroo. My ten minutes is almost up, and the shockeroo's right around the bend.)

So my guru says to me, 'You look more like Barbara Hershey. But do you really think you could survive in Hollywood?'

'Better than in Rochester, New York, in the middle of a blizzard, sleeping on a bare floor without heat, and Mrs Binty suddenly deciding to remodel my apartment.' I frowned. 'If that woman were twenty years younger, I'd wonder if her hormones were off. And those contractors? They're vile. Every morning, seven a.m., a-boomin' and a-bangin' away. They've got the whole place torn up – including my nerves.'

'Well, the pipes burst, you said. There was nothing else to do. And your landlady did offer you a room downstairs with her. Why didn't you take her up on it?'

'Are you kidding? Mrs B's got cats now. I *hate* cats.'

'Cats, *and* dogs, *and* children? I don't believe it for a minute, Jesse. You are nothing but blabber and hot air. By the way, how is Bastard taking all this remodeling?'

'Bastard the Dastardly Dog? He blew the joint. Dogs are like men, you know. When things go sour they slink off in the night.'

Actually, the Flynns had taken Bastard to Arizona for the winter. And it's a damn good thing my neighbors like my dog, since I can't stand him at all. First off, the mutt used to be called Footloose, and I put up with him and a cageful of finches until the owner of them both – a man I loved and lost – conveniently left them behind. The finches chattered all day, so I got rid of them fast. It was that or wring their fine-feathered necks.

As for Footloose, I renamed him Bastard, and he's been with me ever since. Too bad that's not true of certain men in my life.

Too bad it's not true of Marcus Andrelli.

That dash of cold water brought my attention back to the present – to my apartment, and the blizzard outside. I burrowed down into my sleeping bag, wishing the sweats and Arctic jacket I wore were bearskin. My toes, even in Mrs Binty's electric socks, felt numb. The cord to the socks snaked up my left leg and out the top of the sleeping bag. It was plugged into a socket in the living-room wall, one of the few still working in the shambles of my once cozy apartment.

A male voice split the silence of my unhallowed halls. 'Joey, yo! You, there! Get dat ladder ouda my way!'

'It ain't in your way, asshole. Walk around it.'

I sighed. My morning wake-up call: Denny and Joey, Contractors from Hell, arguing all the way up my stairs. My front door opened with a clatter and the two of them barreled in, sabers rattling in the form of saws, drills, nails, wires and pipes.

'Yo, Jesse! You up? Ya got any coffee?'

'Go away.' I dug in deeper.

'Aw, come on,' Joey Martino said. 'Don't be a grump.'

'May your hemorrhoids flourish and multiply.'

'I don't have hemorrhoids.'

'All Italian men have hemorrhoids. It's in the genes.'

'Huh. Real funny. Keep that up, you won't get any doughnuts.'

I peeked out cautiously. 'You've got doughnuts?'

'Bavarian cream, from the Genesee Bakery. They got chocolate frosting.' My stomach growled as he squatted beside me and waved one under my nose.

I sat up and rubbed my eyes.

'Gotcha,' Martino said, grinning.

The coffee was dark, hot, and sweet, just the way I like it.

'You make a mean pot of Java, Joe.' I held my cup in both hands, shivering in the kitchen despite all three sweaters, the Arctic jacket, and double layer of jeans.

'Thanks, pretty lady. You look real glamorous in that get-up.' He spoke from a position at my feet.

'You think you could get that floor fixed any faster? I fell into it twice last night.'

He squinted up at me, his eyes a light tan and concerned. 'You drinkin' again?' An array of nails stuck out of his mouth, making the words a bit mushy.

'No, I am not drinking again. Jeesh. It's just a little hard to walk straight when it's twelve degrees below zero outside and twenty below zero in here. Your knees have a tendency to knock.'

'Be glad you're not in the park like some'a them poor suckers,' Joey said. He stopped hammering long enough to spit out the nails and stare at the little four-inch TV he'd brought with him and stuck on my counter. 'You been listenin' to the news?'

Some sleepy-eyed anchor was droning on about the night's events.

'How could I possibly? I don't even have a television anymore.' I'd stored all my furniture in Mrs Binty's garage and shed, so it wouldn't get demolished along with walls, floor, ceiling . . .

According to the latest progress report from good old Joey, this insanity would last at least another three weeks.

'Thought you might'a heard.' He stuffed another bite of glazed doughnut into his mouth, licking sugar from his lips. 'Some old guy took on a mugger last night in Dwight Square. See, they're tellin' about it now.' He pointed with a sugary finger. 'Thought he might be a relative, seein' as how he's got the same last name as you.'

'Yeah? Well, I don't have any male relatives. They all went and died on me.'

Men will do anything to leave, and just as well, too. My female relatives, Mom and Aunt Edna, were all I could handle. Not to mention Mom's mysterious newish husband, Charlie Browne.

I turned my attention to the news. The anchor, who looked damp and polished, as if he'd just stepped out of his morning shower, continued to drone. 'The would-be attacker chased the homeless woman three blocks before he was caught and subdued by a man police have identified only by his last name,

James. Mr James has apparently been living in the park . . .'

I warmed up my coffee and picked through the doughnuts, looking for another Bavarian cream.

'Saw it on WOKR last night,' Joey said. 'This James guy, he's no more'n five foot two, he takes out after this mugger. Chases him down the street, jumps on his back, and hauls him to the ground. Big guy, the mugger, like a truck – but this little guy, it didn't stop him. He just hung right on till the cops got there and took over.' Joey chuckled. 'Tough little runt. Reminded me of you.'

'Gee, thanks.' I settled for raspberry jelly and watched my breath billow in the air as I bit into it.

'Guy's a hero, now. Guess it pays to fight back.'

That had certainly always been *my* motto. Fight back – with everything, and everyone.

'Yeah,' Joey said, sinking in another nail, 'take no shit from nobody, never.'

'A beautiful sentiment, Martino. Real poetic. You ever gonna get some linoleum laid?'

He looked pained. 'Ya mean vinyl. Nobody calls it linoleum anymore.'

'I do.' *So, call me a relic.*

'You're a relic, Jesse James.'

'I knew I could count on you, Joey.'

I worked for awhile in the living room, sitting in the sleeping bag with eighty pages of screenplay and a red pen. It was a wonder the ink hadn't frozen into cubes. But the screenplay looked good. I hadn't even known if I could do one until last month, when I decided to take a few weeks off from freelancing articles and try it out, see what I came up with. Now I was getting excited. I might even take it out to Hollywood, I thought, when it's done. Sit in the sun! Find an agent! Do lunch!

Important matters first, however. More coffee. I was going for it when there was a knock on the door.

'Get that, will you?' Martino yelled.

'My own door? Sure, massa, anything you say.'

'I'm expecting a delivery of pipes,' he hollered. 'I'd get it myself, but I got my hands full.'

'Right.'

I stumbled from the sleeping bag, script in hand, and crossed the bare living room to my door. As I flung it open, a gust of frigid air blew up my gray wool-carpeted stairs.

'Jesse?' A short, grizzly-looking old bum grinned up at me. He had an upper tooth missing in front, clothes that reeked of booze, a duffle bag over one shoulder, and at least a five-day growth of beard. His matted gray hair looked like it contained an entire family of three-toed sloths. 'Could you –' he began.

'No, I could not', I said firmly, 'I do not have any money.' I might be known around Rochester for helping out at the soup kitchens but none of the bums had ever shown up at my door before.

I planted myself squarely across the doorway and leveled a cold green gaze at the bum. 'I am a writer. Writers do not give handouts, they take them. Look –' I waved an arm at my empty living room. 'I haven't even got a decent place to live. No bathroom, no heat, almost no food –'

'Uh, Jesse –'

'So do yourself a favor, check in at the mission. Here, I'll write down the address.' I scribbled the Fourth Street Mission's address on the corner of a script page.

'See, I was hopin' mebbe I could just come in.'

'Absolutely not.'

'I thought mebbe we could talk.'

'Talk? I don't have time to talk.' I tore off the corner of the script page, and handed it to the bum. Clutching the script to my breast, I started to shut the door.

'For old times' sake,' the bum said.

This scene was bizarre, even for me. 'We don't have any old times. Look, I'm working. Who the hell are you, anyway?'

'Whew! I thought you'd never ask.' The bum pulled a wallet from his back pocket, opening it up. He showed me a driver's license. Then he drew out a photograph, and following that a slip of paper, yellowed, with crabbed writing on it.

'I need you to hide me,' he said, leaning wearily against the doorjamb. He raised a frail, shaky hand and passed it over his eyes. 'I'm real tired, Jesse girl.'

I stared at the license, the faded letter, and the photograph for a long time before comprehending. Then it finally came together.

Holy God.

'Gramps?' I said.

Chapter 2

'Call me a dreamer, livin' on dreams . . . a diet of memories . . .'
'Relic', D.R. Lunsford

'Why didn't you tell me I had a living grandfather?' I bellowed into the phone. 'And why didn't you warn me he was a bum?'

'I didn't know,' Aunt Edna protested from Mill Valley, California. 'But if he's your father's father, it figures he'd be a bum.'

'Not only a bum, but a con. And he's on the run, for heaven's sake. It's *déjà vu*, like when Mom and Charlie showed up with that damned painting last year.'

I need you to hide me, Gramps had said. Mom's almost exact words, back then. 'How did I get this family?' I groaned.

Aunt Edna's voice turned sharp. 'Why is he on the run?'

'It's complicated. But he no sooner arrived in town than he got in trouble in the park. Says he was just hanging out there, waiting for morning so he could come here. But then somebody mugs a bag lady, and good old Gramps runs to the rescue and ends up on the local news.'

'And you don't know what he's running from?'

'Claims there have been two attempts on his life. Something about a sting down in Miami that went bad.'

'Hmmm.' Aunt Edna was smoking and drinking coffee as we talked. I could hear her swallows, and then the *puff, puff*. You could almost see the stray ashes in her frizzy, carrot-colored hair.

'What are you going to do, Jesse?'

'First, I'm having Tark run a computer check. By noon I'll know more about that old man than he knows himself.'

'Where's the old coot right now?'

'Down at Mrs Binty's taking a shower. He's been sleeping in parked cars all the way up from Miami, and I couldn't stand being near him.'

'I thought you people didn't have any running water.'

'Mrs Binty's bathroom is on, now, and so's my kitchen. These idiots can't seem to get one entire apartment working all at once.'

Joey Martino made an offended sound of protest from the kitchen.

'Yeah, well, you know I'm right!' I yelled back.

'What does your landlady think of good old Johnny James?' Aunt Edna asked.

'Mrs Binty is thrilled. You know her. She loves the excitement when I've got trouble.'

'It's the reason she keeps you around,' Aunt Edna agreed.

'So anyway, what the hell am I going to do with this jerk? He's a con man, a grifter. He's spent his whole life being run out of one town or another.'

'By men? Or women?'

'Ha.' I gave a snort. 'What woman would want him? You should see him.'

'That ugly, huh?'

'Just about. He claims to be a master of disguise, and says he just dressed like a bum to throw off anyone who might be looking for him. But he's got that cocky, short man's attitude.

You know how some men hate being short, so they over-compensate by acting tough?'

'You should talk.' *Puff, puff.*

'Listen, at five-four I'm still a head taller than him.'

'But you do have an attitude.'

'I'm a reporter, I need an attitude to hang out with mobsters and hardened criminals. Besides, it'll come in handy when I get to LA. They say attitude is everything out there.'

'You're still coming to California? What about Johnny James?'

'What about him?'

'Jesse, if he really is your grandfather . . .'

'Look, he's been running all these years, and he can just keep running for all I care.'

'That's cold, Jesse – real cold.'

'Yeah, well, tough.'

I shivered as 'Gramps' came through my front door, bringing another burst of ice-laden air. Mrs Binty must have snagged his grubby old clothes and stuck them in the wash. He wore her fluffy chenille robe, the one with the fancy lace collar and pink petunias splattered all over it. His shifty gray eyes looked embarrassed, but the cocky strut was still there.

'Aunt Edna, I'll call you back.' I hung up and returned the phone to the floor, then stood with my hands on my hips.

'Okay,' I said to good old Gramps. 'You've had coffee and a shower. I've heard your story – all about this guy, Barney Noonan, in Miami, and how you bamboozled him out of five thousand bucks. How he's a real nutcase and he's after your hide. Frankly, I don't blame him. And I don't want you here. I'm getting ready to go to LA. In fact, I'm practically out the door.' Which reminded me. 'How'd you know where I lived?'

'I saw an article you wrote in *Newsweek*,' Gramps said, grinning. He hopped up and down on one foot, then the other, hugging the chenille petunias to keep warm. 'I conned your editor into giving me your phone number.'

'Impossible.'

The grin widened. The gap from the missing tooth made him look downright innocent, like an eighty-year-old Dave Letterman. 'Not for me. I told her I was a reporter with the *Miami Sun*, and wanted to talk to you about the subject.'

'What subject? What article?'

'The one about real estate scams.'

I curled my upper lip. 'Of course. Why didn't I know that?'

'Jesse, your father, my son, would be proud. You've come up real good.' The old man's shoulders trembled and a callused thumb wiped away a tear. 'Tell me about him, girl' he said. 'I want to know all about my son, all the things I missed. Do you have any pictures?'

Johnny James looked, suddenly, all of his eighty-odd years. If his story was true, he was a man who'd left his wife and son when the son was only three, then had drifted across the country making it this way and that, sleeping in alleys, bumming food and cigarettes, never staying in one place long enough to make friends. Searching for something and never finding it. Never even knowing, for that matter, what it was.

Tears stung my own eyes. I thought of the wife and child, but also of what life on the road must be like. 'It must have been tough,' I said. 'That kind of life.'

He nodded, brushing moisture from his lashes with the back of his hand, the same way Pop used to do when he was in his cups. 'There wasn't a day went by I didn't think of Mae,' he said, 'and little Johnny.'

'Little Johnny. Yes. And now you're here, after all this time, in my living room. Gramps.'

'I can't tell you how good it feels to see you, Jesse.'

'My only remaining male relative. Family.'

'That's it exactly. I knew you'd see it my way.'

I grabbed Mrs Binty's fancy lace collar with both hands and stuck my nose in Johnny James' face. 'Listen, you old goat! You apparently missed one real important lesson in all those years of grifting.'

'Uh, Jesse –'

'Never shit on your last remaining hope. And never, ever, *ever* con a con!'

Chapter 3

'Call me a schemer, working on schemes . . . I only scheme
what I see.'

'Relic', D.R. Lunsford

'Boy, oh, boy! Girl, you are good! I thought I had you there for a
minute!'

I folded up my sleeping bag, giving it a wrench. 'Dammit all,
my father was never called Johnny. He was *Pat*. Patrick Joseph
John James. Don't you even remember your own son's name? If,
of course, he *was* your son –'

'Now, gal, you can't blame an old man for forgettin' things.
'Course I knew he was Pat, I just forgot –'

'And as for that letter and photograph –'

The snapshot 'Gramps' had handed me at the door wasn't
conclusive. It was of a man and woman who could be him and
my grandmother, both of them twentyish but indistinct, the way
candid snaps were then. The baby in the woman's arms could be
my father, but there was no proving it. The yellowed letter was
something else. It began:

Everything's fine here, Johnny. The boy is well. Please don't worry about us. We miss you, though. I can't wait until you get work and send for us. It's been hard, tending the farm alone.

It went on in that vein: a neighbor had had a heart attack . . . an uncle of my grandmother's had died . . . it didn't look good for the crops this year. An Americana farm wife's letter, it was signed '*Love, Harriet Mae*'. My grandmother's name. And it was written on familiar paper, a blue- and rose-marbled parchment that I recognized as my grandmother's. Pop had kept letters from his mother in a box under his and Mom's bed, and they were on that paper. My grandmother's initials were embossed in silver in the upper left-hand corner: HMJ.

According to family history, my grandmother had come from a wealthy family in Chicago. She'd given it all up to marry a charmer named Johnny James and move to a farm outside Warsaw, just south of here in Wyoming County. Times had been tough. The country was in a depression, and in the third year of their marriage an historic blizzard in upstate New York ruined all the crops. When the sun finally peeked over the hills that spring, Johnny James was gone.

Not a particularly original story. It happened that way all over the country, back in the thirties. But in this case, it struck a personal chord of anger with me. I'd watched Pop on a downhill slide from the time I was able to talk, and no one could tell me that didn't have something to do with having a father who didn't care enough to at least stick around.

'If in fact you are my grandfather, Pop ended up a drunk because of you,' I said angrily. I thumped the sleeping bag into the hall closet and turned to find him right behind me.

'Is that what happened to you, too?' The gray eyes looked uncertain, but his sharp little chin was up. Gray stubble dotted it, like splinters of driftwood. 'You end up a drinker, too?' he persisted, squinting sympathetically at me. 'Because your pop wasn't around?'

My hands tightened into fists at my sides. 'He *was*. He never ran off like some I could name.'

'Bottom of the world, bottom of a bottle . . . it's all the same, Jesse girl.'

'Don't call me that!'

'Is that what *he* called you?'

I folded my arms. 'Get out of here.'

Something came and went in the old gray eyes. He opened his mouth to argue, and then backed off. 'Sure . . . sure thing, kid. I'll wait out in the living room.'

'No. Get out of my apartment, out of my life. I don't want you around.'

I slammed the bedroom door in his face and stood against it, shaking. Then I slumped to the cold bare floor, in my cold empty bedroom, my head in my hands. The old man had triggered something I didn't fully understand.

Outside, wind whistled in icicle-studded eaves. From my kitchen came the ear-busting explosion of hammers and electric saws.

Marcus – where are you when I need you?

I had never felt more alone and afraid.

And why is it, I wondered, that you can be there for a man when he needs you, over and over . . . but when it's the other way around, he's nowhere to be found?

Life could not get much worse.

Chapter 4

I often think dumb things like that – *Life could not get much worse* – only to be proven incredibly wrong.

I sat across from Tark in Marcus Andrelli's apartment, on the round hearth by the fire, drinking coffee. Tark, who lives in an apartment across the way, had set up a small Christmas tree at one end of Marcus' desk.

'I spend a lot of time over here these days,' he'd explained when I commented on the tree. A slight tinge of color had crept up his worked-over face. 'I guess I miss the great Christmases at home when I was a kid.'

My boots were soaked from trudging through six-foot-high drifts between the street and the Rochester Towers. I stuck them closer to the fire.

The penthouse of the Towers doubles as national head-quarters for Andrelli Enterprises, Inc. Marcus has gradually been easing out of his position as head of the mob in western New York – the New Mob, you understand, the coterie of Harvard Business-type grads who make up so much of the Mafia these days. They deal in real estate and corporate ventures, forgoing the old-type violence, including street crime, drugs, and tommy guns.

Well, for the most part, they forgo violence. Sometimes things don't work out as planned.

I was reminded of the first time I sat here, three years ago. I was on the trail of Daphne Malcross, and that was when it began with Marcus and me. Our relationship had seemed, then, like a great and wonderful adventure. Marcus was dangerous, exciting. But more than that, he offered me something I'd never had before, a subtle security that went with being close to a seat of power.

Then, last summer, it all fell apart.

'*Let me know when you're ready to grow up.*' Marcus had said with that cold, proud lift of chin I'd come to know so well. '*Let me know when you're ready to grow up with me.*'

I had never seen him so angry. He'd left town right after that, and ever since I'd been alone.

'Where is he, Tark?' I said now. 'Can you reach him?'

'I can. But do you really want me to?'

I sighed and inched closer to the fire. 'I don't really know.'

'Still afraid?' he guessed.

Tark had known me for three years too, and we'd hit it off right away – the bodyguard who quoted Kierkegaard, and me, the street kid who covered a lifetime of hurts with a boyish swagger and the mouth of a marine.

I'm not proud of who I am and what I have, or haven't, become. But little by little I try to better things. I've been sober, for instance, more than a year this time.

Some days it's easy. Some it's not.

'I could call him right now,' Tark said, tenting his fingers. He gave me a look of steady appraisal. 'Marcus would come home if I told him you needed him.'

'You really think so?'

'I do.'

'But that would mean . . .'

'You'd have to make a commitment?' Tark laughed softly. 'What would happen, Jesse? You'd be happier than you are now? What's so damned scary about that?'

'About being happy? I don't know. I guess I never thought of it that way.'

'Religion,' Tark said positively, swinging to his feet.

'Religion?'

'All that guilt it instills when we're kids. We're not allowed to be happy. It's a sin.'

Tark had come close to being happy with someone awhile back, and it had ended abruptly. It seemed to me there was more silver in his short black hair these days, and a few more lines around the gray eyes.

'You think that's what it is? I'm afraid to be happy?'

He pushed up the sleeves of his expensive black sweats. 'That, and guilt over the past, and your father. Isn't that the real reason you feel uncomfortable with your grandfather around? He's too much of a reminder?'

I frowned and shifted my butt away from the fire; it was getting too hot. 'I just want to be rid of the old goat.'

Tark laughed. 'No, you don't, not really, and he knows it. Didn't you say he's a con? The guy can read people, he knows human nature.'

'Meaning?'

He propped a foot on the hearth and stretched one long, powerful leg, then the other, the way a runner does to warm up. 'Meaning he senses one thing. That you'll help him, if only because you think you've got to make up for what you perceive as past faults.'

'But that's crazy. He can't possibly know –'

'What?'

I couldn't bring myself to say the words: that I'd as much as killed my father – his son, if the old man was who he said he was.

But Tark wouldn't let it go. 'May I remind you that you'd just been nearly raped, Jesse. Your father came after you, to help. It wasn't your fault he was driving drunk.'

Agitated, I ran my fingers through my hair. 'Sure it was. He was drunk damn near every night, and I knew that when I asked

19

him to pick me up on that miserable mountain road. Anyway, we've been over this before. Give it a rest.'

'I would if you would. Your father went off that road years ago. Isn't it time you put it in the past, where it belongs?'

I didn't answer.

'Meanwhile,' Tark said, 'Johnny James may not know the details, but you can bet he's picked up on the fact that, right or wrong, you believe you've got some sort of family guilt to make up for. Hell, if you didn't, you'd have sent him packing when he arrived at your door.'

'It was cold out there,' I argued. 'He didn't have any warm clothes. I may be a grump, but I'm not a monster.'

Tark smiled. 'Nor will you hesitate to pull out all the stops to help him, unless and until you find out he's not your father's kin. Hell, he could be Jack the Ripper, and you wouldn't pass up a chance to beat your breast and do a *mea culpa* on him – just in case.'

I narrowed my eyes to green slits. 'You think you know so much. Well, fine. I certainly wouldn't want to prove you wrong.' I stood. 'Let's see what Big Brother's got to offer so far.'

We crossed to Marcus' long glass desk, to his mega-computer, the best in the state. Next to it, real estate contracts and other legal papers spewed from a fax into a two-foot-deep wire basket – a state of affairs that went on twenty-four hours a day, seven days a week.

I sat in Marcus' swivel chair and began scanning the computer screen. There was a file open that Tark had already labeled JAMES.DOC.

I began reading. 'Holy shit.'

He stood next to me, arms folded. 'You said it. Your grandfather sure can pick 'em.'

The name BARNEY NOONAN was at the top of the screen, in caps and bold. Beneath it was a summarized report from Dave Laker, a Miami crime reporter I knew, with connections. I'd asked Tark to call him while I was on the way over.

'Barney Noonan,' I read aloud, 'retired cop, Miami PD? Gramps actually flim-flammed a cop?'

'Got five thousand bucks out of him, according to Laker. There's more in here. I didn't finish plugging it all in.' He took a folder from the desk, setting it by my right hand.

'This Barney Noonan is one angry mother, Laker says. He's got all his old cronies on the force looking for Johnny James.'

I paged down. 'It's worse than I thought, then. Have you got a macro for the Miami PD?'

'Control, shift, p-l, I believe – palm latitude.'

'Cute.' I punched it in. 'And amazing.' Marcus' computer could access arrest records anywhere in the world. 'Dade County Criminal Court,' I read.

'Several John James arrests,' Tark said. 'It's a common name.'

'But none of them eighty years old.'

'Right.'

'Noonan hasn't made a formal complaint, then.'

'Not yet. Laker says he heard it's a personal thing with Noonan, a matter of pride. He doesn't want it on public record that he got taken this way.'

'Is this old guy really my grandfather? Did you find out about that?'

'Not yet. There's no birth certificate on record in Warsaw County. You're sure that's where he was born?'

'That's what he said, and Aunt Edna seems to remember hearing that, too.'

'Well, a lot can happen to county records in eighty years. If you can dig up the names of old neighbors or friends –'

'"Dig up" might be about right. They're probably all six feet under.'

'And you'd have to find someone who could still recognize him after all this time.'

'No police record anywhere?'

I told the computer to search through all the states, and it started to grind them out. But I already knew the answer. Thousands of John James had been arrested over the years. I could sit here six weeks waiting to find out if anyone of them was my John James.

I paged back up to Dave Laker's info on Barney Noonan. 'Wait a minute. This says Noonan was married, but recently separated.'

Tark consulted his written notes. 'Married thirty years to one Betty Lou Fallon. Old Miami family, loved by all who knew her. Rumors of another man involved.'

'Hmmm. Laker didn't give you a name?'

'No. But apparently this hasn't helped Noonan's disposition.'

I sighed and swiveled the chair away. 'My "grandfather" claims he was shot at last week, and when that didn't work they tried to run him down.'

'Sounds like he was lucky. A couple of years ago Noonan beat up a teenage hooker. Turned out her father was the sheriff of one of those small towns up in Broward County. The kid ran home, did the progidal daughter thing, and the dad went after Noonan. Brought him up on charges of police brutality. Noonan didn't go to jail, but he did have to resign from the force. And he's apparently meaner than ever now.'

'Mean enough to shoot at Gramps? To hit and run?'

'Again according to Laker, there's a story floating around Miami about a guy, a tourist, in town overnight. He was a high school basketball coach, a married man with kids, not looking for any trouble. Noonan picked a fight with him in a bar, and the guy was found the next day, nailed to a tree in the Everglades. His legs had been eaten to the knee by crocs.'

'My God.' My stomach turned sour.

'The way they put it together later, the nails in the hands wouldn't have killed him, but he probably blacked out. By the time he came to, the crocs were busy at his feet. Some locals heard the screaming. They said it was horrible. But sound carries strangely in the Everglades, and it took them awhile to find him. By that time he'd bitten his tongue clear off. Probably from the pain. And fear.'

I stood and crossed over to the oak sideboard, shaking the

blue Thermos pot to see if there was any coffee left. Just a bit. I poured it into my cup and downed it, and the rotten taste in my mouth slowly went away. Setting the cup down, I walked to the window, staring out its broad expanse at the winter sky. A thousand floors below, the city of Rochester stood knee-deep in snow and slush.

'Noonan had powerful friends,' Tark went on, 'who swore he was playing cards with them the night it happened. He was never charged. But there are people who know it was Noonan – people he talked to when he was drunk.'

I began to pace. 'How long was Noonan on the force?'

'Thirty-five years. Came from a redneck hamlet in the Everglades and joined the Miami PD long before they were doing psychological profiles. He'd never make it now.'

'You said he's got pals looking for Gramps?'

'Cop friends everywhere, looking for a wizened little runt of a grifter named Johnny James.'

'Then why aren't they here in Rochester, checking out his so-called granddaughter?'

Tark gave a shrug of his massive shoulders. 'He's probably never talked about family to anyone. But now that he's been on the news here, they'll be on him and you like a cat on a lazy trout.'

'Or maybe not. It wasn't that big a story – strictly local interest. I doubt the Miami stations would've picked it up.' I stared at a wall of photographs over Marcus' desk, thinking.

'You know, I'm sick of this weather and sleeping on the floor. I could use a hit of sunshine right about now.'

'LA?' Tark said.

'Maybe.'

'You really think you can sell that script out there?'

'With ten thousand screenwriters knocking on producers' doors every second of every day? Not bloody likely.' I gave a shrug. 'But it's something to do. Something new.'

'Jesse . . . I'm worried about you.'

'Me? Why?'

'You're drifting lately. You don't seem to know what you want anymore.'

I laughed. 'You mean I did before?'

He gave the fading logs an impatient poke. 'I thought so. You liked investigative reporting, even if you didn't like your job at the *Herald*. Then, when you started to freelance – hell, you liked *working*. What's going on with you?'

'What's going on with me . . .' I yawned and gave a shrug. 'Shoot, I don't know. Sometimes I wish I still drank, so I could be one of those women they do Masterpiece Theaters about – a solitary drunk with a permanently glazed look, schlepping about the house on Sundays with a bottle of vodka, muttering dark thoughts to herself. Or like Peggy Ashcroft in *She's Been Away*. She simply ignored the whole damned world, like it wasn't even there. That was so incredibly great.'

Tark used a small whisk broom on the hearth, sweeping up minute particles of ash. I remembered that his own apartment was always neat and tidy. In fact, he could be downright fussy. The man was the strangest mob bodyguard I'd ever known.

He wiped his hands on a towel from the sideboard, then sat and faced me. 'It's this thing with Marcus. You've lost your anchor.'

'What do you mean, my anchor?'

'Marcus was your best friend for three years. He gave you all the things you didn't get growing up – approval, support, love. He was always there for you.'

'Right. And how long did that last?'

'He asked you to marry him, he bought a house –'

I sighed. 'Look, I don't want to talk about this anymore. It's not why I came over.'

I had come to talk about Gramps. And okay – maybe just a bit to feel closer to Marcus here in his apartment. Around his stuff.

It's funny how we play these games. You know how we all, at one time or another, have secretly driven past a guy's house after we've split up, to see if he's home? I don't do that with Marcus. I don't have to. I just trot on over to chat with Tark.

He stood with a wince and a groan, his knees cracking. 'Damn arthritis. Makes me feel like I'm aging. How about some fresh hot coffee for the road? I'll make it.'

I felt bad for snapping at him. He only wanted to help. I smiled. 'You think you're up to it, old fella?'

Tark rubbed his lower back and grinned. 'I've been too damned inactive lately. I know I wanted out of the mob even before Marcus did, but I never figured on sitting behind a desk the rest of my life. I'm dying by inches this way.'

'Have you talked to the boss about it?'

'Several times. He says we're both getting old.'

I laughed. 'That's crazy. You're what, forty-five now? Both of you.'

'And counting.'

I shook my head, still smiling as he left the room.

Crossing to the wall behind Marcus' desk, I studied the various framed photos there. Some were of family: his mother and brothers, in various poses over the years. The brothers mugged and waved at the camera; his mother looked proper and Old World Italian in a black dress, her dark hair pulled into a tight knot.

One photo was of the house in Arizona, the one he bought there with me in mind. 'We both hate the cold weather,' he'd said last spring. 'I thought we could go there next winter, spend some time alone.'

I wondered if he was there now.

A newer, eight-by-ten photograph hung next to that – a large, gaudy boat in the shape of a swan. The swan was tied up to a dock and painted a godawful flamingo pink. I'd never seen it and, curious, I was just about to call out to Tark and ask him what it was when the phone rang. I heard him answer it in the kitchen, speak softly for several minutes, and then hang up. Moments later he returned with coffee mugs in each hand, looking worried.

'Thanks.' I took one and drank. 'Was that call about business? Do you have to go?'

'No. Not yet.'

Marcus. It was Marcus on the phone.

'How is he?' I said casually.

'Fine,' Tark answered without thinking. Then he gave me a look and an awkward shrug. 'I told him you were here.'

'Did you, now. Well, I guess he didn't want to talk to me.'

'He was in a meeting. I'm sure if he'd had the time –'

'Uh-huh.'

'I left a message for him earlier to call, Jess. I told him what's going on.'

'You mean with Gramps?'

'I hope you don't mind. I thought he might have heard of this Barney Noonan. You know Marcus has connections in Miami.'

From his days with the old mob. I knew. 'And?'

'I'm afraid it's more serious than Noonan's pride, or wanting revenge.'

'You said the man was a psycho. What could be more serious?'

'It seems Noonan owes money to the head of the local mob, a guy named Luis Soldando. If he doesn't come up with the cash by the end of next week, Noonan could be croc fodder himself.'

'No kidding. How much does he owe?'

'Over twenty thou. And word in the Family is, Noonan's broke. He must be desperate to get his hands on that five your grandfather conned him out of.'

I thought for a minute, then gave Tark a calculating look. 'Well . . . if I could manage to hide Gramps out until the end of the week . . .'

'Noonan would no longer be a problem?' Tark shook his head. 'You think Soldando doesn't know by now why Noonan's broke?'

'You're right. He'd figure that five thou was his and come after Gramps for it, once Noonan was out of the way.'

'As I remember, we actually worked with Soldando once, years ago. He was trouble.'

A dull ache began behind my eyes. I rubbed my forehead and drank some coffee, which was a hearty Italian brew, almost making up for the fact that it wasn't laced with brandy.

God, I'd have given anything for a nice warming brandy right then.

We sat in silence for awhile, and finally Tark said, 'Well, what do you think?'

I stretched and looked at the clock on Marcus' desk. Almost noon. It had been quite a day already. 'I don't know. Seems like I'd better get "Gramps" out of the way first. Put him someplace safe. Then maybe I'll just go on down there and deal with Barney Noonan. Maybe I can convince him Gramps ran out on me too. Buy the old guy some time.'

'You'd go to Miami? Alone?'

'Well, I can't sit around waiting for this nutcase to show up. One way or another, he's got to be dealt with.'

Besides, there was something about this whole thing ... this psycho, Noonan, and his minions, threatening an old man. Even if Johnny James wasn't kin, and even if he deserved to take his licks for getting caught in a con, no one deserved the kind of fate that might befall him at Noonan's hands. The whole thing gave me a sick feeling in my gut.

'Thanks,' I said. 'Really, I appreciate the offer. But you know how you accused me of drifting? Suddenly I feel I've got a mission. I'd like to nail this guy – show him he can't mess with people that way.'

Tark smiled. 'And Johnny James? Are you coming around to thinking he just might be family?'

'Let's say I'd hate to disbelieve, and then have something happen to him. You called that one right.'

'Strange, though, him showing up on your doorstep like that.'

I laughed, but the sound was a bit grim. 'Not at all. Weird things happen to me all the time. You ever see *The Sound of Music*?'

'Julie Andrews, Christopher Plummer . . . the Von Trapp Family Singers?'

'Yeah. You remember when she sings that about somewhere in her youth or childhood, she must have done something good?'

Tark nodded.

'Well, somewhere in mine, I must have done somethin' real bad.'

'Maybe it was all those cars you heisted,' Grady North said.

He glared at me over his shiny wing-tip shoes. 'You weren't exactly Kid of the Year.' He swung his legs off the desk – the bright, polished desk with its brass plaque announcing GRADY R. NORTH, LIEUTENANT, HOMICIDE – and crossed his office to lean against a file cabinet. I had just related my theory of bad childhood karma to him.

'We didn't really heist cars,' I argued. 'We merely took them awhile for joyriding. We always brought them back.'

'A fine distinction. I'm just relieved I didn't know you then.'

'Well, how could you? You grew up on the *right* side of Rochester's tracks.'

'Oh, here it comes, the poor-little-kid-from-the-streets routine.'

I scowled. 'Why are you so testy today? I come to you for help and you give me a bad time.'

'You've been coming to me for help more and more lately. Would that have anything to do with the fact that the King of Crime has left town?'

'No, it would not. I thought you and I were friends.'

'That's what you call it, huh – friends?'

'Well, we've known each other for years.'

'Long enough for me to learn I can't trust you anymore than half those crooks out there.' He motioned with his sandy-haired head to the outer office, with its rows of green desks. Plain-clothes cops sat behind the desks, interviewing suspects they'd hauled in. On some of the desks were odd Christmas decorations: a glowing elf with a shoulder holster; a black Santa Claus. One of the female cops wore green and red nightstick earrings.

'Yeah, well, who knows,' I said. 'Maybe all the crooks out there aren't interview*ees*.' The Rochester PD had gone through a major purge in recent years.

Grady's cute, masculine jaw hardened. 'We've cleaned things up around here. My men are beyond reproach.'

'And Marcus is cleaning up his life. 'At least –' I frowned.

'Uh-huh. There's always an "at least". Even you can't defend him without voicing doubts.'

I studied my nails. 'It doesn't matter, anyway.'

'What was that? You're mumbling.'

'I said, it doesn't matter.' I cleared my throat. 'We aren't seeing each other anymore.'

Grady stared. His eyes, ordinarily a warm hazel, fixed on me like stones. 'What's wrong?'

'Nothing. Nothing is wrong.'

He folded his arms. 'You can't commit,' he said. 'That's it, isn't it?'

I didn't answer.

'Well, for what it's worth, I'm glad. He'd never make you happy.'

'Yeah? Well, speaking of happy – how's Sassy?'

'Who?'

'Oh, how quickly they forget. *Sassy*. You were dating her last spring and summer. She still around?'

'*Sissy*.' Grady's chin went up. 'We're still sort of friends.'

'Uh-huh. Friends. Now who can't commit?'

'It's not that. I just can't talk to her, that's all. You know how it is . . . you come home from work at night, you want somebody you can talk to.'

'Not me. I like being alone.'

His look was heavy with scorn. 'You hate being alone. You're miserable and unhappy, and you need a man.'

'Right. All every woman needs is a man. And I suppose you've got one in mind?'

'Anyone but Marcus Andrelli.'

'At least I can talk to him. What's really wrong with you and Sassy? Sissy, I mean. She seemed okay to me. We had a real good talk one day, in fact. About you.'

Grady stiffened. 'What about me?'

'About how you still wear your high school class ring. Sissy thinks that's cute.'

He flushed. 'It's just not working with her. The chemistry isn't right.'

I met him eye for stony eye. 'You know what's wrong with you, Grady North? You think love is all about that first rush of madness, the excitement of the chase. Shit, that stuff doesn't last. What lasts is when you start seeing all the faults, but hang in anyway.'

He raised a sandy brow. 'The expert speaks.'

'Huh?'

'You got selective hearing, too?'

I did the nail thing again. 'I just didn't hear you, that's all.'

He returned to his desk and made a big deal out of toying with a pen. 'Very few people have the kind of relationship you describe, Jesse.'

'Marcus and I do.'

Did.

There was a silence, and I filled it by ogling a couple of the guys from the scuba squad in the outer office. They had just walked in, still in wet suits, minus hoods, and looked absolutely gorgeous – their short, damp hair clinging to their foreheads, their cute little noses red from the cold.

'What's going on?' I asked Grady, my reporter's nose twitching. 'Somebody drown?'

'No. They're having practice drills this week.'

'It's pretty cold out there for that.'

'That's the point. They need to know what it's like in the worst of circumstances.' Grady leaned back in his chair and tapped the pen on the desk. 'Jesse, what do you want from me? Why are you here?'

I drew my attention back. 'I was hoping maybe you'd call down to the Miami PD for me, one cop to another, you know, and see what you can find out about an ex-cop named Barney Noonan.'

'Why?'

'Because he's trying to kill my grandfather.'

A brief silence, then a sigh. 'Jesse . . . I have known you for years. I know your mother, Kate O'Donnell James, a most redoubtable sleuth in Betty White disguise. I have met her mysterious husband, Charlie Browne – though, of course, being a cop, I don't know nearly as much about old silver-tongued Charlie as I'd like to know one day. And I've met your Aunt Edna. If I ever wanted a look at what you'll be like in twenty years, that tough little bird is it.'

He eyed me sympathetically, as if I were three slices short of a loaf. 'Jesse, that's your entire family. You do not have a grandfather.'

'I certainly hope you're right,' I said.

I told him, then, about Gramps. When I'd finished, Grady sat with arms folded, looking glum.

'So, will you help me with this or not?'

He gave me an unhappy look from beneath a troubled brow. 'I know someone in Miami. I'll make the call – but that's all. Do not try to involve me further.'

'Jeez, North, why do you have to be so stuffy?'

'Because your *grandfather* has committed a crime. He's swindled a former police officer, and God knows how many thousands of other poor victims over the years. Dammit, Jesse, you're lucky I don't just haul him in, lock him up, and conveniently lose the key.'

I slanted my green eyes at him and smiled, flirting a little. 'And ruin a beautiful friendship?'

31

He ignored my pitch, and just as well. The two of us, together? No way.

We'd never be able to talk.

Chapter 5

'Gramps? You here?'

'Kitthen,' I heard, which I took to mean 'kitchen'. It was sort of mumbled. I pulled my boots off and dropped my sheepskin jacket to the floor, wishing my old chair was there to unload on. I hate closets; they're an abomination. You have to open doors, find hangers . . . and half the time, things fall on the floor anyway, so what's the use?

I followed Gramps' voice and found that my kitchen now looked like the stage set for a World War II movie, or maybe *Les Misérables*. After the battle, that is, when the bodies are strewn all over the barricades. There was devastation everywhere, and there were two bodies on my kitchen floor – Denny's and Joey's. Neither one looked too pleased. Maybe that had something to do with Gramps standing above them with a pencil in one hand, a yardstick like a rose between his teeth, and a feverish glint in his eyes.

He dropped the pencil and grabbed the yardstick, waving it around. 'See, the thing is, you gotta make sure the corners are square. And that whatchamacallit you've got there isn't always accurate. Now, the eye . . . the eye is the best tool you'll ever find. Cheap, too.'

I threw a little curve into the conversation, deflecting the bad energy that rolled in waves from Denny and Joey. 'Gramps, did anybody ever tell you that you look like Willie Shoemaker?'

He frowned and shook his head. 'Never play the horses, girl, you can't control the outcome. Grifting, now? Grifting depends on skill. Only thing you can count on, skill.' He grinned at Joey. 'And the eye.'

Joey groaned. Denny just hoisted himself to his feet, hiked his work pants over an abundant belly, and left. 'I'll be downstairs,' he muttered over his shoulder. 'See if I can wheedle de old lady ouda some crullers.'

I took Gramps off Joey's hands and into the bedroom, closing the door so we wouldn't be heard.

'Old man,' I said. 'I know everything.'

He swallowed, his Adam's apple bobbing nervously. 'Everything?'

'I know the guy you're running from, Barney Noonan, is an ex-cop. I know he's out for bear. And do you know why?'

He looked nervous, shifty-eyed. 'Not 'xactly.'

'It seems there's an angry mobster after him. You swiped money Noonan needs to pay this guy back and save his own skin.'

'You don't say.' For some reason, I thought Gramps looked a bit relieved.

'Now listen, old man. I want you out of the way while I deal with all this. I've decided to send you to LA.'

I shrugged off his protest. 'You can get lost in the crowds there. And after I deal with Noonan, I'll be coming out there, and if you need some help, I'll get you settled in an apartment.'

Provided he was still around, and hadn't run off by then.

'Just one thing,' I said, 'I need that $5000, and I need it *now*. I'm taking it with me to Miami.

Gramps shook his head. 'Girl, I ain't got any money. I ain't got nuthin'. I swear.'

'Don't give me that. What about the five thousand you took from Barney Noonan?'

'I'm telling you true, gal, it's gone. See, what I did was, I put it all into a pigeon drop. Then I had to leave Miami before I could get my share back.'

'A pigeon drop?'

'Yeah, but with a new twist. You get some mark – in this case, it was a guy I met in the park in Miami – to put up money for some 'investment' that you tell him is gonna pay off big. But you have to put your own money in the bank along with his, so it looks on the up and up. The account's under both names so he doesn't get worried, especially in these days of *60 minutes* and *20/20*, with all the best scams bein' exposed in public for all the world to see.'

I folded my arms and glared, and he paused and stuttered, but not for long.

'S-so anyway, what happens is, the, uh, the mark . . . he puts his five thou in. And then you put yours in. And it's okey-doke, see? Because you've got the mark's signature on a special sort of carbon you've slipped in, and you palm that and transfer the sig to a withdrawal slip along with your own, and there ya go – you've got ten thousand bucks in your pocket.' He grinned. ''Course, you gotta get out of town fast.'

'Apparently too fast this time, if you couldn't even hang around to make your score.'

Gramps shook his head sorrowfully. 'Almost killed me, leavin' that sweet little pot behind.'

I didn't know whether I believed him or not. But I'd already made reservations from Marcus' apartment – one for Gramps to LA, and one for me to Miami. Thank God the airlines were in the middle of a fare war. I'd guaranteed both discount tickets with my Visa card, which I'd been saving for a rainy day.

It seemed that rainy day was here.

'All right.' I sighed. 'I'll pay for your damned ticket. I'll figure out something. One way or another, old man, I'm getting you out of my hair . . .'

Gramps stood in my bedroom looking humble. 'LA, huh? Ain't been there in years. I sure appreciate what you're doin' for me, Jesse girl. I don't know what I'd do or where I'd go, if it wasn't for you.'

'Yeah, well . . . in the meantime, you just stay inside and keep your miserable hide out of sight. If Noonan finds you here, God knows what he'll do.'

'I will, I will,' Gramps promised. 'And I'll pay you back, girl. Honest.' His old gray eyes focused on me earnestly.

'You most certainly will,' I said. With any luck at all, the old coot was lying about that five thousand, and I'd find it in a sock somewhere.

He was still giving me more shit, more 'family is so important, gal' stuff, when it all fell apart.

Chapter 6

I heard the footsteps on the porch, first. Heavy, thudding steps. Then voices. A knock on my downstairs door exploded quickly into pounding.

I shoved Gramps aside and headed for the stairs. 'Stay here. Whatever you do, don't come out.'

I ran down the stairs, staying close to the wall. A lace curtain covered the etched glass of the door leading onto the wide porch. It wasn't likely they could see in, but I could see them. *God damn.* Becky Anderson, my nemesis from the *Rochester Herald*, and her nasty little cohort, Nicky Ludgett, Ace Photographer Sludge.

Behind them was Petey Dorken with his video-cam. Petey was freelance; he followed reporters around hoping to tape something he could sell to local TV news.

What the hell did they want?

Becky had been trying to move out of the society pages and into stories of more substance in recent months, a major shift for her. When I worked for the *Herald*, she was kind of a mincy, snotty little thing who dressed in heels and blouses with prim little bows and got off on being the Total Woman. Which I used to think was just as well, since she certainly had no balls.

But Becky had been changing. She'd toughened up over the past year or so, and lately it seemed she'd do anything for a story. I'd heard, in fact, that she'd irritated staffers at the *Herald* with her new competitive frenzy, and they'd begun to cut her out of assignments whenever they could.

I watched Becky through the curtain. One delicate pale hand rose and pouffed out an equally pale coiffure, as she turned slightly to offer her best side to Petey's camera.

Ah, maiden, thy name is vanity. That at least hadn't changed.

From behind me, Gramps spoke. 'What's goin' on?'

'Dammit, I told you to stay up there!' I glanced beyond him and saw Joey standing at the upstairs door.

'You got trouble?' He looked like he'd come barreling down if I said yes, and I didn't want that. 'No, go back to work.'

'Who's that girl?' Gramps said. 'Why's she fluffin' her hair like that?'

'It's a tic from the eighties, a holdover. Now hush.'

Becky began pounding again. 'Jesse? Look, I know Johnny James is in there. All I want is an interview.'

'What's she want with me?' Gramps whispered.

'I can't imagine. Go on back up, I'll talk to her.'

'I'm not leavin' you alone with that pack of hungry wolves,' Gramps said stubbornly.

'They're not wolves. They are three very minor newspaper people. Now, *go*.'

'I'm not leavin'.' His stubbled chin went up.

'Jeez! Then stay behind the door.'

I opened it just as Becky was raising her delicate fist to pound again.

'Jesse!' She flashed her rather vacuous smile my way. 'Good morning.'

'What do you want, Becky?'

Her glance shifted to a spot behind me, where Gramps had disobeyed orders and stepped into plain sight. Becky thrust out a hand. 'Mr James, I'm so happy to meet you! As soon as I heard you were Jesse's grandfather, I knew we simply had to meet.'

'Becky, what the hell's going on? How –'

'I never reveal my sources, Jesse. You know that.' She flashed the baby blues at Gramps. 'But you, Mr James, are definitely the hero of the day. After that act of bravado last night, saving that woman in Dwight Square . . . I must say!'

Gramps was the picture of aw-shucks humility. 'Naw, anybody would've done the same.'

Becky fluttered her lashes. 'No, but you, you are the one who did it. You are a very brave man.'

Gramps blushed.

'I absolutely must interview your grandfather,' Becky said, turning to me. 'He's a real hero, Jesse. Of course, it's too bad WOKR got it on *News at Eleven* first, but never mind. I'll bet I can get Charlie Nicks to let me do a feature . . .'

The self-confident smile faltered. Behind the carefully erected façade I could see that Becky needed a story, and needed it bad. I could also see how she'd slant it. The news didn't lie in Gramps being a hero; it lay in his being a bum – and kin to a high-profile ex-*Herald* reporter, one with a local mobster (albeit semi-retired) for a sometime lover and friend. Becky would take that and build on it, and by the time she was done Gramps would be larger than life: a loser who finds religion, a parolee gone straight, a prodigal son returned to a less than reputable fold.

In short, a character worthy of capturing the imaginations and hearts of a vast readership hungry for sensation. Next thing we knew we'd be in *USA Today*, for all the world and Barney Noonan to see.

I glanced at Nicky Ludgett, who was lifting one of three cameras strapped around his neck. He looked like a large rubber ball in a rumpled green windbreaker over brown pants, both with stains and a size fifty-two. The ball had a white face and was topped with greasy black hair.

'Jesse! How goes it? Long time no see.'

I moved to block his view of Gramps. 'No photos, Nicky.'

He held the camera to his eye. 'Just one, okay?'

'Absolutely not.' I shoved my hand over his lens and appealed to Becky. 'Look, my grandfather isn't well. As soon as he's feeling better, I'll call you. We'll get together.' I started to close the door.

'Nothing staler –' she began.

'Than yesterday's news, I know. Spare me the cliché.'

The door was nearly shut, and I thought we were home free. But then the blue eyes narrowed, and Becky surprised me by aggressively sliding a foot in to keep the door from closing.

'Just one photo, Jesse?' she pleaded, her determined body halfway through. 'One of the two of you together.'

'No, dammit!'

I tried to ease her out without hurting her. But a determined Becky was a force to reckon with. She planted her feet wide apart, boot heels digging in. I might as well have tried to topple a tree.

Becky's cornflower eyes appealed to Gramps. She smiled artlessly, as coral-tipped nails fluttered through her hair. 'It's just that I don't understand, Mr James. You're the hero of the day. Everyone's talking about your adventure in the park last night. How could you possibly be afraid of a little old photograph?'

At the same time Nicky leaned on the door, his immense weight shoving me back. 'You don't mind a little photo op, do you, old fella? Our readers will love it.'

I shoved the door hard, slamming it against Nicky's arm.

He gave a loud 'Yipe!' but raised his camera and snapped.

'Stop that!' Gramps yelled, flinging his wiry little body at Nicky. He knocked me off balance, and the door flew back against the wall with a bang. Gramps hurtled out onto the front porch. I followed, reaching for his arm to yank him back inside.

'Gimme that camera!' Gramps shouted.

'No can do.' Nicky smiled placidly, holding the Leica high out of Gramp's reach. He snapped several times in rapid succession, backing down the porch steps, then slip-sliding on the icy sidewalk as he ran away.

I started after him. But movement caught my eye from across the street. I turned, looked, and drew back.

'Gramps. Get inside.'

He followed my gaze to the sidewalk in front of Mr Garson's house.

A man stood there, hands in pockets and hunched as if cold and shivering. He was taking in the scene – and he wasn't from the neighborhood.

In the first place, he had a deep tan. In the second, he was dressed in a light windbreaker, more fit for sailing than today's below-freezing temperatures.

As I turned to shove Gramps out of sight, Mrs Binty appeared at her porch door. 'What on earth is going on, Jesse?' She was even tinier than Gramps, with sharp, birdlike eyes that pierced through Becky, then turned enquiringly to me.

'Go back inside, Mrs B. *Please*.'

She hesitated, bewildered. Gramps took her arm and whispered something to her, easing her back over the sill. He stood in front of her, forming a shield. Down the street, Nicky was taking a final shot. Petey Dorken stood beside him, scanning with his video cam.

The man across the way simply stood there, watching.

I turned on Becky, my voice shaking with anger. 'This is *National Enquirer* shit! Dammit, Becky, how could you?'

She smiled a suddenly less-than-vacant smile. 'Well, now, Jesse . . . everything I know I learned from you.'

I told Mrs Binty I'd explain later, and she seemed to accept that. I also told her to keep her doors locked and not open them to strangers. I indicated the man across the street and told her to particularly not let him in. She nodded, her eyes excited and shining.

The truth is, Mrs Binty delights in the now and again trouble that surrounds her only boarder. She'd be telling the neighbors an embellished version of today's events within the hour. '*I wonder what Jesse's up to this time! There were reporters and photographers all over, and land's sakes, she just about knocked them down!'*

Gramps and I stood at my living-room window, looking out through the heavy flowered drapes I'd left up to ward off the cold. The guy with the tan was in a car now, a light blue Chevy compact with rental plates. I'd seen it earlier, parked half a block down the street. Now it was directly across from the house. He was sitting behind the wheel, motor running – probably for heat. It had steamed the windows, but he'd wiped a spot to see through.

'Not even trying to be subtle,' I said.

'That he's not, girl.'

'I'd say he's from Miami, wouldn't you?'

'No doubt about it.'

'You ever see him before?'

'Might have.' Gramps rubbed his chin stubble.

'What do you mean?'

'Gal, I just ain't sure. I'm thinking he might be the guy who tried to shoot me down in Miami. He was inside a car and it was goin' pretty fast, so I only got a quick look. But he's got the same blond hair, same tan.'

'Hmmm.' I was chilled clear through, and I hugged myself for warmth. 'Well, he had plenty of opportunity to get you, out there on the porch. My guess is he's just checking out the territory. Otherwise, he'd be up here by now, instead of down there.'

'Maybe he's waitin' for somebody.'

'Barney Noonan?'

'Could be.'

I dropped the curtain and we stood back. Gramps' frown turned into a grin. He clapped me on the back. 'You gave it right back to those reporter folk, gal. You have my admiration.'

'Thanks. I'd rather have had your support.'

He sounded offended. 'I did okay.'

'Old man, if you'd listened to me and stayed out of sight, I might have been able to convince them you'd already left town.'

Irritated, I headed for the kitchen. Denny and Joey were downstairs, attacking the kitchen floor from below. They were out of the way, but still a presence; I could feel the force of their hammer blows beneath my feet.

I shook the coffee pot. Not much left but dregs. 'You want this?' I said.

'No, you go ahead.' But the old guy was still blue from the cold, still shivering. I poured the steaming dregs into a mug and handed it to him. 'Here, I've had enough.'

'I don't –'

'Will you please . . . just take it!'

He grabbed the coffee and chugged it down. His nose grew pink again. 'That was nice of you, gal. Thank you.'

'You're welcome.'

'So, what's next?'

'I guess I've got to rethink things. Between Becky's story and our friend over there . . .'

'He's mebbe just the tip of the iceberg, don't you think?'

'Exactly. Noonan may have people watching the airport by now.'

I thought of the Andrelli jet. If it wasn't in Kyoto or points east, north or south, shuttling Marcus' business cohorts around, Tark might be able to commandeer it for me.

But that'd be even more visible than public transpo. Besides, I didn't like asking Marcus for help these days.

'Let's get out of here awhile,' I said. 'Test the waters with the Tan over there.'

'See how sharp he is, ya mean?'

'Can't hurt. But I want you to stick close and do as I say.'

'Sure thing, gal. And listen – long as we're goin' out, I could sure use a bite to eat.'

I peered down at his thin frame. 'I didn't . . . when was the last time you ate?'

'Yesterday sometime, I guess.'

'Mrs Binty didn't offer you something this morning?'

He shrugged. 'I didn't want to impose.'

'Old man, you are one big fat riddle to me.'

He grinned. 'I could say the same for you, Jesse girl.'

Gramps didn't have warm clothes, so we rummaged through mine on the floor. He ended up wearing my old navy anorak with the fur-lined hood. It was a size eight, but big on him. He also wore a pair of my Nikes, since his own tennis shoes were still soaked from last night in the park. Mine were encrusted with mud and too big, so they flip-flopped. Put that together with the splinter-like stubble, and Gramps looked pretty much like he'd picked through a dumpster of Goodwill rejects.

We crossed the few feet to the driveway and my old Dodge Dart. The sun was out now, the snow melting, but it still felt a thousand degrees below zero. My boots crunched as I walked on the street side, shielding Gramps – one eye on the Chevy for a window cracked open just enough to allow a weapon to poke through. But the car stayed sealed up tight. Our visitor made no moves.

At the Dodge I unlocked the passenger door first and let Gramps in. Then I looked across the way to the Chevy, thinking.

'You stay here,' I said.

Gramps followed my glance. 'You're not –'

'Relax. I'll be right back.'

He made a move to get out. 'If you're doin' what I think you're doin', I'm comin' too.'

'*No.* If you want my help with this, you stay here. Understand?' I slammed his door.

He opened it again and grabbed my sleeve. 'Gal, if that's the guy who shot at me, you think he won't do the same to you?'

'No, I think he won't. The fact is, he hasn't. And I want to know why.'

Gramps shook his head worriedly. 'I don't like this, not at all.'

I turned and walked across the street, hoping he'd do as I said. The Chevy's windows were defrosted now. The motor was still running, and the radio – a talk show – blared. I pounded on the driver's window with my fist. 'Open up!' I yelled, so he could hear. 'Roll your window down!'

The radio noise faded. The window opened and a face appeared.

Up close, he was older than I'd thought. Deep lines circled the eyes and mouth, and the cheeks were sunken. He didn't look ill – more gaunt, the way runners sometimes get. The eyes were alert and wary.

I leaned a hand on the top of the car. 'You look pretty cold in there.'

No response.

'Nice place, I hear, Florida.'

Still no response.

'Palm trees, sunshine . . . the Busted Flush.'

He blinked. 'The what?'

I grinned. 'John D. MacDonald? Never mind. Shit, nobody reads anymore. Noonan send you here after Johnny James?'

He gave a shrug.

'You must be a low man on the totem pole.'

The sharp eyes narrowed.

'I mean, he's right over there. You could've picked him off anytime.'

He shrugged. 'I can wait.'

'That's what I mean. Only a grunt would have to wait around in weather like this.'

Ego. Always the weak spot.

It worked. His jaw clenched; you could almost hear the teeth grit. 'Noonan knows what he's doing.'

'What *is* he doing? Why are you here?'

'Let's just say the old man's not disappearing again. Not before Noonan wants him to.'

'Uh-huh. And when Noonan's ready, he'll just forgive and forget? Let my grandfather go on his way nice and peaceful, like?'

The guy's laugh was sarcastic.

'That's what I thought.' I smiled at him then. 'You all alone up here?'

'You wish.'

'Noonan's got everything covered? Airport, bus stations, hot air balloons . . .'

'. . . police, highway patrol,' he added smugly.

'Shit, he's bought them off, too?'

Miami shrugged.

Well, there's always somebody looking for an extra buck. And much as Grady liked to believe the department was clean . . .

Out of the corner of my eye, I saw Gramps get out of the Dodge. I hurried it up.

'We're heading for the Water Street Grill, downtown,' I said, giving Miami the address. 'Thought I'd let you know, so you won't get lost.'

The guy actually took out a pad and pencil and wrote it down.

'Well . . .' I gave a friendly pat to the car's roof. 'Have a nice day.'

'Thank you.' Miami shivered and rolled the window back up.

Jeez, criminals. Sometimes they're geniuses, sometimes not.

I motioned to Gramps to get in the Dodge, and began walking back. He stood beside the car until I got there, and didn't climb in till I was behind the wheel.

'You are the orneriest man I've ever known,' I said.

'I was gettin' worried.'

'Well, you don't have to worry. We're not slab material. At least, not yet.' I started the motor and put the defroster on full blast.

'What'd he say?'

'Says he's been sent here to make sure you don't leave town.'

'Pretty much what we figured, then. Is Noonan on his way?'

I revved the motor so it wouldn't stall. 'He wouldn't say.'

I cranked the radio dial, pulling in some mellow jazz. 'We've got to get creative.'

'Creative, huh? You got somethin' in mind, gal?'

'Not yet. Can't think on an empty stomach.' I backed out of the drive. As we passed Miami, I gave him a friendly wave.

'Boy, what I wouldn't give,' Gramps said, 'for a nice thick steak and baked potato. Maybe top it off with some sour cream, butter, chives . . .'

'Sounds expensive,' I said. 'You buying?'

'Not me.' Gramps gave a mock pouf to his stringy gray hair and batted his eyes. 'I'm the hero of the day.'

Chapter 7

I don't know if there really is more crime in Rochester, New York, than any other city of its size. But for a population of only roughly 250,000, there are a hell of a lot of serial killings, random murders (the kind where a guy walks into a convenience store or bar and shoots two or three people on sight), and family or gang shootouts. Sometimes the family *is* the gang.

There have also, lately, been several suicides directly linked to the recession. Three major companies that were founded here – Xerox, Bausch & Lomb, Kodak – have been laying off. And it used to be that jobs were sort of handed down, family to family. If your dad worked at Kodak, it was almost certain you'd get a job there too. That no longer happens so much.

So you have this beautiful city on the south edge of Lake Ontario, with its nationally known and respected GeVa Theater, its art museums, concerts, big-name stars and politicians coming to town to wheel, deal, and perform. And then you have the dark side. The dark side swings from graft and corruption in the police department, which in recent years saw a major upheaval, to the fact that the department actually needs a scuba squad whose main duty some days is to dredge the Genesee River for jumpers.

Such were my dim and desultory thoughts as I sat across from Gramps at the Water Street Grill. It was late afternoon, between the lunch and dinner rush, and we'd lassoed a window table overlooking the river. On the opposite bank the scuba squad was out in full force. I watched long enough to know they were having another drill. There was a paramedic truck, and scuba and medical gear lined the bank clear up to the brick warehouses that had been converted to apartments. But there was a casual air in the way the guys interacted, laughing and talking back and forth. It was clear no one had fallen or jumped.

I'd brought Gramps here because I knew the Water Street from when I worked at the *Herald*. It was in a good, downtown neighbourhood, the dining room not too accessible from the street. I figured I could think here without having to worry too much about Gramps.

Although, Miami's actions seemed to match his story. We'd parked in the *Herald* lot a block away, and he'd followed on foot without giving us any trouble.

I checked Gramps out across the table. Here at the Water Street we were among the nine-to-five types, with white tablecloths and a Victorian-decorated Christmas tree. Neither one of us had dressed for the occasion. But then I suspected that neither one of us ever dressed right, anyway.

My "grandfather" cast an uneasy glance over his shoulder. 'Can't wait for this whole thing to be over, girl. What makes you so sure they ain't in here?'

'They?'

His skinny shoulders moved beneath the denim shirt. 'Barney Noonan . . . or one of his killers.'

'They wouldn't try anything in here.'

He didn't look convinced. And I couldn't help feeling sorry for the old man. He must have spent his whole life looking over a shoulder, never knowing when someone he'd conned might show up for a piece of his hide. And now he had this psycho after him, this Barney Noonan, who nailed people to trees for sport.

Gramps passed on the steak and trimmings and ordered a

Meg O'Brien

pasta dish, one of the most expensive on the menu. Mentally counting the cash in my pocket, I ordered a corned beef on rye. It came with mayo, Swiss cheese, lettuce and tomato.

'Should've gone to Harrigan's,' I grumbled. 'Damned *nouvelle cuisine*. Don't they know a *real* corned beef on rye's got nothing but mustard and maybe just a little cheese? Actually, I don't like cheese on corned beef and rye, but . . .'

Gramps was clearly not listening. His pasta swam in fabulous shavings of fresh Parmesan, tomatoes, garlic and basil. He shoved forkfuls down his gullet while my mouth watered. Now and then he made little moaning sounds of pleasure, smacked his lips, and sighed.

His beverage, and mine, was water. 'You want wine or beer?' I had asked.

Gramps frowned, disapproving. 'Never touch the stuff. Gotta keep the mind clear.'

'You reeked of booze at my door this morning.'

'Part of the con, gal. I bought a cheap bottle of red and dumped it on my clothes. You know . . . so I'd fit in at the park last night.'

'Fit in?'

'Sure. If you're just an old drunk, people figure you ain't got nuthin' of value. They leave you alone.'

'Old man, do you always play a part?'

'Sure I do, girl. So do you.'

'I do not.'

'Girl,' he cackled, 'you *are* a part. A walking, living part.'

'You don't even know me!' I tapped my nails irritably on my water glass.

'I know your type. There are only so many types in the world, like so many stories, so many cons. And you're just like me.'

'Hah. I am not at all like you.'

'Oh? Then tell me this, girl. You got more than one scam up your sleeve right this minute, don't'cha?'

I fixed him with a cool look. 'All I've got is getting you out of my hair. After that I'll be just fine.'

50

Gramps showed me all but his missing front tooth, grinning through pasta and basil. 'You're gonna miss me, gal.'

We finished up and I paid the bill. Then we walked outside into the dusk, bracing ourselves against an icy wind. Miami was in front of the Marine Bank across the street, and I noted he'd picked up a green plaid scarf somewhere, and a watchcap. He still didn't look happy. Gramps and I headed down the street toward the *Herald*, with him in tow.

Gramps looked up at the new, ugly sign atop the otherwise lovely, historic, pre-Civil War graystone. *Rochester Herald*, it proclaimed in blazing red neon. The sign looked like a head wound on a duchess.

'How come you don't work there anymore, gal?'

'Got fired. And I quit.'

'Both?'

'Well, they fired me, then wanted to hire me back later, but I said no. I figured I was better off working on my own.'

'So you sell these stories – freelance, you call it – to magazines like that *Newsweek*, and *Time*?'

'Those, and some papers around the country.'

'You make good money at this?'

'Not much. But it keeps me honest.'

The old man fell silent, and we trudged on, toward the short bridge over the Genesee River. A patrol car was parked along one curb, and behind it a black and white van marked ROCHESTER POLICE DEPARTMENT – SCUBA SQUAD. A city news reporter I knew slightly stood at the far end of the bridge, taking notes about the ongoing drill.

'. . . live here?' I heard Gramps say.

'What?'

'I was askin', you plan to live here all your life? What're you thinkin', gal? You've gone a mile away.'

We were about midway along the bridge, and I steered Gramps over to the side. 'Let's stop a minute.'

We leaned against the cement parapet, looking down at the

icy floes and at the scuba squad – some of whom were now in the water. Gramps gave a shiver, even though my anorak hood nearly covered his face. Poor guy. He was all hunched up, trying to keep warm as the cold wind sailed up his thin pants legs.

'Somethin' happen down there?' he asked.

'No. They're just practicing. In case something does.'

Gramps hopped back and forth from one foot to the other, his teeth chattering. 'I sure wouldn't like that job.'

'They're adventuresome guys. They get a lot of press.' I gave him a look. '*Real* heroes of the day.'

'Well, they can have it. Let's get back to the car, girl. My old Florida bones are rattlin' so hard they're about to break.'

'You know,' I said, still looking down, 'it's funny about the Genesee River. It's one of maybe only three in the world that runs north.'

'That so? Can we go now?'

'And the current is running pretty damned fast.'

'Uh-huh.' His scrawny body shook against my arm.

'Makes it kind of hard to find a body,' I said. 'Unless, of course, it gets snagged on roots or something along the way. Sometimes they end at the Upper Falls and don't get found until spring.'

'Jesse?'

'Hmmm?'

'Can we do this guided tour some other time?'

I glanced up and remembered the Coppertone Kid, watching us now from half a block away.

'Right,' I said. 'Let's go.'

Inspiration's a funny thing. There are times, those lucky times, when it comes all at once, in a flash, when the only thing left is to turn a thought into a plan.

This, it seemed, was one of those times. So we didn't go back to the car. Instead, we went inside the *Herald* building, up to the fourth floor, to the city news room that used to be my home. Gramps kept giving me sly looks in the thirties cage elevator, those 'watcha cookin' up, girl?' looks, but I didn't tell him what I was thinking. Not that he wouldn't like it. My guess was he'd fall into place with nary a grump.

There were possibly seven people in the city room, which held thirty or so desks. One computer keyboard stopped clacking as we entered, and a strong female voice came from behind a tumbled pyramid of files. Atop the pyramid was the only bright spot in the entire office: a tiny pink Christmas tree with silver balls.

'Jesse? Jesse James? Girl, is that really you?' said the voice.

'I wish people would stop calling me *girl*,' I muttered.

'What?'

'Nothing. Hi, Jen. Where's Charlie Nicks?'

'Doctor appointment,' she called out. 'Should be back any minute.'

I dragged Gramps with me and peered over Jenny Taylor's files. 'Are you really here behind all this shit, or are you just a tape recording of Jen?'

She grinned, leaning back in her chair. A pencil with a fuzzy purple 'troll' head was stuck through her tight black hair. Her eyes were brown, like her skin, and her cheekbones more Indian than Afro. Jenny's mother was an Apache, her father a black professor of political science from Boston.

'You really want to see Charlie?' she asked.

'No, just making sure the coast is clear. Why's he at the doctor? What's wrong with him, anyway?'

'Charlie? Too many doughnuts and coffee.'

'High blood pressure?'

'Nope. Fat. Charlie Nicks is fat.'

'I *know* Charlie's *fat*.' The *Herald* should open its own doughnut shop; I'd gained ten pounds myself while working here. 'Is that all?'

Jenny took the pencil and stroked her cheek absently with the fuzzy end. 'Ain't that enough, girl? Even his pink balding head is fat. Not to mention his mind.'

'Tsk, tsk. What have we here, an attitude?'

'No more than usual. I think I'm getting backwash from all the wrath our ignoble editor still feels toward you. I'm learnin' to fight back.' She looked behind me. 'So this is your grandpa, Jess?'

He peered through the anorak fur and shuffled his feet.

'How'd you know?' I said.

'Heard about your little contretemps with Becky Anderson and crew.' Jenny's mouth quirked.

'Amazing woman, that Becky.'

'Truly. Amazinger every day. So, to what do we owe your presence here in paradise today?' Jenny glanced around the grim, ancient office ringed by glass cubicles where the editors sit. I've always figured news editors have to sit in glass cubicles so people won't throw stones at them. Either that or so those of us with brains can keep a sharp eye out and thus prevent them from making total fools of themselves.

'I've got a favor to ask,' I said.

And Jenny owed me one. I was the first to break the story about corruption in the Rochester PD. Somebody came to me, *à la* Deep Throat, and we had secret murmurings in dim corridors. That led to interviews with cops. Most were ordinary working stiffs, some not too bright, and coping with the recession in a less than legally acceptable way. When their supervisors' rocks were upturned, many were shocked to find themselves being prosecuted. There was a lot of paranoia. The few cops who had talked to me lurked in dark corners, hands in pockets, chins invariably jerking over their shoulders to see if anyone with a video cam was around.

When I went to Charlie with that first piece, he was scared to death. 'The *Herald* won't touch this,' he said. 'It's a can of worms.'

I'd threatened to give all my notes to a journalism class at Roberts Wesleyan. Those fresh-faced wonderful young men and women of integrity would descend upon the story like locusts.

The upshot was that R. D. Chastain, our fanatically puritan publisher, who had himself threatened to fire me several times on other matters, overrode Charlie Nicks. The story saw light, went nationwide, and won me an award. And that's the story of my life: always somewhere between celebrity and doom.

When I left the *Herald* later, there was still plenty of follow-up to do. I turned my sources over to Jen, who was new then, down from Boston, and she carried on. It helped to boost her career. Jenny Taylor's byline is now standard fare in the *Herald*.

'A favor?' she said now. 'Name it, girl. Anything you want ... long as it doesn't include cohabiting with Charlie Nicks.'

'Please.' I closed my eyes against the horrible thought.

Gramps shuffled impatiently again, and Jenny said, 'You want to sit down, Mr James?' She shoved a stack of handwritten notes off the chair next to her desk. They scattered across the aisle. Jen slid her feet up onto her desk and leaned back. 'Hell, it's almost Christmas. I wasn't gonna do that story anyway.'

Gramps sat heavily, as if to rest his weary feet. He'd pulled off the hood, and his hair stuck up in cowlicks. Out of old habit, it seemed, he licked an index finger and reached up, awkwardly smoothing them down, like a kid trying to look good for his eighth-grade teacher.

I sat on the edge of the desk, close enough to talk without the rest of the office hearing. 'Jen, I need you to call somebody at the police department. I'd like to know this week's schedule for the scuba squad drills.'

'The Glamour Patrol? That's easy enough.' Her eyes turned shrewd. 'But I don't get it. Why don't you call over there yourself? You've got plenty of contacts at the PD.'

'If it comes from you, nobody'll think twice about it. They'll just assume you're doing a routine piece.'

'So you don't want them to know you're asking,' Jen said.

'You got it.'

'Not even your old pal Grady North?'

'Especially not Grady North.'

'Uh-huhhh.' Jen thought a moment, reached for the phone, then paused with her hand on the receiver. 'Just one thing. You gonna tell me why I'm doin' this, girl?'

'Maybe,' I said. 'If you'll please just stop calling me girl.'

Chapter 8

'Street kids, a hardline bunch . . . Have a knuckle sandwich for
lunch.'

'Street Kids', D. R. Lunsford

We came out of the city room to find Miami lurking in
the corridor. He was smarter than I'd given him credit
for; I'd actually thought of sneaking Gramps out the
back way, past the presses in the basement – if only as a
test.

Instead, we shared the elevator, all three of us. And the ride
down was truly bizarre.

There was silence at first, as the antique lift descended to the
first floor. I placed myself between Miami and Gramps,
wondering if I'd misjudged Miami's intentions. The stress got
so bad my head ached. Was he planning to pull a gun and take us
both out?

I'd picked up a few self-defense techniques from Grady when
he was teaching it over at the high school and I mentally got
ready. But our companion just stood there, like a faithful dog at
our heels.

'How's it goin'?' Gramps finally said, breaking the silence. His tone was casual, friendly. He might have been talking to an old pal.

Miami shrugged. The lines in his face moved downward, like a pug's. 'Could use some warmer clothes, I guess.'

'Boy, do I know what'cha mean.' Gramps bobbed his head in agreement. 'I ain't used to this at all.' He gave a shiver, and Miami looked morose.

'You got a room somewhere?' Gramps said.

'A room?'

'Yeah. You got a good hotel?'

'No . . . not yet.'

'Well, golly, you ain't plannin' to sleep in that car, are ya? It goes down below zero at night around here. Lordy, it was colder than a nun's tit in that park last night.'

'Gramps –' Another minute and he'd be inviting the guy to move in.

But he gave me a quick, sly grin. Damn the man, he was playing a game with Miami, like a cat with a rubber mouse. This was relaxation for him.

'Say, you need a warm place nearby. I hear there's hotels out by the airport, not more'n ten minutes away.'

'Really?' Miami perked up.

'Bet you could still get a room. Middle of the winter, things're slow. Not like Miami.'

'No . . . not like Miami at all.'

They both nodded sorrowfully and were silent again.

I was glad when the elevator stopped and let me out.

From the *Herald*, our little three-party caravan headed for Jimmy's pool hall on Genesee Street, next to Harrigan's Bar & Grill. Along the way I told Gramps the idea that had come to mind as we stood on the bridge over the Genesee River.

'You want to *drown* me?' he said nervously.

'Not precisely.'

'Whew. That's good to hear. For a minute there –'

'But I need some help to pull it off.'

'Well, sure, gal. If there's anything I can do –'

'Real help,' I said. 'People who know what they're doing.'

Just before we reached the pool hall, a driving snow began, and my car heater quit. The old Dodge seats became thrones of ice. I had to feel for a spot at the curb; by the time we reached it, visibility was nil.

Once parked we left Miami to fend for himself. Gramps and I stumbled through Jimmy's door with numb faces, limbs like chunks of frozen granite, and breath that billowed out like steam from an old Lionel train. We stamped our feet, knocking the snow off and making a racket.

A small sea of black faces near the door swiveled our way and checked us out. I nodded to Syracuse Slim, who took me for an entire week's pay one night when I was still young and stupid and thought I could outshoot the master. It was an expensive lesson and worth every penny – in terms not only of pool but of life. Nowadays I make sure I've got the skills to beat people at their own game before I enter the play.

Slim nodded back, and everyone relaxed and returned to hustling.

I led Gramps to the back room, where at one of four tables a muscular young black man stood by with a cue. His name was Percy Greene, he was about seventeen, eighteen, and had a zigzag hairdo. Rack 'Jack', another black kid about the same age, stood in leathers and studs with a cue in hand. A third man leaned over the table, sighting a ball. His rear end was pointed my way. It was a nice rear end, clothed in natty white pants that were clean and neatly pressed, with razor-sharp creases. A soft white shirt with billowy sleeves complemented dark skin. The rear end swayed as the player moved into a better position. He pulled his arm back, paused, and was just about to smack the ball into a corner pocket when I whacked that part of the anatomy that was pointed my way.

Rack and Percy, who had seen me coming, grinned. Abe swung around, cue raised, ready to let his assailant have it.

'Shit, should of known it was you.' His eyes were an amazing blue-green, and irritated. 'You just ruined my best shot of the day, lady.'

'You should be out working the streets, anyway,' I said. 'What are you doing inside on such a lovely day?'

Abe Denton glanced through smoky windows to the mini-blizzard.

'The people with money to steal,' he complained, 'are inside by their fires, drinking expensive bourbon. Business is mighty bad today.'

'Been bad for weeks,' Rack agreed, creaking leather as he shrugged. 'You just get a good scam going, and winter comes along.'

'Slows down your getaway.' That from Percy – the Three's designated getaway driver.

I grinned. 'I've got somebody you should meet. A soul brother.' I turned to Gramps. 'Gramps, meet the Genesee Three.'

We sat at a table and ordered coffee all around. The Three don't drink these days, and neither do I. Drugs? Who knows about these things. Rack used to do pot. Abe's been clean as a whistle for months. Percy, now – lately he's been into food. We all have our obsessive compulsions. But drugs aren't something we talk about. I take the Genesee Three as I find them, and for me, they've always been good friends, guardian angels, and even – now and then – cohorts.

It drives Grady North mad. He'd like to lock the Three up. Hell, Grady would like to lock everybody in Rochester up. Cut your hair like Al Pacino, and he'll toss you in the slammer. But the Genesee Three keep peace in the neighborhood, even while they're ripping it off royally. The other hoods look up to them, listen to them, and fear them. When the G-Three say "Cool it," they do.

Grady's smart enough to see that as a blessing – albeit mixed.

'So, you're Jesse's grandfather,' Abe said, cradling his coffee mug with long, slender fingers. The green eyes assessed

Gramps, who was starting to look tired and not a little edgy. He kept shifting his skinny bottom on the chair. 'How long you gonna be around?'

'Hard to tell,' Gramps said.

'Not long,' I said.

Abe looked from Gramps to me and back again, smiling slowly. 'Heard you helped old Nettie over in Dwight Square last night.'

'You mean the bag lady?' Gramps gave an elaborate shrug. 'Wasn't much.'

'Was for Nettie,' Abe said.

He took a deep swallow of coffee, picked up a paper napkin, and dabbed at his mouth. It wasn't exactly a prissy gesture, but delicate. Abe's a bit of a dandy. He sees himself as kind of a black man's Cary Grant. Every now and then, he even slips into a British accent. Put that together with all-white clothing, like Tom Wolfe, and you get the picture.

'You know, Abe, you add real class,' I said admiringly.

'Yeah? To what?'

I made a gesture that took in Rack, Percy, myself, and Gramps. 'The family.'

Abe grinned and folded his arms. 'We family today, Jess? You must want something.'

I sipped my coffee. 'A little assistance,' I said casually. 'No big deal.'

'Uh-huh. When's the last time I heard that?'

'But this time it's not illegal.'

'Everything you do is illegal, lady. 'Least by the time you get to us with it.'

'No, really. I want you to work a con with me, but it's not what you'd call strictly illegal.'

Rack gave a snort. 'Your friend Grady North in on this?'

'No.'

He laughed outright. 'Like Abe said, illegal.'

I frowned. 'What, you guys don't have anything better to do than harass me today?'

Percy got in on it then, and we'd been through this before, the kidding around, the banter. A lot of people think we're serious when we do it. For me, it's simple fun – like having brothers. It tests my wits and mettle.

But Gramps didn't look happy at all. His face had a scowl, and a nerve over his cheekbone throbbed. I tried to catch his eye, but Percy was saying, 'Sure, we got better things to do – almost anything, in fact, than mess with the likes of you.'

'Oh, the likes of me, is it now?' I said.

'Trouble,' Perce gibed. 'You are trouble, lady, with a capital T.'

And that's when the old man lost it. He jumped to his feet, knocking his coffee cup over. It tumbled to the floor and rolled. Dark splatters appeared on Abe's white pants leg.

'Yeah, well, I know trouble when I see it!' Gramps said in a raised voice. 'And I don't like a lady bein' talked to that way. We're gettin' out of here, Jesse girl. You and me, we can manage just fine without these . . . these boys.'

The Three and I looked up, our jaws dropping in unison. A silence fell, so thick it cut like a blade through the smoke-filled room. There were alert black faces pointed our way, no longer friendly.

The word 'boys' hadn't gone over well.

Holy shit. I could only hope they'd see Gramps' 'slur' as generational rather than racial.

Gramps realized belatedly, I guess, what he'd said. He didn't look away from the Three, and he didn't back off. But he paled, and his Adam's apple quivered.

Abe's quiet eyes looked down at his pants leg, then moved back to Gramps. They rested on the skinny frame, the chin that trembled but remained high. I fancied I could actually hear the soft fall of snow on the roof.

Finally, Abe just shook his head and laughed. He raised his coffee mug in a gentle toast.

'Your kin, Jesse. Your kin for sure.'

Rack took it up. He stood, the studs on his jacket glimmering under the green-shaded overhead lights. He circled behind Gramps, studying him from side to side. 'That be about right,' he said. 'Same temper. Same don't-give-a-damn. Plus, he's short.'

'Same big nose,' Perce offered.

'What? I do not have –' I began heatedly.

And finally everyone laughed.

Our coffee had been warmed, our tensions cooled. Gramps had apologized. 'Guess I been on edge. Didn't mean nuthin'. But I don't like a lady not bein' treated right – understand?'

'Gramps, hush. I told you, we were kidding.'

'I know, I know. Just don't like it, that's all.'

It seemed clear there was more to Gramps' outburst than simply nerves. Was there a woman in his life? Someone he felt protective about? I made a mental note to ask questions later when we were alone.

Meanwhile, I gave the Three some background on our problem, and outlined my idea for Gramps' watery denouement. When I was finished Abe said, 'Just so we're clear on this, lady, what you're proposing is most definitely illegal. First off, calling in a false alarm on a drowning could be construed as an intentional perversion of the truth that takes advantage of the public. That alone is felony fraud. You get all of us in on it, you can add conspiracy.'

'Abe,' I said, 'you're beginning to sound like a lawyer. This is scary.'

'Well, I've got responsibilities now. I don't fall into scams these days without thinking out the consequences.'

'What responsibilities?'

He didn't answer. I looked at Rack and Percy. Rack gave a shrug. Perce scooped some popcorn out of a bowl and munched, staring glumly out at the snow.

'Okay, so you've got responsibilities. Abe, are you turning me down?'

'No. But I don't want to end up in jail, either. If we do this, we'd damn well better do it right.'

'We could just distract this Miami tail,' Rack offered, 'sneak you both to the airport.'

'No. I've already discarded that. It's not good enough.'

'You want to tell us why not?' Abe said. 'Seems to me you're holding something back.'

'I . . . it's just that it's more complicated than this one guy. There's someone else.'

'Who?'

'His name's Soldando. He's Miami mob, and Noonan owes him money. If he doesn't come up with the cash by the end of the week, Soldando's taking him out.'

'Shit. So Noonan's desperate. He'll pull out all the stops to get his money back from Gramps here.'

'On the other hand,' Rack said, 'if Noonan's dead by the end of the week, he won't be anymore trouble to you.'

'I thought of that. But suppose Soldando finds out that the reason Noonan couldn't pay him was because Gramps had swiped Noonan's money? Soldando might come after Gramps then for it. No, I think it's better if Gramps is "dead". That way, they'll both be forced to deal with me.'

Gramps shook his head. 'You're crazy, girl. Downright loco, thinkin' you can mess with those guys alone.'

'Not at all. I've had a bit of experience with the mob.'

'With Soldando?'

'No.' I exchanged glances with Abe.

'Jess, you might say, has connections,' Abe told him mildly.

'Still don't like it,' Gramps said.

'You don't have to like it,' I said, an edge in my voice. 'You asked me for help. Now let me work it out.'

Abe turned to Gramps, his calm words like oil on water. 'Mr James, you are an unknown quantity to me. Are you sure you can handle *your* part of what Jess has in mind?'

Gramps made a sound like a grunt. 'You mean, over at Harrigan's? Piece of cake, friend. Piece of cake.'

'And Jess, you'll have to talk to the cops at the river. You sure you can do that?'

'You mean am I a good enough con?' I decorated the words with sarcasm.

'Chip off the old block, seems like,' Gramps muttered.

But Abe still looked worried.

We sat staring at each other, although each of us was really looking into our heads. There were long moments of silence.

'Okay, I've got it,' I said. 'Rack – you'll call in the false alarm.'

He nodded.

'Tell you what. Make sure it goes through homicide.'

'Homicide? Why?'

'Get Grady North on the phone. Don't tell him who you are. Just tell him the jumper left a wallet on the bridge, and the ID in it was my grandfather's. I'm betting he'll take over.'

'What about the scuba squad?' Abe said.

'Officially, of course, they'll be in charge. But you know Grady. He just pushes his way in, and pretty soon he's running things.'

'I'm not sure I see the benefit of having North on board,' Abe said.

I smiled. 'The felony fraud angle. When I was doing the series about corruption in the police department, I learned that it was difficult to prove fraud if the other person – quote, unquote – 'had the ability or knowledge to protect himself from it and didn't exercise a due degree of caution'.'

'And?'

'And Grady North has known me for years. Given all the times I've conned him in the past, he just plain shouldn't trust me now. It's his own damn fault if he doesn't exercise a due degree of caution.'

'Which brings up a major point,' Perce said. 'What if he does? You'd have to put on some terrific act. What if he sees through it?'

'Perce is right. It's a risk,' Abe warned.

'I need a risk,' I said. My eyes met Abe's and I saw that he knew what I meant. I'd been numbed-out long enough, since Marcus left. It was time to see action again.

Gramps spoke up. 'This North person. He's in homicide?'

'A lieutenant. He grew up on the force.'

'Well, if we're gonna involve him, why not just report my drowning as a homicide? Say I was pushed. It'd fit with the set-up, and that'd really put the guy in charge.'

I shook my head. 'He'd be all over us with an investigation. That's the last thing we need.'

Abe steepled his hands and tapped his nails against his teeth. 'It's still a legal risk.'

'Well, if it helps –' I grinned – 'I know a good lawyer.'

'Who?'

'Dieter.'

The Three looked impressed. 'No shit,' Rack said. 'How do you know him?'

Hugo Dieter was the big-shot lawyer who'd saved several top cops from prison sentences for fraud and corruption.

'He's the one who explained this loophole to me in the first place. 'If it's concealment of a matter which a person of ordinary skill or vigilance might discover, it does not constitute fraud,' he said.'

Abe shook his head. 'I still don't know . . .'

Percy, chomping on popcorn again, looked glum. 'This Miami tail. You really think he'll believe your grandfather's dead, spread his wings, and fly on home?'

'If we play our parts right. Meanwhile, Gramps will be toasting his buns in LA.'

Another mutter from that direction.

I looked at each of the Three in turn. 'C'mon guys . . . you know how long it's been since we had any real fun?'

'Fun, she calls it,' Rack said.

'A regular trip to Disney World,' said Perce.

'Now, there you go! You help me pull this off and I'll treat you all to Disney World after. I'll even get Tark to commandeer the jet to take us there.'

'Sounds great. If we're not all in jail.'

'Jeez, Abe. You were never this skittish. What's going on?'

Rack looked at Abe and smiled. His tone was lightly teasing. 'Abe's got a girl,' he said.

'A girl? No kidding. Who?'

'Her name is Elena. They're living together.'

'Abe, that's great. When do I get to meet her?'

He sighed. 'Lady, I'm keepin' her as far away from you as I can.'

'Hey, I'm hurt.'

But he was smiling, and I wasn't hurt, not really, just glad to know he was with someone now.

'I'm just tryin' to straighten out my life a little, Jess. Not take on anything too heavy.'

'I understand. Abe, I'm sorry. I didn't know. If you really don't want to do this, it's okay.'

He hesitated, exchanging looks with Rack and Percy. Finally, he said, 'No. We'll do it. Just make sure North doesn't catch on, okay?'

'I'll do my best. I promise.'

'So. You get airline tickets yet?'

'I did. The earliest I could get Gramps a seat to LA was seven-forty-nine tomorrow night. I'm heading for Miami right after.'

'Guess that's it, then.' Abe sighed and raised his coffee cup again. 'To tomorrow.'

'To tomorrow.'

I glanced out the window and saw that it was getting dark. 'Let's summarize. Gramps and I will be next door at Harrigan's by noon tomorrow. You'll be over here. And Miami, I'm betting, will have gotten tired of lurking outside in blizzards. He'll come into Harrigan's for something warming.'

'But if he doesn't –' Gramps began.

'Don't worry.' Abe gave us that slow smile. 'We'll get him in there. Maybe pay some kids to harass him. One way or another, your man won't like life on Genesee Street. Not at all.'

'Sounds perfect. Now all we need is a bit of luck,' I said.

Abe's green eyes slid my way. 'Luck ain't got nothin' to do with it. And you're gonna owe us, lady. Big time.'

Chapter 9

Love is a worrying game.
When will it come? When will it go?
I don't want to feel the pain.

'Go On', Katherine Ketner

'Jesse girl, who is this?'

I raised a mittened finger and rubbed dust from my frozen nose. 'What?'

'This guy in the picture.'

We'd gotten home from the pool hall an hour before, and were in Mrs Binty's garage. Gramps had been helping me drag out suitcases, a chore complicated by the fact that I'd stored a bunch of junk in them that needed to be unpacked now. Other odds and ends were parked on bookcase shelves.

While I sorted through an overnighter, Gramps had picked up a silver-framed candid shot of Marcus and me. We stood with arms around each other, my head on his shoulder, at Marcus' cabin on Irondequoit Bay last summer. Tark had snapped the picture when we weren't looking.

That was the thing about Marcus and me – all too often, we weren't looking. Not at the obvious, anyway, at the fact that it was nigh impossible for us to be together.

'It's just a guy I used to know,' I answered.

'How come you put it face down on the shelf?'

'Did I? I didn't notice.'

Gramps studied the photo. 'You're smiling. Ain't seen you smile like this since I been here.'

'You haven't given me much to smile about, old man.'

'But he did?'

I dropped books onto a box of Mrs Binty's and heard glass shatter inside.

'Damn!' I wondered what had broken. 'Will you stop poking into things? I've never known anyone so nosy in my life.'

Gramps lifted a sly brow. 'Struck a nerve, did I?'

I shoved the hapless box into a corner, next to an old Victrola gramophone that had belonged to Mrs Binty's mother. I would have to tell her about the breakage. I hoped it wasn't something irreplaceable.

'So, where is this guy?' Gramps said.

I gave a snort. 'Off in Europe, most likely, buying himself a kingdom.'

Gramps' eyes lit up. 'He's got money?'

'Tons, but you're never going to see it. He'd spot you coming a mile away.'

'So you had a good thing going and couldn't handle it. Is that it?'

I brushed my hands on my jeans. 'What the hell are you talking about?'

'The good life. You felt too guilty to enjoy it.'

'That's dumb.'

'No, it's not. You like to think of yourself as one of the people, I'll bet. Part of the masses, the common man.'

'Yeah, right. I love being broke, wondering where the rent money's coming from.'

'Sure you do. It makes you feel one of *them*.'

'Them *who*?' I shoved my dusty hands on my hips and glared.

'The creative types, the starving artists. Even though you've sold out.'

'You're crazy, old man. What do you mean, sold out? I gave up a steady income at a full-time job so I could be free to do work I love.'

'Well, Missy, so far as I can see, you ain't been doin' it.' He put the photo back on the shelf.

I opened my mouth to argue, and then shut it. Damn his hide, the old guy was right. And he wasn't saying anything Tark hadn't said earlier. The thing I'd been best at lately was floating.

'Well, I *am* going to do what I want,' I said, 'and I'm going to do it soon. I'm writing a screenplay.'

Gramps hooted. 'A screenplay? What do you know about screenplays, girl?'

'Not much – but I'm learning.'

He shook his head. 'Look, now, don't get me wrong. I don't mean t'make fun of you, girl. But I've known some people in Hollywood in my time, and believe you me, if it's freedom you want, you ain't gonna find it there.'

'You're free when you're doing what you want to be doing,' I argued. 'And right now, I want to write a screenplay.'

Gramps looked at me shrewdly. Thin gray hairs fell over his furrowed brow. 'What's this screenplay about?'

'Hah! You think I'd tell you? You'd steal my idea and sell it.'

'Jesse . . . Jesse girl,' he said sadly. 'How can you think that?'

'Old man, you would steal my teeth if you could get to them. Now help me drag these suitcases into the house.'

'Your grandfather's right,' Joey Martino said wisely. He snapped a plumb line down my living-room wall. 'It's time you settled down and either got yourself a good job or a good man. Somebody who can give you a nice home, take care of you like a woman oughta be taken care of.'

'I don't believe this. When were you born? In the year 1200? And what business is it of yours, anyway?'

Damn Johnny James. He'd started all this, and then he'd gone off. I didn't even know where he was.

'Don't get testy, I'm just showin' interest. Hey, Denny, you got that wallpaper ready yet?'

'I hate wallpaper,' I said.

Joey shook his head. 'Can't help it. Mrs B wants it done. Case you ever decide to leave, the place'll be nice for the next tenant.'

'That's crazy. I've been here for years. I'm not giving notice, and I do *not* want *wallpaper*.'

'Tell dat to de old lady,' Denny said. He finished pasting the first strip and held it up, slapping flowers and butterflies all over my sanctuary, *my wall*.

'It's not even living-room paper,' I complained. 'That stuff's for bedrooms.'

'Tell dat to de boss,' Denny said again.

I sighed. 'I already did. It reminds her of something she had as a kid.'

Or maybe not.

Mrs Binty was getting worse. Her memory, always a bit hazy, tended to get things wrong. It was possible this wallpaper only reminded her of something she'd seen in a neighbor's kitchen last week. Meanwhile, my once dark, woolly, winter cocoon was on its way to looking like an Impressionist's version of a French *tuilerie*.

'So anyway,' Joey went on, 'you still goin' out to LA? Not that's it's any of my business,' he added pointedly.

'Maybe. Someday.' I stepped close to stare at the paper on the wall. 'Joey, these butterflies look like the *Moth That Ate Tokyo*. Couldn't you talk her into something else? Before it's too late?'

Joey shook his head. 'I think she's sendin' you a message.'

'What kind of message?'

'She's worried you'll get to LA and never come back. She's tryin' to say she doesn't care, she'll decorate the place any way she wants, and the hell with you.'

'Mrs Binty? She doesn't think like that. She's not that mean.'

'Not mean. Just insecure. And maybe a little proud. Why don't'cha talk to 'er about it?'

'At least get outa da way,' Denny growled, holding up a second strip, 'before I slap this right over ya and we never find ya again.'

'Tiny little thing like her?' Joey scratched his belly, grinning down at me as he took his end. 'Could happen.'

It was past six. Joey and Denny had left for the day, and Gramps and I were watching *Penny Serenade* – 1941, Cary Grant and Irene Dunne – on my old nineteen-inch television, which he had insisted on dragging up from the garage. 'No sense leavin' it down there,' he'd said. 'Looks like this makeover's gonna last awhile.'

I surreptitiously dabbed at my eyes with a paper napkin, as Irene pressed valiantly on through the turmoils of married life. Gramps pretended not to cry. But glancing at him sideways, I'd seen moisture in his eyes.

I decided it wasn't so bad – for a day or so, anyway – having him around.

Used to be I'd drink when twilight fell and I found myself alone. Then I got sober, and those hours between four and six were even worse. If I'd finished work for the day, I'd hide in my nice soft armchair and watch old movies, dreaming of life in a better place, a better time. A time when people went to nightclubs with marble pillars, and when they danced in black chiffon and sequins – on the ceiling if they damn well pleased.

It was an era, if you believe what you see on celluloid, when Mr Blandings could afford to build his dreamhouse, when Claudette Colbert could ditch life in the city to raise chickens in *The Egg and I*, and when pirates in all their lusty, bloody splendor roamed the Main.

Then the fifties arrived, and so far as I'm concerned the entire female population went mad. I mean, why would any woman in her right mind want to trade in fantasies of Fred Astaire and a date at the Coconut Grove for a station wagon, a

Maytag washer, and vacations at the Holiday Inn (Kids Under 12 Free)?

See the USA, in your Chevrolet . . .

Television. That's where the descent into madness began.

'Why'd you take this to the garage in the first place?' Gramps had asked, huffing as he carried up the set, which was half as big as him.

'It was my way of concentrating on work. I was planning to use this time to hunker in. No distractions.'

He shot me a look. 'Then I happened along. That what you're sayin', girl?'

'Whatever.'

I'd strung an extension cord to the TV from the one outlet that worked, and we sat on folding chairs from the garage. I'd also brought down kerosene lamps from the attic and lit them, putting two in the living room, one in the kitchen. The heavy drapes were closed at every window, and for the first time since all this mess with the construction began, my apartment was actually rather warm.

'Sometimes I wish I'd lived back then,' I said, sniffing, when the movie, with its requisite three-hankie ending, was over. 'Seems like life was a lot simpler then.'

'Everything's simple in the movies,' Gramps said. 'It's the three-dimensional stuff that gets you in the end. The kind you can't rerun.'

I couldn't help smiling. 'Watch it, old man. You're starting to sound like me.'

Gramps got up and headed for the door. 'Stay here, girl. Don't move. I'll be right back.'

Curious, I heard him go down the stairs, then through the outer door. There was a knock below at Mrs Binty's. I watched the beginning of *Mrs Miniver*, and was just getting to the part about the rose contest when Gramps came back with a couple of wide, deep pans, and a steaming tea kettle. He set them on newspapers, on the floor by our chairs.

'Shoes off!' he ordered briskly. Sitting down, he removed his, then his socks.

'Corns,' he groaned, stretching out his toes. 'Darn things are painful. You want to take care of your feet, Jesse girl. Sometimes they're the only transportation we've got.'

My feet, in fact, hadn't been the same since I'd done full-time waitress work to get through Ithaca State. So I took off my shoes and Gramps and I sat and soaked our feet. His were a bit smaller than mine . . . but astonishingly, we had the same kind, right down to the wedge-shaped little toes.

'If you still doubt who I am, girl, that should settle it,' Gramps said with a chuckle. 'You can't deny genetics.'

'On the other hand, if you really wanted to convince me you were my grandfather, I wouldn't put it past you to have a toe transplant.'

Gramps looked pained, and we went back to watching *Mrs Miniver*.

Later, he cooked dinner – his speciality, he said: hobo stew.

'Learned how to do this over a campfire outside the Chicago freight yards,' he told me, browning chunks of beef in my cast-iron Dutch oven, then adding potatoes, carrots, onions, and a dash of water and flour. 'Nineteen and forty, I think that was.'

'Smells great,' I said. 'Where'd you get all this food?'

'Went shoppin' earlier, gal. Noticed you didn't have much in the house.'

'Really? I thought you didn't have money.'

'Don't. I found a twenty-dollar bill in your jacket pocket.'

My eyes widened. 'And you didn't ask me? You just took it?'

'What, you don't like my stew?' He laid on an injured tone.

'Oh, for heaven's sake,' I muttered. 'Never mind.'

As the stew bubbled, Gramps talked me into helping him carry wood up for the fire. 'Be nice to eat dinner by a real fireplace. Haven't done that in years.'

I dropped my load on the hearth, puffing from the run to the shed and then back up the stairs. 'Guess I haven't bothered with it much lately.'

'You mean since he's been gone?'

'Hmmm?' I crumpled newspapers, then laid the kindling, and over that a nice symmetrical pyramid of logs.

'Don't play deaf with me. You been grievin' since that guy in the picture's been gone?'

I lit the fire, then stood and wiped my hands on my jeans as it blazed. 'Marcus has nothing to do with it. I've been busy, that's all.'

'Hah. You've been lonely, gal. It's a darned good thing I showed up.'

'You ready for tomorrow?' I asked as we ate with our plates on our laps. Stan Getz played his buttery sax on my portable radio, and the fire crackled cheerfully.

'Lookin' forward to it,' Gramps said.

'You're not nervous at all?'

'Well, there's no tellin' what the guy from Miami will do, not for sure. But I got a pretty good fix on human nature. And so do you, gal. Most people believe what they see. I think you take that and add those three friends of yours playin' their parts, and it should go off without a hitch.'

Actually, he looked more excited about the prospect than nervous.

'You've been doing this sort of thing all your life, haven't you?' I said.

'Pretty much, I guess. I was only twenty-three, you know, when I left your gramma and went off to look for a livin'.'

'Twenty-three? That's all?' I knew my grandfather had left home back around 1930 – but I'd somehow never pictured him as being so young then. He wasn't much more than a kid.

I remembered myself at twenty-three, deep into the bottle, losing jobs every six months – heading straight downhill, with nothing at the bottom but one more Genesee Screw.

'A lot of people hit the road back then,' Gramps said. 'Wasn't any work in the factories, and the banks were takin' away people's farms. Your gramma's family had money, and they were one of the few who managed to hang onto it when the Great Depression hit. So they helped us out, and we paid up our bills and held on.'

He made smacking sounds with his stew. 'But I hated it, gal. Hated takin' their money and not bein' able to take care of your gramma all by myself. Then when the blizzards struck that year and we lost all our crops, I guess I went a little crazy. Figured I'd go look for some way to make a livin' in the city, and then I'd come back some big hero or something. Make your gramma proud.'

'You loved her, then?'

'Your gramma? Shoot, Jesse, she had this way of touchin' my cheek . . .' He reached out with the back of his hand, the red, chafed skin barely grazing my face. I felt a shock of warmth, as you do when a person's chemistry is the same as yours. The way it happens sometimes between lovers – or family.

'Mae's hand,' he said, dropping his gently, 'was so soft you hardly felt it. But it lingered, like an angel's kiss.' The old eyes grew dreamy. 'Jesse girl, the day I left, Mae touched my cheek that way, the tears runnin' down her own in rivers. 'You take care of yourself, Johnny,' she said. 'We'll be together again soon.'

His voice caught. And for a moment I couldn't help feeling sorry for him.

But then I remembered Mom's stories about my grandmother, and how she'd waited all those years for Johnny James to return, struggling on alone.

'Promises, promises.' My voice had an edge of bitterness.

Gramps set his plate on the floor and stared into the fire, leaning forward with elbows on his knees. 'Well, now, that's not exactly how it was, Jesse girl. See . . . I did go home once.'

I looked up, surprised. Beneath the flannel shirt his wiry back was rigid with tension.

'Lordy, but I was excited,' Gramps said. 'I'd been workin' at sellin' things door to door, and there wasn't any money in that.

But then I figured out a scam. Might've even been my first, in fact. It was pretty small potatoes. But I remember I had a few dollars in my pocket from that, and instead of sendin' them through the mail to your gramma, I hopped a train in St Louie and came on home. Didn't even tell her I was comin'. Thought I'd surprise her, see?'

He fell silent, staring at his hands. There was a slight tremor in them.

'What happened?' I asked.

'Well, now . . . I got there round dinner time. And I stood outside the dinin'-room window of our little farmhouse, lookin' in.' It seemed like a world of troubles weighed the skinny shoulders down. 'You know, gal, my memory isn't always so good anymore. I mean, I can't always tell you what happened last week. But I sure can remember every detail of that night. Just like it happened yesterday. I remember it was spring, and the dinin'-room window was open. There was a fresh white curtain blowin' just a little in the breeze, and the table was set with a lace cloth, and with the old crystal glasses and china that belonged to Mae's gramma. In the middle was a huge bunch of lilacs –'

'Lilacs?'

'Your gramma's favorite flower. A great big mass of them there was, and it seemed like I could smell them all the way through that window. And there was this crispy-lookin' pork roast on the table, and mashed potatoes with gravy, and apple sauce. My, oh my, your gramma was a good cook. My stomach started growlin' almost as much as my heart was achin' – just to touch her, you know? So I moved up closer to the window to tap on it, surprise her, let her see I was back –'

He broke off, his voice catching. 'And then I, uh . . . I saw him, sittin' there in my old chair, across from Mae.'

'Saw who?'

'Walter . . . Walter Bucks. A neighbor, used to be my best friend. And there he was with Mae, him in a nice new-lookin' suit, and her so purty, the lamp light soft on her face. And I thought, well, ain't that good. Mae hasn't been alone. Walter's been lookin' after things while I've been gone.'

Gramps' mouth worked, but he couldn't seem to get the next words out. I listened to Stan play a riff of bluesy notes, while Gramps gathered himself together. Finally I prompted him again.

'What happened?'

He sighed. 'Jesse girl . . . what happened was I stood there watchin', just drinkin' in the sight. And I was just about to raise my hand and tap on the window, surprise them both, when Mae . . . well, she reached over and touched Walter's cheek. The same way she used to touch mine.'

The old shoulders moved in a gesture of defeat. 'I knew it was over then. I just turned right around from that window and walked away. Never looked back.'

Anger swept my pity away. 'You just left? Without even talking to her? Old man, if you loved her, why the hell didn't you go inside and fight for her?'

His voice grew tough, defensive. 'Fight with what? The paltry little amount I had in my pocket? And me still wearin' my worn-out old farm clothes, with newspaper inside my shoes to fill in the holes, while Walter's there with his farm next door, lookin' so prosperous and like he could give her the world?'

Horrified, I felt tears sting my eyes. 'Maybe the world wasn't what she wanted, old man! Maybe she'd rather have had you.'

Gramps fell silent. But he looked at me shrewdly, and finally he said, 'You're mighty hot under the collar about somethin' that happened all those years ago. You sure it's *me* we're talkin' about here?'

I threw up my hands. 'Oh, never mind! Hand me your dish, I'll take it out. It's time we got some sleep.'

We slept on the floor by the hearth, me in my sleeping bag, him wrapped up in a heavy quilt. For awhile I watched him in the fading firelight, his scrawny chest rising and falling, a strand of stringy hair stuck to his damp cheek.

If the old man wasn't lying – and I had to keep in mind that he might be lying – he had given me a gift tonight.

No one had ever told me things about my grandmother. None of the important things, anyway, like the fact that she cooked a wonderful pork roast, or laid a table with good family linen and china. (Hell, I'd never known our family had any good china.)

Or, that she loved lilacs . . . my favorite flower.

No one ever tells you the important things, it seems.

Chapter 10

At nine-thirty the next morning I went down to see Mrs Binty. She had been deep-frying doughnuts for hours. It used to be cinnamon rolls, but last Halloween she got this great new recipe from Toni Langella's mom and there have been hot, homemade doughnuts all over the place ever since. That can be either a blessing or a curse.

'I'm getting fat from all this,' I complained as I helped her carry coffee and a heaping plate of crullers into the front room.

'Nonsense. Those are the same nice bluejeans you wore last winter, Jesse.'

'But they're tight now. And I'm too short to be this fat.'

Mrs B., whose feet barely touched the floor when she sat in her armchair opposite me, raised a birdlike brow. 'You've been a size eight ever since I've known you, dear. That could hardly be called fat.'

'Even so . . . maybe I can worry it off.'

I leaned over the fireplace and poked at logs until they were blazing. Despite a heavy tunic-length sweater over my pants, I'd nearly frozen just coming down the stairs.

'Speaking of trouble –'

'Were you, dear?'

'Where's that miserable cat?'

'Samantha ran off, dear, the minute she heard you coming.'

'Thank God.' I'd gotten her trained at last. 'And Gramps?'

'Your grandfather? Why, I don't know.'

'He's not down here? I thought he must be taking a shower or something.'

'No, dear, I haven't seen him yet this morning.'

Damn. Gramps and I had eaten breakfast together around eight, standing at the kitchen sink. We'd had leftovers: tender hunks of stew beef on crusty rolls, with coffee. 'You eat this kind of breakfast a lot?' I'd asked.

'Only when I'm lucky, gal. Only when I'm lucky.'

But I hadn't seen him in the last hour. I crossed to the front windows, pulling back lace curtains and looking up and down the snow-covered street. Miami was across the way, motor running, windows steamed.

Even with the heater on, had he really slept in that car instead of taking a room? This was one motivated employee.

But why hadn't he followed Gramps, wherever the hell he'd gone? 'He couldn't have gotten far,' I mused, 'without a car or money.'

'That never stopped you,' Mrs Binty pointed out.

She was right. My wheels were always getting stolen or breaking down; over the years, I'd become intimate friends with the RTD.

Now and then, however, I get to borrow Mrs Binty's ancient Olds. It's sturdy and strong, and has less than 8,000 miles on its pristine engine. At the moment it was parked in the Flynn's garage next door, while my furniture took up space over here. But if I could think up a way to steal Mrs Binty's Olds without her ever finding out, I would. I covet that car like a newly widowed man covets a neighbor's wife, for its workhorse value alone.

'He's such a delightful man,' my landlady said. 'Your grandfather. So charming, and a brilliant sense of humor.'

'Uh-huh.' Gramps must really have laid it on.

I sat across from her, and she leaned forward anxiously, almost spilling her coffee. 'You're not still going to Los Angeles, are you, Jesse? I'm sorry about all the mess and bother upstairs. I've been meaning to run up there and see how it's coming along –'

'No, everything's fine, really. They're doing a great job . . .' I hesitated. 'I did want to talk to you again about that wallpaper. It's a bit, uh, busy, don't you think?'

'Wallpaper?'

'All those . . . butterflies?'

Mrs Binty looked confused. She set her delicate china cup on the table and shook her head. 'I don't remember ordering wallpaper, dear. No, I'm quite sure I didn't, in fact.'

'Butterflies, big as dinosaurs?'

She shook her head firmly. Then, in the wink of an eye, confusion became chagrin. Her lower lip trembled.

Reaching over, I took Mrs B's hand and held it gently. 'You said the pattern was something you remembered from when you were a little girl.'

She leaned her head back and closed her eyes. 'I don't remember it now,' she said tiredly. 'Not at all.'

I moved a finger lightly over the thin, papery flesh and gave her hand a light squeeze. 'Hey, it's great wallpaper, now that I think of it. Brightens things up on a day like today.'

Outside, snow was blowing about in frantic tornadoes of white. Inside, storms of frustration raged behind Mrs Binty's closed eyes. You could see it in the way her facial muscles twitched.

She sat straight and gave me a determined look. 'I'll go up there right now. I'll have them tear it off.'

I could imagine the bill she'd get for that. 'Don't you dare. I'm starting to like it. Honest.'

What was I saying? 'Maybe if you just told them to stop.'

She didn't look convinced, but finally she nodded. 'Yes, that's what I'll do. Right away.' Then her mind shifted, and her lip trembled again, though she obviously tried to still it. 'You never did tell me. Are you going to Los Angeles, Jesse?'

'No. At least, not right away.'

'But you are going?'

I gave a shrug.

'Will you . . . will you come back?'

I smiled and put more certainty into my voice than I felt. 'Of course. Nobody *lives* in LA. Not if they can help it.'

'Well, you said you were writing a screenplay. Isn't Los Angeles where screenwriters live?'

'I'm not a screenwriter, I'm a dabbler.'

'I just don't . . .' My landlady's voice faded. 'I don't know where I'd find another friend like you.'

'Me too. You.' I drank my coffee, ate a cruller, and hiked on back upstairs – wondering with every step how I'd break it to her, if I did decide to stay in LA.

Chapter 11

Gramps and I were supposed to be at Harrigan's by noon. It was eleven-twenty-five and the old guy still hadn't returned. I had a terrible sinking thought, and went to the closet in my bedroom, yanking open the door.

Sure enough. His duffle bag was gone.

My first reaction was anger: *Dammit, he's bailed on me at the last minute.* My second – one I nearly didn't admit, even to myself – was a fleeting sadness that he'd left.

I was looking out the window, picking up the phone to call Abe at the pool hall, tell him our scam was off, when I saw Grumps trudging along the sidewalk, his face a ruddy red from the cold. I watched him approach, realizing that he hadn't taken my anorak, but wore his own unlined denim jacket. He must have bought it second-hand; it swallowed him up and left far too many air pockets to be filled with chill winds from Lake Ontario. He hadn't worn my boots, either, but his old canvas tennis shoes with the cut-out spots over each little toe, for the corns.

I stood at the top of the stairs as he thumped snow off. Folding my arms, I tapped a foot, and by the time he started up I'd worked from worry to anger, like a mother whose missing kid has just been found.

'Where the hell have you been? You shouldn't be wandering around alone. What if Noonan's here by now? What if they'd gotten hold of you, and I wasn't there? And how did you get past the Tan, anyway?' *Tap, tap.* 'Get in here. You're letting in a draft.'

Gramps eased past me and shivered his way into my living room. His tone was offended. 'I may be over eighty, gal, but I ain't exactly stupid. I been takin' care of myself a mighty long time.'

'I don't care. As long as you're under my roof –' I broke off, horrified at hearing Mom's voice come out of my mouth. 'Look, I just want to know where you were. What were you doing?'

'Takin' a little walk, that's all. Lordy! Where's the fire, anyway?'

'Forget the fire. Where exactly is your duffle bag?'

He headed for the kitchen. 'Took it to the airport, of course. Put it in a locker so's it'll be there when I get there tonight.'

'Are you telling me you walked all the way to the airport? In this weather? I don't believe it.'

'Why not? It ain't that far.'

He was right; I'd done it a few times myself. Straight out Brooks and you're there – a pleasant jaunt, spring or fall. But in a near blizzard? The old man's determination, and cunning, astounded me.

'Anyway, you gotta plan these things ahead, gal. It's the little things that can trip you up, the details.' He poured himself a cup of black coffee and swilled it down.

'But I would have done that for you. I'd've gotten it to you later, somehow.'

He shook his head. 'They'll be watchin' you, gal. No sense in takin' the risk they'd see us together.'

'You risked Miami following you to the airport. And come to think of it, just how did you give him the slip?'

His pale gray eyes went crafty on me. 'I got my ways, gal.'

'What ways?'

'Nothin' you need to know.'

'Old man, you're not as smart as you think. They've got

someone watching the airport. If they saw you put that duffle bag in a locker, they'll know you're planning to fly out soon.'

'Well, now, that doesn't matter, does it? What I'm plannin' this mornin', that is? Not if we play our parts right at Harrigan's. Ain't that the whole point?'

I sighed. He was absolutely right.

Even so, it was a risk I'd rather he hadn't taken.

And what the hell was so important in that duffle bag? The missing five thousand dollars? I wished I'd gotten a look inside it while I'd had the chance. *Stupid.* I'd been so caught up in Gramps' stories last night . . .

Still angry, I went to the closet for my anorak, where Gramps had hung it the night before. I stood there thinking, and finally I took out an extra scarf and two sweaters. The old boy was looking blue again; his blood must have really thinned out since living in Florida.

I'd be glad when he was safely in LA.

'So this is the Harrigan's you been talkin' about,' Gramps said, looking around from our booth toward the rear. 'Used to be owned by an ex-cop?'

'An ex-cop who was crooked. Except for Grady North and a few others, cops don't come here much anymore. It's a reporters' hangout now.'

It was the same old Harrigan's though – stained glass over the bar, blue-tinted windows across the front over a waist-high, used-brick wall.

That was from inside. Outside, there was more graffiti than ever, and kids hung out dealing and whoring. Usually, there's some nineties version of *West Side Story* going on. Skin tone aside, the kids all want to be George Chakiris these days.

Hypothetical question: did *West Side Story* set things up for all time? Did it glamorize gangs so much that we now have this takeover of our city streets? Except that what we have is a bastardization: Hollywood gone amuck. And gangs are so 'in' now in Hollywood, I hear you've got to fit them into every screenplay in order for it to be commercial. It's the nineties version of the obligatory car chase.

So let's see now . . . how to fit the Crips and the Bloods into a story about an aging grifter and his granddaughter who is so smart she outwits him at every turn . . .

As for Genesee Street, I still walk down here at night alone, but that's only because the Genesee Three have put the word out that anyone who even touches a hair on my chinny-chin-chin will have their balls fried in oil and served up for brunch in the morn. I wouldn't advise most honest citizens to come waltzing down here at night without a billy club and ten canisters of mace at hand.

So you can see, I feel honored.

Gramps must have been reading my mind. 'You just love it, don't you, girl?' He peered at me knowingly across the table.

'Love what?'

'Livin' in the city. Takin' risks. Knowin' anything can happen, that when you wake up in the morning life may turn out to be a whole different pot of stew from yesterday.'

'I guess I like that. Why? What's wrong with it?'

'Not a thing.' Gramps cackled through his Harrigan's Special, salami and cream cheese. 'Not a thing. Just means you're more like me than you think.' He wiped his chin with the back of his sleeve.

I frowned, still irritated from earlier. 'Didn't anyone ever teach you any manners?'

'Manners ain't much use on the road, girl.'

'And will you stop calling me *girl*?'

'Somebody has to remind you of your gender.'

'Now what the hell does that mean?'

He waved a skinny hand. 'Well, look at you . . . always in jeans and some boy-jacket or shirt. Don't you ever wear a dress?'

Used to – when I went out with Marcus. Now and then.

'Dresses are for Barbie dolls,' I said.

'Men like to see a little leg, girl.'

'Yeah? Well, men can suck ice water.'

'Holy Mother Mary!' Gramps gave a fake shudder. 'You really think you're tough, don't'cha?'

'I don't think it, I know it. Now eat your sandwich – the one *I bought you* – and aren't you glad I'm independent and *masculine* enough to pick up the tab?'

I chomped down on my own lunch, for once a *real* corned beef and rye.

We'd finished eating. I checked my watch: twelve-forty-seven. Miami, whom we'd left freezing his tush off in the street, still hadn't come in. The guy was tough, I'd give him that. I'd have sworn he'd have joined us by now.

Meanwhile, the scene in Harrigan's was as usual. Harve was mixing drinks at the bar and talking to a couple of sports reporters I knew from the *Times-Union*. One, Hank Crebbets, sat sideways on his stool. He glanced my way and gave me a smile and a half-wave. I nodded back. Every few minutes someone new drifted in, the usual crowd from the *Times* and its esteemed competition, the *Democrat-Chronicle*.

My gaze slid to Becky Anderson, one of Harrigan's regulars now. I'd thought it odd at first, the Total Woman suddenly having lunch nearly every day on Genesee Street. But then I realized she came here to watch me – to do what I did, in an effort to be more like the person she perceived me to be.

I'd found that truly touching. For about ten minutes. After that, it became a downright pain.

Until now.

Becky was eating a sandwich that was fat with sprouts. She pulled some out, laid them delicately on her plate, and flicked a nervous look at Gramps and me. Probably wondering if, after yesterday, I'd be coming over to pop her one in the nose. I surprised my nemesis by flashing a smile her way.

Then my side vision caught movement at the door. Coming through it was none other than Mac Devlin.

What the hell? Mac never hung out here. Not anymore. But he was in fact coming through Harrigan's door, and this was someone I hadn't expected to see, someone who could get in the way.

Shit. Mac headed for the bar, then looked our way and paused. He veered and came toward us. The corners of his mouth tilted into his best sardonic smile, the square jaw lifting in a cocky way that had turned a few hearts – including mine, last spring. He wore the same leather jacket that I'd first seen him in, with the silver wings on the lapels. His pilot's cap was at a jaunty angle.

The eyes were something else. There was a new wariness, and perhaps even some leftover hurt.

Not that Mac would express it aloud. He was far too macho for that.

'Hey, now,' he said with a jaunty grin, as he slid into the seat beside me. 'Haven't seen you in a coon's age, gal.' He looked at me, then at Gramps.

'Mac. Hi. This is my, uh . . . grandfather.'

Gramps stretched out a hand across the booth. 'Johnny James. Pleased ta meet'cha.' His eyes bounced back and forth from Mac to me, full of speculation. *Aha, a man in the picture, at last*, I could hear him thinking.

Sorry, Gramps. You're a few months late for that one.

'Nice to meet *you*,' Mac said. 'Seems to me I read about your exploits in the paper last night.'

'Wasn't nothin',' Gramps said, grinning. 'A little adventure, that's all.'

'I guess adventures run in the family.' Mac gave me a pointed look.

'She lead you a merry chase?'

'Don't know how merry,' Mac said.

Gramps' expression was sympathetic. *Know just what you mean.*

'Can we move this conversation along?' I said crossly.

But it was true I'd led Mac Devlin a merry chase. All the way from Rochester to the Thousand Islands to Arizona and back last spring – only to leave him high and dry at the end. One more man who thought I was poison these days.

Still, you don't get off scot-free. Sometimes in the late afternoons, in those hours between four and six when I can't drink anymore to forget, I remember the Thousand Islands, and lying in Mac's arms beneath a sky full of springtime stars. I also remember thinking I could explain to Marcus what happened, later, and the hurt that passed through his eyes when I tried.

I never want to do that again, never want to see that kind of pain or be the cause of it again.

'Mac has a charter flying service here at the airport,' I told Gramps. 'He also works for the Davies School for Executive Bodyguards. The first time I met Mac he blew me up.'

Gramps looked startled, and Mac laughed. 'Fake explosives. Jesse was doing research out at Davies, and part of my job was to rig a building to "blow up" around the students, see how they'd react. It was pretty much smoke and mirrors.'

'Smoke and deafening noise would be more like it,' I said, smiling at the memory. 'My ears tingled for a week.'

'You learn that sort of thing in Nam?' Gramps said.

'Actually, I did more flying in Nam.'

'Seat o' the pants sort of thing?'

'Skimmed a few trees.' Mac allowed with a grin. 'Learned to fly growin' up in Oklahoma though.' He turned to me. 'You're lookin' good, gal.'

Mac, come to think of it, had always called me gal. Between him and Gramps, I was beginning to feel like Pippi Long-stocking.

I wondered briefly what it was about some men that they insist on doing that even now, when it's not 'politically correct'. Maybe they're wistful sometimes for the days when they brought home the bacon and found the little woman in an apron, baking cookies in the kitchen.

Hell, I'm wistful for those days sometimes myself. Not that I've ever actually known them – except in those old forties movies. When I was growing up, Mom waited tables to keep us in food while Pop drank. He'd lose one job after another, stumble around the house with his bottles of Genny beer, and

I'd clean them up and haul them out to the trash before Mom got home. That was about as close as I'd ever come to being a 'housewife', and a codependent one, at that.

Then I started to get a mind of my own, and I couldn't stand it that Mom didn't *do* something, that she didn't leave him, make a better life for herself, and me. I started hanging out on the streets with the kids in our neighborhood, mostly boys whose family situations were similar to mine. We heisted cars, jumped off bridges, hopped freight trains – all of us looking for some thrill, something that got our juices running, that told us even in the midst of a living death that we were indeed alive.

I looked at Mac Devlin, at the gray eyes similar to Gramps' in a way, but younger of course, and still a bit cautious beneath the cocky smile as they met mine. I'd involved Mac in one of my scams last spring, and the result was that he nearly died.

My eyes slid down to my watch. *One-oh-five*. Almost showtime.

'Mac . . . Gramps and I were talking. Do you mind?'

The smile faded. The eyes grew cool. 'As a matter of fact, I'm meeting a client at the bar.' Mac turned to Gramps, extending a hand. 'I hope we get to talk again, Mr James.'

'Me too,' Gramps said. 'Later, maybe?'

'Right.' Mac shoved his pilot's cap back with a finger and stood, not even giving me another look. His back was proud and stiff as he walked away.

Gramps leaned toward me. 'Boy, oh boy . . . you sure know how to decimate a man,' he said softly.

'Decimate? What kind of a word is that for a hobo?' I muttered. 'You been reading books on the road, old man?'

'I know more about things than you think, gal. And there's somethin' between you and that Devlin guy, ain't there?'

Used to be: Marcus Andrelli. But that was long ago and far away.

I frowned at my watch. 'One-oh-eight. Where the hell is Miami? Abe promised he'd have him in here before one-fifteen –'

I broke off as the Coppertone Kid came through the door, right on schedule, slapping his hands against his upper arms to warm them. He looked around, saw us, and took a seat at a table so close I could almost feel his icy breath. Unzipping his brown parka, he sneezed, grabbing a paper napkin off the table to cover it. Beneath the parka was a thin tropical-print shirt. Miami pulled his watchcap off, revealing sun-bleached hair that was parched-looking and flattened down. The tips of his ears were red.

Harve came over from the bar to take his order. 'Coffee,' Miami said. 'Nice and hot, and plenty of it.'

'Sure,' Harve said. 'I'll bring you a pot.'

He glanced over at us. 'Get you anything else, Jesse?'

'I'll have another cup.'

He looked at Gramps.

'Me too.'

'Be right back.' Harve walked away, his red hair bright as flames in the meager light that seeped into the bar. I checked out the scene again, now that our one-man audience had arrived.

Mac had met up with his client, someone I didn't recognize, and they'd left together. For that I was glad. Hank Crebbets, the *Times-Union* sports reporter, however, was still at the bar. That was good. There were other people on stools or at tables, most of whom I'd known for years. Perhaps twenty-five souls, all told, a few of them former co-workers from the *Herald*.

In her corner, Becky Anderson had finished up her lunch and was standing.

I looked over at Gramps, felt my adrenaline start to run, and raised my voice a bit. 'You've got something on your chin, old man. Wipe it off.'

He lifted a napkin and dabbed with it. 'Girl, you are the most critical person I ever did know.'

'And you're a slob. God, I will be so damned glad when you're gone.'

'You think so, do you?'

'You are trouble, old man. And I'm sick of it.'

Gramps stuck out his chin. 'Trouble, is it now? Gal, you don't know the meanin' of the word.'

'Like hell. Since you've been here I could write a dictionary.'

'Now, I remember back in seventy-five –'

I slammed down my coffee cup. 'I don't give a shit about seventy-five! I've been listening to your damned stories for twenty-four hours, *ad nauseam*.'

His voice rose to a whine. 'Little girl, you oughta be ashamed, talkin' to yer own grandpappy that way. Yer own kin.'

'And don't give me anymore of that 'kin sticks together' shit! Where were you when my father was growing up? Where were you when he needed somebody to teach him how to be a man?'

He flushed. 'Now don't go blamin' me for that. If his mama had done a better job –'

I half rose from the booth and grabbed his shirt by the collar. 'Don't you dare say a word about my grandmother. She did the best she could – after you ran off and left her alone to raise *your kid*.'

'All right, all right!' He threw up his hands to fend me off. 'Don't get yourself all in an uproar.'

I gave a flick that sent him back against the booth. "You really think this is funny, don't you? You think you can waltz into town and act like you never did anything wrong, and I'll welcome you back with open arms. But it doesn't work that way, old man. The things you did sixty years ago have tainted my whole fucking life!'

Harve appeared with the coffees, and I saw that the entire assemblage had turned our way – not only Miami, but Becky Anderson, who had paused in the act of putting tip money on her table, her nose twitching like a pointer after a big fat bird.

'Easy, now,' Harve clucked like a mother hen. He set the coffees down. 'Let's just have a peaceful day, here, okay? How about if I bring you both some nice warm soup?'

'I don't want soup,' I said, folding my arms and glaring at Gramps. 'I want this good-for-nothing bum out of my life.'

'You know I ain't got no place to go,' Gramps whined.

'Jess?' Harve turned to me, his expression worried. 'If your grandfather needs a place to stay, there's the back room here –'

'No.'

'I just might take you up on that,' Gramps began.

'I said *no*. This is my territory, my home, and I'm telling you, I don't want you here.'

The phone began to jangle at the bar. 'Look, I gotta go,' Harve said. 'You two gonna be all right?'

'We're fine,' I said.

'Well, I don't want you killing each other while I'm gone.'

'I said, we're *fine*.'

He left us, casting an uneasy glance back. It wouldn't be the first time an argument blossomed into a fistfight in here.

Gramps and I stirred our coffees.

'I know I ain't been good company,' he said appeasingly. 'If I didn't have so many worries . . . and if *Asshole* over there would just leave me alone –' He cast a sullen glance at Miami, who was looking wary and depressed.

'I'm just doin' my job,' Miami said.

'Yeah, well, just so you know, Noonan only sent you up here because you're no good for nuthin' else.' Gramps' tone was scornful.

Miami half rose, shoving back his chair. 'You wanta say that again?'

'Yeah, I wanta say it again. You're good for nuthin', Asshole. Got it?'

I slapped my hand on the table. 'Stop it, old man! There, you see what I mean? You can't leave things alone. You've got to pick and pick till you've got an open wound.'

'I didn't open those wounds of *yours*, gal. That Andrelli fella did. You gonna take that out on every man you see?'

'You old –' *Dammit, this wasn't in the script. For a moment, I was speechless.*

'See, you ain't got nuthin' to say to that.' Gramps cackled. 'You know I'm right.'

Heat rose in my face. 'You are out of bounds, old man.'

'Sure I am. Everybody's out of bounds with you. You got yourself so locked-up tight, ain't nobody can get through.'

'Shut up,' I said softly. 'Stop this now.'

He gestured to Miami. 'You and what's-'is-name over there – you'd make a good pair. Both of you numb. *Hee-hee.* 'Course, *you're* numb in the heart. With him it's the nuts.'

Miami's chair screeched on the wooden floor. 'That does it. Outside, asshole.'

'You gonna make me?'

'I am.'

'You and who else?'

'Oh, for God's sake. You're both acting like a couple of kids.' But I slid from the booth, relieved. We were back into script again.

'You stay out of this,' Miami warned. 'This is between the old man and me.'

I planted my hands on my hips. 'I don't remember giving you a choice.'

Miami reached for Gramps. I stepped in and grabbed Miami's arm, then came down on his instep with the heel of my boot. He howled and doubled over, grabbing for the foot.

Gramps yelled from beside me, 'Stand back now, gal. I can handle this turd.'

'The hell you can! Go away, old man, get out of here. *Now.*'

Miami straightened and pulled back an arm. I saw the fist coming, but couldn't get out of the way fast enough. He caught my cheek with a glancing blow. I stumbled back.

Gramps, who was almost two heads shorter, let out an angry bellow. He threw a punch at Miami that landed in the solar plexus. Miami *whuffed* and doubled again. But the guy was like one of those birds that keeps dipping its beak in a water glass. He kept bobbing back up. Before he could land a return punch, I caught his arm, gave it a twist, and kicked the back of his calf. He yelped and tried to break away. I hung on.

'That's it, gal, keep him right like that!' Gramps hopped up and down, fists in position and a thumb flicking at his chin. He took aim.

But before he could swing, Harve yelled out from the bar. 'That's enough! – all of you! Quit it. Right now!'

I saw him reach for the billy club he keeps there, the one that Pat Harrington used in the old days, to break up fights between cops. Harve leaped over the bar, red hair flying, and headed our way. By now everyone was watching with fascination.

Becky stood several feet away, visions of bylines clearly dancing in her head.

Harve got between Gramps and Miami. I loosened my hold on Miami and stood back, raising my hands, palms out. 'Okay, okay, Harve. It's cool. Take it easy.'

Miami glared at me and rubbed his calf. 'I'll get you for this.'

'Listen to the big man!' Gramps taunted. He was still bobbing up and down on his toes like an old prize fighter. I wouldn't have bet two cents on what might happen if a bell sounded anywhere nearby.

'Shut up, Gramps,' I said.

He weaved closer.

Harve pushed at his shoulder. 'Enough, now! Get back.'

'He still has to apologize for hittin' my grandgal.'

'I ain't apologizin' to nobody,' Miami said sullenly. 'You and your fucking granddaughter can eat shit.'

Harve spun around then, his face flaming as bright as his hair. He pointed the billy club at Miami. 'Listen, I don't know who you are, sewer mouth, but nobody talks about Jesse that way.'

'Yeah!' Gramps advanced behind Harve.

'Say you're sorry,' Harve ordered. He jammed the billy club against Miami's throat.

'For God's sake, stop it, all of you!' I yelled.

This had gone far enough. Where the hell were the Genesee Three?

Harve leaned against the club, giving it all his weight, and nearly knocked Miami off his feet.

Miami pointed a finger in Gramps' direction. 'You're not

gettin' away. Noonan knows where you are. And that bitch broad is goin' down with you.'

Gramps bounded forward, pushing Harve aside, and landed a solid punch on Miami's chin. Miami grunted. His face screwed up in pain. He checked for blood, then doubled up his fist and swung.

Gramps danced away, just missing it. 'C'mon . . . c'mon,' he taunted again, rubbing his fingers together.

Harve tried to move in, but I was closer. I grabbed for Miami, my arms around his waist. 'Stop it! And you, old man – damn you, you've done it again! You are nothing but a goddamn screw-up.'

There were crowds of people around us. Reporters scribbled furiously. Out of the corner of my eye I spotted Abe and Rack coming through the door. *Thank God*. Rack still carried a pool cue from Jimmy's. I shouted at him. 'Help me stop these idiots before somebody gets hurt!'

They surged forward and into the fray. Abe got Gramps from behind with an arm around his chest. Rack grabbed Miami away from me, jabbing the tip of his cue deep into the Tan's fleshy neck.

Harve stood back, looking cheated out of the action.

Abe addressed Gramps and Miami in a slow, deceptively soft voice. 'Gentlemen, you are in my territory. I would consider it a kindness if you would wrap it up now and go home.'

'In a pig's eye!' Gramps sputtered.

'Please, Mr James. Make it easier on Jesse, if you do.'

Gramps turned uncertainly to me.

'The only thing that would make it easier,' I said coldly, 'is if you were out of my life.'

Miami squirmed. Rack gave a jerk to the pool cue. 'Bet this thing could fit down your throat and all the way to your toes.'

'Look, I'm just the messenger,' Miami said quickly. 'You don't shoot the messenger.'

'Seems you have a bit of a mouth on you, messenger.' Rack

smiled at Abe. 'Maybe we should just step outside and wash it out.'

Abe nodded. 'Do that. I'll get Jesse's grandfather out of here.' He had a grip on Gramps' shoulder that was making him wince.

Rack shoved Miami out the door. Abe waited a few moments, giving them a head start. Gramps turned to me with a grin of bravado mixed with uncertainty. 'You sure handled that guy, Jesse girl.'

'You are goddamned lucky I was here,' I said angrily. 'You could have gotten yourself killed – and no telling how many others.'

The grin faded. 'He was a lightweight, girl. He wasn't no match for us.' His voice quivered. 'We make a real team, don't we? You and me?'

'I told you, I don't want to team up with you. A man who'd leave his wife and child and never call once in sixty years to see if they were even alive? You're a loser. You'll never be anything else. Old man, I've worked my ass off to forget I've got blood like yours running through my veins. Now, will you get the hell out of my life?'

Gramps flinched. His frail body trembled. He glanced at the people who surrounded us, listening – some of them still writing furiously. His face flushed with embarrassment.

'I guess I knew it wouldn't work,' he said, his voice no more than a croak. 'Like they say . . . you can't go home.'

I folded my arms and didn't respond.

A heavy silence fell over the bar, thick with sympathy now for Gramps, the underdog. If looks could kill, I'd have died on the spot.

Abe said softly, 'C'mon, Gramps. I'll take you home.'

'Ain't got a home,' Gramps said heavily. 'Guess I ain't got one anywhere, now.'

Abe picked up the thin denim jacket from our booth. 'Here, put this on,' he said. Gramps sort of shuffled, bent over, as Abe let him to the door. At one point he paused, looked back, and said shakily, 'Grandgal?'

I turned my back. The door opened and closed. Cold air swept in.

My eyes met Becky Anderson's on the fringe of the crowd. She gave me a look of cold contempt, then turned on her heel and headed out into the street.

'There's nothing more here to see now,' Harve said briskly. 'Everyone back to your seats, please. Free drinks all the way around.'

There were less than a dozen people left, those few who hadn't run at the first hint of trouble for fear they'd end up in the midst of a shooting spree. A couple of reporters had disappeared; the others returned to their stools or tables good-naturedly.

I sank into the booth again, my head in my hands, nerves shot.

Harve touched my shoulder. 'Can I get you something, Jesse? More coffee?'

I wanted a drink. A belly-soothing, nerve-smoothing drink. I wanted it more than I'd ever wanted anything in my life.

'Maybe some of that soup,' I said.

The soup was potato and leek, thick with butter and cream. I gulped it down and eventually my hands stopped shaking. People who'd been staring went back to their own business.

Pulling out my notebook I drank coffee and pretended to work, as I often did here. But I couldn't stop thinking: how much of my tirade against Gramps was real, coming from somewhere way inside? Just as his had turned real, had mine, too?

That's the thing about insults. Even when they're planned – a farce – the truth can all too easily out.

It seemed like hours before the call came. Every time the phone rang I kept thinking it was for me. Finally, an hour and ten minutes later, it was.

Harve picked up. 'Harrigan's.'

I saw him nod. 'Yeah, she's here. Sure.' He raised his voice. 'Jesse? For you.'

'Who is it?'

He spoke into the phone again and listened.

'Grady North,' he said.

I crossed over, taking the receiver and standing by Hank Crebbets' elbow.

'Grady? What is it?'

I listened to him talk.

'Oh, my God . . .'

I could feel people listening, ears perking up. 'I'll be right there.' I set the phone down and leaned weakly against the bar.

'What's wrong?' Harve said. 'Jesse, you okay?'

I turned and ran for the booth, grabbing up my notebook and purse.

'Jesse, what's wrong?'

'The river. Somebody saw him . . . they called it in . . .'

I nearly broke my neck on the treacherous ice as I ran for my car.

Chapter 12

I stood on the river bank near the First Federal plaza, a few blocks south of the *Herald* and the Water Street Grill. There were several squad cars in the nearby street, an ambulance, a rescue truck, and a van marked ROCHESTER POLICE DEPARTMENT, SCUBA SQUAD. Milling about me were over a dozen cops, some in wet suits.

Becky Anderson and Nicky Ludgett had already arrived. Becky was interviewing onlookers as Nicky snapped away like a hungry hawk. Steve Bates from the crime desk appeared right after me. They always send him out on jumpings. He's an old-time reporter – not too factual, a bit of a drunk.

The water was murky and gray, with huge floes of ice that sped upstream so fast, they might have been propelled by an underwater turbine. Wet snow had begun to fall in the last hour, and the wind chill index, according to the car radio, was thirty degrees below. I shivered and hugged myself, frozen to the core.

'Jesse . . .' Grady North came up behind me. 'I'm so sorry.'

Off to the side, Nicky Ludgett moved in for a reaction.

'It . . . it must be very cold down there,' I said, not taking my eyes off the water.

Grady stumbled around verbally, trying in his awkward way to be gentle. 'Jesse, the person who called, the one who saw him jump –'

'Who was it? Is he here?'

'No. The call was anonymous, came from a phone booth outside First Fed. Jess . . . the thing is, the call didn't come in time. The witness said he had trouble finding a phone, and that was more than thirty minutes ago. Even if your grandfather survived the fall, there's the temperature of the water, and the current . . .'

'I know.'

'They've got boats out all along the river looking for him. And a couple of divers went down. But to keep them in the water, given the circumstances . . .'

'Doesn't make sense. I know.'

Grady, who had been there in much the same way when Pop died, put a hand on my shoulder. I turned and shoved my face against his coat.

'I was just getting to know him,' I said. 'Do you know what he did last night? He cooked the most wonderful stew, and we watched old movies . . .'

Grady smoothed my hair. 'Do you know why he did it?'

I pulled back and saw Becky edge closer – her notebook, pen, and thin leather gloves soaked from the pelting snow. 'It's all my fault, Grady. Dammit, it's all my fault.'

'What do you mean?'

'We had an argument.'

'You and your grandfather?'

'Yes. Just now, at Harrigan's. I told him he was a loser, and I yelled at him. I told him to get out of my life.'

Grady looked up at Becky and at Steve Bates, who had now followed her over. He turned us away from them slightly, lowering his voice. 'This fight. Did it have something to do with the trouble you were telling me about yesterday?'

'Yes. And I lost it. Dammit, Grady, first Pop, now him . . .'

'Jess, I'm sure –'

I shook my head. 'You don't understand. It's the middle of the goddamned winter, Grady, and he didn't have any place to go. The poor old guy was at the end of his rope. And I tossed him out on his ear.'

Grady was silent. He knew my background; he knew how often I'd screwed up and hurt people who didn't deserve it. So did Becky Anderson. No one could honestly argue with me.

Joe Rodriguez, the head of the scuba squad, trudged up from the edge of the river. He was dressed in a heavy ski parka and hip-high boots.

'Jesse, hi. The uh, the jumper . . . I hear he was your grandfather?'

I'd interviewed Joe a couple of times in the past, as a reporter. His dark eyes were sympathetic.

I nodded.

'I'm real sorry. We'll keep the boats circling awhile. And we're searching the banks all along the river. But if he hasn't surfaced by now . . .'

'Why don't you go on home,' Grady said gently. 'I'll call you myself if we find anything.'

We walked back up the bank toward the group of cops. Joe talked to them, just out of earshot. I saw a few heads nod. But their mood was somber as they began to fold up equipment: medic boxes, a stretcher, inhalation machines. They seemed reluctant to give up. One young cop in a wet suit said, 'I wouldn't mind going down . . . take one more look around.'

Joe Rodriguez shook his head. 'There really isn't –' He glanced apologetically at me. 'As soon as there's a break in the weather, we'll start again.'

The cop nodded reluctantly. He joined the others in carrying equipment back to the van. The beat cops began to drift off to their squad cars. Several of them knew me and stopped to offer condolences. Their words were awkward, but sincere. I thanked them and accepted their gruff pats on the shoulder for as long as I could. But by this time I was drowning, myself – in guilt. This wasn't the lark I'd blithely envisioned it to be.

Shit, what had I done?

A dry drunk – that's what they call it when you come up with wild schemes and dreams, every bit as insane as if you were floating on an eighty-proof high. I kept forgetting that.

The wonder was that I'd gotten Gramps and the Three to go along with me.

Grady and I walked toward my car. When we were out of earshot of the press, I said, 'I need something to do. Did you get that information on Noonan I asked you for the other day?'

He reached into his inside coat pocket and pulled out a long, thin envelope. 'I brought it with me. Actually, I thought at first that this thing here today might be Barney Noonan's handiwork. But it turns out a couple of people saw your grandfather jump. No question of it being a homicide.'

'Really?' I struggled to hide my surprise. 'Who else saw it?'

'A couple of street people. They were sitting on those benches over there when it happened.'

But Rack had turned in a false report. And Gramps wasn't anywhere near here. Did the homeless guys just *think* they saw it happen? Or did they lie, hoping to be part of the drama?

I looked down at the envelope Grady handed me, and shoved it inside my jacket to keep it dry. 'Thanks.'

He put an arm around my shoulders and gave me a hug. 'I wish I'd been able to meet your grandfather, Jess.'

A young reporter I vaguely knew blocked our path. He was jittery, anxious to run off and call in his story. 'Lieutenant North, how long you think it might be before he turns up? I mean, if the river freezes, you think the body might not surface before spring?'

'Excuse me,' Grady said coldly. He elbowed the reporter out of our way and hustled me to my car.

Nicky, who had been snapping furiously, called after us. 'Jesse! Just one full-face shot, okay?'

I didn't even yell at him. I just stared. At him, and at Steve Bates, who hadn't missed a word since my arrival on the scene. If this had been for real, I wouldn't have found a moment of privacy in which to grieve.

'If I can do anything else,' Grady said at the car, 'just call.'

'I will. Thanks.'

I watched him walk back to Joe Rodriguez, and felt another wave of remorse. I wanted out of here; I wanted to hide.

I wiped snow from my windshield with my sleeve, then crawled into my car. I was sticking my key in the ignition when Becky Anderson came up to my window and tapped on it.

Now what the hell? Reluctantly, I rolled the window down.

'I know, Jesse,' she said. Her bright blue eyes were hard as sapphires.

'Huh?'

'I know what you're doing. I know he's not dead.'

Oh, shit.

'That's crazy,' I said, my mouth dry.

'Remember when we worked together on the *Western Free Press* and you were looking for Daphne Malcross? I remember the sleight of hand you pulled to get that story. This is just one more scam, Jesse, I know it.'

'Becky, you think I'd have that old man jump –'

'Of course not. I don't know where your grandfather is, but he's not in that river.'

I began to sweat, despite the frigid temperature. I had to tell her something – get her off the scent before she blew the whole deal.

Nothing came to mind. Nothing at all. Except, 'Fuck off.'

I began to roll the window up.

'Oh, no, you don't!' Becky jammed her purse in the opening to stop it. 'Whatever you're up to, Jesse, I want an exclusive when it's over. Either that, or I go over there right now –' she nodded toward Grady and the other cops – 'and I tell them what you've done.'

I leaned on the steering wheel, staring despondently through the windshield at the wiper blades going whish, whish, whish. Grady would have my ass if he even suspected Becky's accusation was true. I might even be brought up on charges – and then I'd never get to Florida tonight.

Besides, I'd promised Abe. He couldn't be involved.

'Okay,' I said finally, sighing. 'You've got me, Becky.'

'You'll give me the exclusive?'

'Yes.'

She nodded, the eyes hard, sure, certain.

'You're damned good,' I said, 'I'll also give you that.'

'Remember it,' she said.

Chapter 13

Becky and I had a little talk, and after that I drove slowly through slush and occasional icy patches, watching for Miami, behind me. But he was nowhere in sight. I had to trust that he hadn't followed Gramps from Harrigan's to Marcus' apartment with Abe. Percy had driven, and he was good at ditching tails, so I wasn't honestly worried.

Becky Anderson was something else again. Could I trust her not to talk until this was over? Possibly. The story I'd promised her was bigger than the fact that Gramps was alive.

But would she trust me?

Oh, what a tangled web.

When I pulled into Mrs Binty's driveway, I saw her watching for me out the window that opened onto the porch. By the time I got to the porch steps she was outside shivering, a green and yellow knitted shawl pulled tightly around her shoulders.

'Hi,' I said. 'Got any coffee?'

'Jesse, I just heard on the news. Your grandfather . . .'

'I could really use something hot,' I said.

Lines of sympathy scored her face. 'I'm so sorry.' She touched my arm. 'Come inside.'

She led the way into her kitchen, where the scent of cinnamon still lingered from that morning's doughnuts. A large plate of them sat on the round oak table, stacked high. Christmas decorations were out now: Santa Claus salt and pepper shakers, potholders in the shape of trees, a red and green tablecloth.

I sat tiredly in a high-backed oak chair. Mrs Binty placed one of her delicate cups on the table, filled to the brim with steaming coffee.

She sat down and pushed the doughnuts toward me, along with a bright red napkin. Bless Mrs Binty. She believed food to be the best drug in town. Often, she was right.

'That poor, poor man. Jesse, you must stay downstairs with me now. It's nice and toasty here, and besides, dear, you shouldn't be alone.'

I picked up the coffee and sipped. I hated lying to my landlady, but I was afraid to trust her with the truth. She would promise not to tell, of course. But given her problems with memory, would she remember that promise later? What if Miami, or any of Barney Noonan's henchmen, showed up at her door?

'Do you want to talk about it?' she asked gently. 'Some people say it helps, but then again, others say it hurts too much.'

I dropped my cup with a small clatter. 'Oh, for heaven's sake. It's not like I knew him all my life or anything. And I don't even know for sure he was my grandfather. The man lied through his teeth – what little he had left.'

'Jesse!'

'It's true. Showing up like that after all these years, bringing me all his troubles.'

Her voice grew even more gentle. 'One doesn't speak ill of the dead, dear.'

'And that's another thing I never understood. Why can't people speak ill of the dead? It's not like they're going to hear it, or anything.'

Mrs Binty tsked. 'You waste so much energy trying to prove how tough you are. If you'd put all that to use in some productive way . . .'

I hadn't any answer for that.

Mrs Binty picked up a pile of red wool, a scarf she'd been knitting for a grandchild. 'How are your mother and Charlie, dear? Knit one, purl two.'

'They're in China right now, supposedly touristing. If I know Charlie, he's knee-deep in some nefarious scheme.'

A long silence. 'I suppose, now that your grandfather's gone . . .'

'What?'

'You'll be going to Los Angeles after all?'

I shrugged. How to break it to her that I was leaving tonight? And did it matter if anyone knew I was heading for Miami, not LA? Noonan would find out soon enough that I was there.

On the other hand, I'd prefer taking him by surprise.

'I suppose you could spend Christmas with your Aunt Edna,' Mrs Binty said with a sigh. 'Doesn't she live near Los Angeles?'

'If you call an eight-hour drive to Marin County 'near'. It's like traveling from Baltimore to Boston back here.'

'Still, dear, the world is such a lonely place these days, and one needs relatives, especially after a loss. If you feel you need to go . . .'

'Johnny James was no loss, Mrs B.'

'Eat a doughnut, dear.'

We sat in companionable near-silence, with only the click of knitting needles and the sound of the coffee pot as its automatic warmer turned on and off. Even Denny and Joey had stopped their relentless pounding upstairs.

'The thing I like about your doughnuts,' I said finally, pulling one apart and nibbling at the edges, 'is that they're crispy and brown on the outside but moist inside.'

Mrs Binty looked up from the red scarf. 'You have to fry them quickly, I think, to get that. You can't let them sit too long in the oil.'

'Mom used to try to make doughnuts when I was a kid, but they were always hard as rocks. You had to dunk them before you could bite into them.'

'Like biscotti,' Mrs Binty reflected. 'I've always wondered if they were first discovered by an Italian mother who got a bad batch of cookies.'

I laughed. 'How's that coming along?' I nodded toward the scarf.

She held it up so I could see the length. 'It's for Christmas. I have such a short time left to finish . . .' She glanced away and sighed.

'What?'

'Oh, I was going to make one for your grandfather, too. It's strange. He wasn't here any time at all, but I miss him.'

All of a sudden she doubled over, dropping her knitting and covering her eyes. Her shoulders shook, and from deep inside her tiny frame came a sad little cry.

'Mrs B?' I was shocked – stunned – to see her like this. I got up and ran around the table, kneeling to put an arm around her shoulders. 'What's wrong? What is it?'

She shook her head and made an effort to pull herself together, laughing softly. 'I don't know.'

I wiped at her eyes with a napkin. 'Is it Christmas? Are you worried about being alone?' We had always spent the holiday together – she and I, and even Marcus these past two years. He'd arrive in his limo, bearing packages of every size and shape, and I'd go on about that a little, accusing him of spending too much, of showing off.

But to be fair, his gifts were always thoughtfully chosen, like the electric comforter for Mrs Binty last year. She loved slipping into it when she sat on cold winter nights by the fire, reading. And that was another thing Marcus had given: books by all her favorite romance authors, enough to last her a month or two. He and Tark had wrapped them each separatedly one year in colorful gift wrap, so she'd have the fun of being surprised at every one. Then, later, Tark had come over, and Toni from next door . . .

I came back to the present as Mrs Binty said, 'There are just so many changes lately.' She took the napkin and dabbed at her eyes. 'I'm not very good with changes, I suppose.'

I sat on the chair closest to her, and held her other hand. 'I've put you through a lot since I moved here, haven't I?'

'Oh, Jesse, don't be silly! I've loved having you here.'

'Still.' I'd had people coming and going – mostly men, and mostly going – and now even I was threatening to leave.

I guess I'd thought it wouldn't matter. I do tend to think I won't ever be missed.

I dropped her hand and rubbed my forehead. 'Mrs B, please don't cry.'

She sniffled. 'I'm all right. Now don't you go feeling sorry for me.'

'No, what I mean is, there's really no reason to cry.'

Her chin went up bravely. 'Of course there isn't, dear. I'm fine.'

I sighed. 'What I'm trying to say is, I'll be home for Christmas. I promise.'

'You will?'

'Absolutely. And . . .' Oh, what the hell. 'There's something else, Mrs B. Gramps isn't dead.'

It was worth the risk, just to see light come back into her eyes.

Chapter 14

'Sorry about your grandfather,' Joey Martino said in my kitchen. 'Heard it on the TV.' He pushed his thick black hair off his forehead and checked me out for emotional bruises.

'It was on TV? Already?' I checked my watch. The timing wasn't bad.

'News break, right after *The Guiding Light*.'

'Oh.' I poured myself a glass of water and glanced at the little black and white TV. Geraldo was interviewing two people who, put together, must have weighed a thousand pounds.

'You watch *The Guiding Light*?' I said.

Joey shrugged, his face turning pink. 'Nah. It was just on.' Uh-huh.

'You look pretty worn out,' he said. 'Anything I can do?'

'You could leave me alone. Even better – you could stop it with that godawful wallpaper.' I peered into my near-empty fridge, then slammed the door.

'We already have. Jeez! You are the testiest woman alive. I try to offer a little sympathy . . .'

'I don't want a little sympathy. I want to make a phone call.'

'So here.' He shoved the phone my way. 'Why don't you just plug it into the living-room jack?'

'It's not comfortable out there. At least here I can sit on the counter.'

He shook his head and lowered himself to the floor, stretching out full-length on his stomach to eyeball the new kitchen vinyl for bubbles or something. You'd have thought he was Michelangelo, all the time he was taking.

Then I realized he was watching me. Trying to figure out if I was hiding my grief and would burst into tears without warning, I supposed. I tried to look suitably morose and punched in Marcus' number at the Rochester Towers.

It rang twice, then the machine came on with the Andrelli Enterprises announcement. 'Tark?' I said when it was over. I waited a minute to see if he'd pick up.

No answer. That was odd. He was supposed to be there to keep an eye on Gramps until his flight tonight.

There was a timid knock on my front door. I hung up.

'Jesse?' a soft voice called out. 'You home?'

'In the kitchen.'

Sneakered footsteps crossed the bare living-room floor. Toni Langella poked her head in. 'You okay?' she asked cautiously, fingering her long, dark hair.

'Sure I'm okay,' I said crossly. 'Why wouldn't I be okay?'

Toni circled around Joey and climbed nimbly onto the opposite counter. She sat with her knees drawn up and sticking out of the holes in her jeans. 'I was watching *The Guiding Light*. There was a news break, and they said . . . they said your grandfather . . .' Her voice went soft. 'I'm sorry, Jesse.'

'Jeesh, does everybody around here watch *The Guiding Light*?'

She smiled and gave a little shrug, knowing she wasn't supposed to answer. 'He was such a nice man.'

'You met him?' That was a surprise.

Toni's dark eyes lit up. 'He came over yesterday. We had a long talk.'

'You and my grandfather had a long talk? About what?'

She giggled. 'About you, of course. And boys.'

'About me – and boys?'

'Well, not in the same breath, of course. But he told me how neat he thought you were, and how it was so good to be here with you after all these years.' She fell silent. 'I'm sorry, Jesse.'

'Thanks.' I sighed. 'What about boys?'

Toni was fourteen and a gymnast, on her way to the Olympics if boys didn't interfere. Lately, she'd been trading hours at the gym for hours on the phone with girlfriends, during which she'd adopted the annoying teenage habit of giggling – about boys.

'Well, Gramps –' She hesitated. 'I hope you don't mind, he told me to call him Gramps. Anyway, Gramps said boys at my age only want one thing, and that I'd better give it to them or I'll never be able to hang onto one.'

'Toni!' I was shocked. 'That old –'

She giggled. 'I know, that's what I thought he meant too. It turned out he was talking about sports. "The trouble with most women," he said, "is they don't learn about sports, and they're always complaining when a guy wants to watch football or something."' She flipped her hair back and laughed. 'I told him my problem is that the boys I know complain about me working out so much at the gym.'

'Well, Gramps wasn't the most liberated of men.'

'Oh, he was just old-fashioned. He didn't mean anything by it. And he sure was proud of you.' She gave me a compassionate look. 'Were you down at the river?'

I nodded.

'Was it awful?'

I shrugged. 'It was cold.'

Her expression was wise beyond her years. 'It was awful.'

We were silent for several moments.

'Did they . . . did they find him yet?'

'No. They said . . . it, uh, might be a few days. Maybe even longer. The weather, you know. And the current.'

She sent me a consoling glance. 'Mrs Binty said the other day that you're going out to California.'

'Later. Not right now.'

'Will you be here for Christmas?'

'Yes.'

She smiled. 'I'm glad. I'd have missed you.'

'Me too.'

Joey Martino hoisted himself to his feet and stood, hands on his hips, scowling at us.

'Look, if you two are gonna get all schmaltzy, would you mind doin' it in the other room? I got work to do.'

Chapter 15

I had to leave for the airport by seven, so after Toni left I finished packing. I tried Tark again a couple of times, but still no answer.

I wasn't seriously worried. If there'd been any problem about getting Gramps to Marcus' apartment, Abe would have called. But according to Joey, there had been no messages. I did try to reach Abe at his place, just to double-check. He wasn't there, or at any of his usual hangouts.

I'd have to trust that Perce would get Gramps to the airport in time. My job was to see he got on that plane.

It was twenty before seven, and I didn't want to get there too early. I sat in the window seat in my bedroom, looking out. The street had been cleared, but in the yards there were still high drifts. In Mrs Binty's yard the old lilac bushes were weighted down with snow. Roses were bare sticks.

Winter is an ugly sight, a sight I hate – in fact, I hate November and December anyway. I always seem to lose people in December, one way or another. My mind drifted, accompanied by the drip of the water faucets a few feet away in my bathroom. Drip . . . drip . . . drip . . .

The hot and cold faucets in my bathroom have always been reversed, and when I first moved into the top of Mrs Binty's house I used to scald myself every time. I'd turn the faucet on thinking it was cold, and hot water would come steaming forth. After a while I got used to it, and now when I'm at somebody else's house I always get it backward.

I guess that's the way it is with relationships. You get used to things being a certain way, used to someone being right in place where they've always been, and when it's not like that, you get all twisted up.

Like, with Marcus not being around anymore. And Gramps leaving now. They had both moved into my life quickly, upturning emotions, raising old ghosts, making me feel things I'd avoided for years.

In the days before Marcus came along, I wouldn't have known love if it walked up and smacked me in the face. When he did come along, it took awhile to recognize it for what it was. I had spent years intellectualizing, working relationships out in my head instead of my heart.

'I'm not in love with you,' I had said in those early days to Marcus. 'I love things about you – your strength, and knowing you care. I love the way you always tell me I can do things, even when I think I can't. But I'm not "in love".'

I was twenty-nine at the time, just turning thirty. How could I be in love with a man fifteen years older, I had reasoned – a mobster, someone Grady North had spent the majority of his career on the force trying to put behind bars?

And how could I be in love with a man whose lifestyle was so opulent, so vastly different from mine? If nothing else, my odd determination to align myself with street people, welfare mothers, and the downtrodden (that wonderful, combustible, ethnic hodgepodge of "real people", as I saw it), made it embarrassing to be in love with a man of such wealth and position as Marcus Andrelli.

Declaring love also meant giving up the option to gallop off with the True Prince when he came one day. And I wanted all the options open, all the magic still forever to come. I wanted to wake up each morning knowing I could be whatever I wanted to be, do whatever I wanted to do.

I thought loving Marcus would somehow prevent that.

So I told him, 'I am not in love. I care about you, I enjoy being with you. I love the way our eyes lock over other people's heads in common understanding and humor. I feel happy when you appear at my door. And I miss you when you walk away.'

It was only later, more recently, that I learned the truth: that love isn't always convenient, and it isn't always smart. It often makes no sense at all.

Herbert Shipman said it in a poem: 'Across the gateway of my heart, I wrote No Thoroughfare. But love came laughing by and cried, "I enter everywhere."'

So if I now realize, deep in my heart of hearts, that I am indeed 'in love' with Marcus, why aren't we together? I don't know. Perhaps because when he gave me that ultimatum last summer, it was all too new. From old habit, I was still afraid of scalding myself – of getting hot water when expecting cold.

Now that I know all this, of course, it's far too late. But that doesn't stop me from checking out every black limo that passes, hoping for his license plate – or calling in from wherever I am to check my messages and see if he's called.

Sometimes I miss him so much, a great lump rises in my throat, making my collarbones ache. I want to say, 'I'm sorry I hurt you, sorry I lost you. Please forgive me. Please come home.'

That's what I want to say. I don't know why I can't.

Chapter 16

At seven, I took a cab to the airport and sort of loitered off to the side of the American Airlines gate, my collar pulled up to my chin, a slouchy rain hat pulled down over my eyes. Trying to be careful – though I hadn't seen Miami, or for that matter anyone else who looked as if he were scouting the airport for one Johnny James to appear. It seemed as if our scam had worked, and by this time Miami might even be on his way home to report that Gramps was dead.

I watched the line of passengers boarding flight 203 for LA. Most had gone through the gate already, but last-minute arrivals brought up the rear. They included an elderly man in a wheelchair, and a young woman with a baby in a small collapsible stroller. Behind her stood a skinny kid of about fourteen with long blond hair and thick glasses. He carried a backpack and wore a Dodgers cap, a heavy warm-up jacket with a high collar, and earphones attached to a Walkman that was clipped to his belt. A couple of Tootsie Roll Pops stuck from his upper pocket, and one from his mouth.

A typical LA dude, heading home, one would think. Unless one knew the 'kid' was Gramps.

'By the time I finish with him you won't recognize him,'

Rack had assured me yesterday at the pool hall.

'Swell. Then how will I know he's there?'

'Look for the Tootsie Roll Pops.'

The disguise was great. And Gramps was great. He'd made it to the airport in time and according to plan – just when I'd begun to think that maybe he'd skipped, and that Tark, who never did answer his phone, was out scouring the town for him.

My eyes stung. When all was said and done, I kind of liked the old guy. And he was right. I'd miss him.

As the line thickened and lengthened, as it began to move, I edged sideways to the window that overlooks the runways. I stood there a few moments so I could see, in the window's reflection, Gramps move through the gate. 'Bye, old man,' I whispered to myself. 'Safe passage.'

After everyone had boarded, and there still seemed to be no tail lurking about, I picked up my carry-on and hightailed it down the hall to a US Air gate. I dragged a ticket out of my deep coat pocket and handed it to a smiling clerk.

She scanned it. 'Miami, flight 602,' she confirmed. 'Any luggage?'

'Only this.'

She did her bit with the ticket and handed it back. 'Better hurry. Flight 602 is boarding now.'

I slid into my window seat, shoving the denim coat and my carry-on beneath and praying the middle seat hadn't been booked. That's the thing about flying. You get stuck sitting next to people you would never in a million years have anything to do with at home. Or with somebody perfectly nice but with blue hair and a Grandma's Brag Book stuck inside her huge flowered purse. That's always good for a straight eight-hour chat.

There were late arrivals here, too, but there was also a delay getting clearance, as there often is in winter. Passengers kept piling in, making futile searches through overhead compartments for room to stack the most incredible things. 'Carry-on' used to mean an overnight case. Now they're bringing on everything from fishing rods to skis to luggage with wheels that only a body builder can lift.

When the number of arriving passengers dwindled to none and no one had taken either seat next to me, I began to relax. I'd have room to stretch out sideways and ease my still-frozen bones as I studied Grady North's report on Barney Noonan.

There hadn't been time for more than a quick glance earlier. But I'd seen enough to prick my interest. There were juicy tidbits even Tark couldn't have unearthed by computer, the kind of inner-circle gossip that takes place between cops.

I reached down to pull the report out of my bag, and heard a commotion at the front of the plane. A fat, rosy-cheeked woman trundled down the aisle laden with a shopping bag and an overflowing paper sack. She wore an old woolen coat that might have been from a Salvation Army thrift shop, and her packages knocked several people in the head as she passed. They glared and inched away. 'Sorry, sorry, sorry,' the woman muttered, her heavy makeup running, glasses steaming. Strands of graying brown hair fell damply from beneath a black felt hat.

Oh, no. Please, God, don't let her sit next to me, I prayed. She will talk with a drawl. She will call me 'honey' and 'chile'. I just know it.

Maybe it was a public holiday in heaven. Or maybe God thought I needed to pay back a karmic debt. Whichever, all my fears came to pass. (What a person fears, appears, Samved would say.) The woman dumped a bunch of bags down next to me, one of which smelled like rotting cheese. From another poked a length of unwrapped white hots.

Her own bulk, she dumped into the aisle seat. 'Whew! My legs aren't what they used to be,' she wheezed.

God, a wheezer.

I turned and stared deliberately out the window, sending a message: I am not your friend. Do not talk to me. Not a word.

But I could still hear her settling in. Rummaging through bags. I heard paper unwrapping, and the cheese smell got worse. My stomach lurched. The plane began to taxi.

Staring straight ahead, I tried to still the nauseous flutters. My peripheral vision caught thick cotton stockings below the coat's hem, and a lumpy arm beneath too-heavy clothing.

I felt a flicker of remorse. The poor woman was probably somebody's grandmother. She'd be flying to Miami for her annual winter visit, and when she arrived little kids would be climbing all over her yelling, 'Gramma, Gramma, what did you bring me?' She would babysit and bake cookies, and people would love her despite the fact that she made a horrible seatmate on a plane.

Which did not mean I wanted to talk.

I sensed her looking at me and steeled myself for the inevitable opening gambit. It took less than sixty seconds in coming. 'Would you like to see a picture of my cat?' the woman asked.

I shook my head. 'Sorry. I don't like cats. Or kids. Or dogs.'

My seatmate let out a cackle. 'I know you don't, Jesse girl. Anyway, that's what you claim.'

Oh, my God.

'Gramps?' I said.

Chapter 17

'Shhhh . . .'

The apparition at my side grinned at me through carmine lips.

'I will not shhhh!' I looked around nervously, then lowered my voice. 'What the hell are you doing here? How did you get here?'

He grinned through layers of makeup that gave the illusion of added pounds to his face. 'Want a Tootsie Roll Pop?' He pulled one out of the woolen coat.

'I saw you board that flight!' I hissed. 'I watched that Dodgers jacket and that blond wig all the way through the gate. And where the hell did you get that outfit? And the makeup? Not to mention all that padding?'

'It was in my duffle bag, girl. Remember, I put it in a locker this morning?'

I was still staring, trying to believe it was really him.

'Shoot, Jesse girl, disguises are the easy part. I been doin' this for years.'

'But how did you get on this plane?'

The sly old eyes peeked out from above steamy glasses. 'Kid, I been walkin' this road with you all the way. Shoot, I booked my ticket to Miami soon as I heard you'd booked yours! Even asked for this seat so we could be together.'

'But I didn't tell you –'

My mouth fell open. My travel agent. I'd used a travel agent whose number was in my address book, which had been in the kitchen drawer since Gramps had arrived.

'Where'd you get the money for another ticket?' I demanded.

'I told them to put it on your account, girl, same as yours. And I canceled the one to LA. Now, don't go gettin' all upset, I'll pay you back.'

I glanced uneasily around. 'Dammit, Gramps, I went to a hell of a lot of trouble to set up that fake drowning. Have you any idea what Grady North would do to me if he ever found out? Not to mention that it cost the city a fortune to get the scuba squad out there. I could go to jail for fraud. I didn't risk that so you could end up on some slab in Miami.'

Gramps sighed and sat back with a satisfied smile. 'It was beautiful, girl. The best part bein' that breakneck ride in the Three's van with Percy at the wheel, slippin' and slidin' all the way in the snow. Shoot, that kid can drive! And then hidin' out at the top of the Rochester Towers in a penthouse owned by a mobster, havin' the time of my life ... You know, girl, you could have it real good with that guy. The bathroom alone must've cost more than any house you'll ever be able to afford – all those gold fixtures, towels as thick and soft as all get out –'

'Yeah, well, money doesn't buy everything.'

'Maybe not, but it sure makes a nice down payment.'

'Oh, God, forget it! Just forget it! You are never going to get within shouting distance of Marcus Andrelli. I have not allowed you into my life so you could scam on my friends.'

Gramps shifted laboriously in his seat, the layered clothing and padding making it difficult. 'Scam ...' he said thoughtfully. 'Now there's a word you'd know about.'

'Dammit, old man, if Noonan spots you in Miami –'

'You didn't spot me, did you?'

'No . . .' I studied his disguise again. 'You know, for a little guy, you actually look tall this way.'

'Optical illusion. When people are overweight they look taller. And when they lose weight, people always think they got short.'

'I never thought of that.'

'Most people don't,' Gramps said with a grin. 'That's the beauty of the con, girl . . . that's the beauty. So how did it go after my untimely death?'

'Awful. I can't tell you how hard it was to put on that act for my fellow scribes. And then to lie to all those people, to Grady, Toni, Joey . . . and poor Mrs Binty. She honestly misses you, though I can't see why.'

'A real lady, that woman, a right real lady. Makes a man want to jump on a shiny white horse and save the day.'

'Yeah, well, you're not jumping on any white horses, old man. When we get to Florida I'm hiding you out in my motel, and you will not set foot out the door till I'm finished with Barney Noonan. Understand?'

'My, oh my, those eyes. Did you know they're just as green as your grandmother's were, Jesse girl? And just as sassy, too.'

'Don't sweet-talk me, old man. And will you please stop calling me girl?'

He cackled. 'Tell ya what. I'll trade ya.'

'For what?'

'For you not callin' me old man.'

I thought about my screenplay the rest of the flight. It had taken on another twist. This time, the granddaughter of the aging con, who is too lazy to work for an honest living, sets him adrift on a boat to Haiti, in a brilliant move to rid herself of him once and for all.

It was eighty-nine degrees in Miami, hot for this time of night and year. The airport, even at one a.m., was filled with snowbirds in print shirts, carrying straw totes. Gramps, puffing along with his shopping bag and groceries, fit right in, except for the heavy winter coat. I stayed twenty paces behind all the way, so I could keep an eye on him.

We took separate cabs, to be on the safe side, and I got to the Lonely Palms motel first, as my driver was faster. Scratch that. My driver was a maniac. He spoke non-stop into a static-filled radio, cussed in a foreign language, and ignored red lights entirely. When he finally came to a halt at the motel, I almost landed on the floor.

He leered as I handed him the fare. 'Hey, pretty lady, you wanna fock?'

I rolled my eyes. 'No, I do not wanna fock,' I said tiredly. 'Jeesh.' So this was Miami.

I had somehow never made it down here before. The travel agent had recommended the Lonely Palms, and it was just about what I'd expected for the price. The rooms were built in a fifties style, with full-length slatted glass 'jalousie' windows front and back for a cross-breeze. No air conditioning. That was okay; after Rochester weather, I didn't want air conditioning, anyway.

I checked in under Mom's maiden name, Kate O'Donnell. Gramps was to register under an alias, alone. I did all the settling-in things, and when I finally heard him come into the room next to mine I looked in, which proved to be a pain.

'What took you so long?' I said suspiciously.

'Nothin' girl. Traffic, that's all.'

'I don't believe you.'

He was peeling off layers of makeup. 'Well, now I never thought you would.'

He was no more forthcoming than that, and I finally just warned him again to stay put and not wander off anywhere. He tried to get me to stay and go over 'our' plan together. I told him I was far too tired, and managed to escape, closing the connecting door firmly. Then I lay naked on the lumpy bed and basked in the balmy night temperature, letting it warm my bones. Light from a neighboring bar poured through the jalousie slats, creating neon strips on my stomach that bent and traveled up the wall. Turning sideways, I could see a small pool with underwater lights, and hear a radio. Michael Bolton was going on about not wanting to love some girl who didn't love him. Imagine not loving Michael Bolton. There was no one swimming in the pool. Litter bobbed on its murky blue surface. Newspapers and empty styrofoam cups drifted across a concrete patio. A dry old palm clattered.

Seedy. The place was downright seedy, thank God. It suited my mood.

I stretched and sighed. What was I going to do about Gramps? My original plan wouldn't work if he was spotted down here. I had thought that with him safely out of the way at Aunt Edna's, where no one would look for him now that he was 'dead', I might sneak up on Barney Noonan, catch him unaware.

Well, best-laid plans, and all that.

So there I was, in a chintzy motel room in Miami with My Wonderful Plan, on the one hand . . . and on the other, the things that happen when you're not looking.

It's the latter that will get you in the end.

Every time.

Chapter 18

The telephone rang. Sitting up, I was disorganized, expecting to wake in a sleeping bag, shivering, with the phone on the floor. But my blurry sight revealed darkness through slatted windows, and a blue-lit pool. Then I realized how relaxed my muscles were, not tight from having to fight off below-freezing temperatures all night. I peered at the cheap little bedside clock: four-oh-three.

I lifted the receiver cautiously. Who besides Gramps knew I was here?

'Hello?'

'Miss O'Donnell?'

'No, uh . . . yes. Who is it?'

'This is the office. There's a message here for you. The guy who delivered it said it was urgent.'

Urgent. Now what the hell? Tark knew where I was, but he'd have rung straight through. Did Noonan already know?

I rubbed my face. Too soon. It's starting too soon.

'I'll be right there.'

I pulled on a pair of shorts and a sleeveless tee and followed the cracked cement path to the office. It was lined with dark, rubbery plants and dry, dying palms that whispered warnings from hidden corners. There was no moon, no stars – the lights of the city were still too bright for that. Someone told me once that there's a bar on every corner in Miami, like there's a grocery in some cities. And that there's a crime committed in the city every minute. My figures may be off, but they were close enough to make me glad to finally get past the loaded-down dumpsters, then a couple of big rigs, and arrive at the office.

The male clerk was in rumpled PJs and surly. Handing me a white envelope, he said, 'He paid me twenty bucks to wake you. But I'm not gonna do this every night.'

'Right.' I patted my pocket. 'Then I won't give you this fifty for waking me every time I've got a message.'

I ignored his glare and made my way back through the warehouse-type lot of the motel. In my room, I tore the envelope open. It was typewritten.

If you want to know what's in
store for you in Miami, come
to Room 301 of the Tropic
Shores Hotel, 3002 Hibiscus
Drive, Star Island, right
away. Come alone.

It was unsigned.

Barney Noonan? This Tropic Shores Hotel wasn't the address I had for him. Tark had learned through contacts down here that Noonan lived in Miami, on Bonita Street, just outside the Coconut Grove area.

A set-up, then? More than one murder victim had been lured to a hotel room only to be shot in a dark hallway by someone who was never even registered. It was a more or less common occurrence in all large cities.

Damn. Noonan must know I was here. Did he know, too, that Gramps was alive?

I jumped into the shower to wake myself up. Then I pulled white cotton shorts on with a clean sleeveless tee, and running shoes. In a hip pack, I stuck a few accessories . . . a Swiss Army knife, a can of mace, a few other odds and ends. I checked the map I'd picked up at the airport and saw that Star Island was just off the MacArthur Causeway, on the way to Miami Beach. I called a cab that took me to an all-night Rent-a-Wreck lot. The clerk was slow and sleepy, so it took longer there than I'd thought it would. Anxious to be on my way, I cased the lot for the perfect car and found it: a drab, anonymous Chevy Chevette, its gray paint dulled by time and salt air.

Fifteen minutes later, at six-thirty-three by the dashboard clock, I crossed Bridge Road to Star Island and entered another world: luxury homes, streets lined with healthy green palms, softly lit gardens. A bright salmon streak meandered across an indigo sky. Sprinklers cast a false morning dew over lush vegetation; gardeners were already working. Along the way I passed no corner bars, nor did I see high-rises, or other hotels. I assumed I was now in the land of the tastefully rich.

The Hibiscus Drive sign was small and discreet, set off from surrounding neighbors. I almost missed it at the far end of East Star Island Drive. Turning, I entered a two-lane drive lined with shrubbery and palms. Tiny lights rimmed either side, pointing upward to shine on the tips of the palms as if they were Hollywood stars spotlighted for the occasion. After a minute or two the road opened up to a wide green lawn, and beyond it, a white, oversized mansion, actually quite small for a hotel. A small, softly-lit sign on the lawn bore the name in elegant script: *Tropic Shores*.

I slowed and looked about me, getting a feel for the territory. Three-storied rooms spread sideways from a center lobby area. White shell paths wandered through gardens with vibrant green shubbery, manmade brooks, and more palms. A semicircular drive led to a dark green awning where a valet parking attendant held a stance of respectful attention.

Rather than solicit a glare of disdain for my little Chevette, I self-parked in the proffered lot, passed the valet with a smile and wave in his direction, then climbed several marble steps to the lobby. Inside were two smartly dressed clerks behind a desk, and a bellman, all three standing alert and ready, despite the hour. There wasn't any gold bullion actually showing, but you could almost smell it.

Barney Noonan, I thought, must have done well for himself, despite Gramps walking off with his cash. Drugs, probably, the number-one contribution to the gross national product down here. If Noonan was into drugs, that could account for his bad temperament as well, and for his need to show everyone he dealt with that nobody made a fool of Barney Noonan.

I did wonder, however, why he was so upset over the loss of five thousand dollars. Surely that would be a paltry sum compared to what it cost to stay here.

Or did he stay here? Was I right in the first place, and this was nothing but a trap?

I passed the clerks and bellhop by as if I had every right to be there and knew exactly where I was going. On the first floor, down a long corridor, I found the kitchens. I strode through them, smiling at sleepy cooks and fruit salad preparers. 'Hi. Service elevator?' I called out as I breezed by.

'That way.' A sleepy cook pointed off to the left, barely looking at me.

'Thanks.' I picked up half a cored apple on my way out the door.

Munching the apple, I found the elevator and pressed the button to the second floor, rather than the third: a minor but sometimes helpful diversion, in the event anyone may be watching. As it rose, I took the last munch of apple, balanced the core on the brass rail around the elevator, and removed the Swiss Army knife from my hip pack, opening the large blade. Then I put it into the pocket of the lightweight cotton jacket I'd worn. Small defense against anyone armed with a gun at more than three feet away, but closer up it might give me a fighting chance. Guns are seldom an option for me.

A soft ivory glow above my head indicated a stop at the second floor. My stomach clenched as the doors whispered open. I stepped cautiously out and glanced up and down an empty hall. At each end was a sign marked EXIT. I followed the plush flamingo carpeting to the stairs. They took me up one floor to the third. Opening the door into the hall, I eased through slowly, nervously. No one in sight. I followed the room numbers in the obvious direction . . . 320, 318, 316 . . . expecting at any moment to be bushwhacked.

There is nothing like walking down a long hotel corridor with no access to a hiding place on either side to turn one's belly to jelly. You listen for everything, from the smallest sound to the largest – like the snick of a door opening softly behind you, or an elevator bursting open to empty itself of passenger with automatic weapon, the spray of bullets stinging your heels as you run.

Except that, as in nightmares, there really is no place to run.

No doors opened behind me. With my spine so knobby and tense you could have scrubbed a day's wash on it, I reached the central elevator again and stood flat against the wall, hand in my pocket over my puny weapon. I could see now, that at the end of the hall on this floor the corridor didn't end, but turned to the right. Counting out in my mind, I judged that 301 must be in that direction – round a corner, where I could not see. If Noonan wanted revenge against Gramps through his family, rather than money, he would try to get me there.

I tiptoed past the remainder of the rooms, pausing now and then to listen. I heard nothing – no alien breath up ahead, no other warning sounds. Reaching the end, I stopped, took a deep breath, and shot a quick glance round the bend.

Less than a hundred feet away, between me and what I figured must be Room 301, two people stood talking quietly: a maid and a bellhop. From here they looked Latino, though I thought I heard an English word or two. I drew back out of sight and hesitated, sweat making my hand slippery on the knife in my pocket. The hairs on the back of my neck felt as if they rose.

The maid, I recalled, had a cart. Attached to it had been a large white laundry bag. On top of that I'd caught sight of a large white plastic box, the kind that might hold cleaning utensils – or weapons.

Which was it?

I had only two choices, as I saw it: keep going or turn back. I wanted, more than life or death or peace on earth, to turn back. The older I get, it seems, the more I value life. Things I did at twenty-nine I no longer do. Chances are no longer always taken. They call it 'learning discretion'.

The truth, I think, is closer to fear.

What finally decided my course was that I wanted Noonan even more than he wanted Gramps, or me. I wanted the thing over and done with so I could go off to LA, and Gramps could stop worrying and do whatever he'd do when he no longer needed me anymore.

I stepped into the hall. The two Latinos looked up, then quickly away. I began to walk toward them, a friendly smile on my face, but my hand on the Swiss Army knife in my pocket. 'Morning. Beautiful day, isn't it?'

The maid slid her hand into the white box. My stomach went into spasms. Sweat rolled toward my eyes. I tightened my grip on the handle of the opened knife and began to draw it out.

The maid's hand appeared holding a trigger – on a bottle of cleanser, 409.

'No English,' she said. 'Sorry.' She began to spray and wipe the molding around the door behind her.

Holy shit. I wiped my now-flowing forehead, wondering how close a person could come to cardiac arrest and still be upright.

The bellhop merely smiled, and somehow I made it to Room 301. It was the only door in this corridor. A suite, then? And it would face the ocean, if I had my bearings right, rather than the road. It would have a certain privacy. Isolation. This wasn't good news.

On the other hand, I'd made it intact this far. Maybe all Noonan wanted to do was talk.

I took a deep breath, glanced back down the hall and saw the maid and bellhop watching me. They were not smiling now.

Dear God.

I raised my hand to knock, and hesitated. Finally I stood slightly to the side of the door, in case bullets flew as it opened. Rapping three times, I gripped the toy weapon in my pocket, wishing arbitrarily that I'd brought a Luger.

The door swung to.

Silence. No bullets.

I cricked my neck to risk a look round the corner.

'Are we feeling shy today?' Marcus Andrelli said. He grabbed my arm and pulled me in. Then he put his arms around me, which was just as well since my knees weren't working anymore.

Chapter 19

One thing about that kind of weakness, it passes pretty fast. The legs come back and so do the wits.

'What the hell?' I pushed away angrily. 'What are you doing here? What kind of game are you up to now, Andrelli?'

He turned and crossed the large living area, pulling open a wall of curtains to let in the first pink rays of dawn. He was wearing white pants and a white shirt, the sleeves rolled up. His dark hair was damp and curling over his forehead. He looked thirty rather than mid-forties, except for the tired eyes. There were newspapers and business files scattered about a desk top.

'No game, Jess. I just didn't think you'd come any other way. You must admit, you've been avoiding me for months. So when Tark called me in Puerto Rico and told me you were coming to Florida, I thought it might be a good idea –'

'What do you mean, I was avoiding you? You said you didn't want to see me. "I want time to get over you." That's what you said.'

'Well, I was angry. And hurt.'

I walked away and stood with my back to the window, arms folded. 'Huh. The only thing hurting you was a sprained ego, when I said I wouldn't marry you. And it didn't take you long to disappear.'

The dark eyes flared. 'Dammit, Jess, we might have had a good life together. I couldn't just sit around and brood about that.'

He strode angrily to a breakfast bar and picked up a pitcher of juice. Pouring into a cobalt blue glass, he held it up to me questioningly. I shook my head. Marcus drank the juice in one long swallow, then slammed the glass down.

'I don't understand what you want from me,' he said. 'I've done just about everything you ever asked of me, including pulling out entirely from the Lucetta family. I've cleaned up my business practices and worked my ass off the past couple of years to build a power base that none of the mob can touch. I'm all but free of them now.'

I folded my arms. 'All but free. Funny how that statement doesn't fill me with confidence.'

'Look, can we table this for now?' His voice, and eyes, softened. 'It's good to see you, Jess. I've missed you.'

I turned away, looking out the window. There was a view of the bay toward the east: pink glitter on water from the rising sun. Along the shore to the left lay a small white sand beach, possibly man-made, with cabanas and gaily colored umbrellas. Directly below, however, was a wide green lawn that stretched several yards to the bay. Docked there was a godawful, huge wooden boat, painted in a garish flamingo pink. The same one, I thought, that I'd seen in the photo at Marcus' apartment.

'What is that thing?' I said.

He stood behind me, his hand on my shoulder, gently caressing. 'I said I've missed you, Jess.'

'I heard you. What's that boat?'

'Jess?' He turned me around and kissed the tip of my nose. 'This is where you say, "I've missed you too."'

I flushed and mumbled something unintelligible, even to me.

'And we're right for each other, you know that,' he said.

'I don't know anything of the kind,' I argued, pulling away. 'For heaven's sake, Marcus, we've been over this before. Why do we have to do it again? It's not you, it's me. There. Is that what you want to hear? Do you need to be let off the hook, yet again? Well, here it is: the higher you climb in the business world, the more you need someone to travel beside you, not someone like me. I'd pull you off course every time.'

'That's a smokescreen,' he said irritably, 'and you damn well know it. Jess, you're the one who put me on course.'

'Maybe. Or maybe you were heading that way before you even met me. You were retired from the mob, remember? And I drew you back into it with all that business about Daphne.'

'It was Daphne who drew me back into it. Before we ever met.'

'Even so.'

'Even so, why do you keep throwing up walls like this? Why do you insist on putting me up on a pedestal and seeing yourself as one of the minions below? That's all it is, Jess, a wall of your own making. Do you do it on purpose? So you won't have to commit to anything?' He threw up his hands. 'Hell, I don't care where we go with this anymore. I'm not asking for marriage, we don't even have to live together. Let's just *be* together, make some sort of promise to each other.'

'We can't. It'd never last. We're too different,' I said. 'You want different things.'

'And that's nothing but a romantic illusion you harbor.'

'Romantic?'

'Yes. That oddly puritan conscience of yours tells you that you should want to be down there with the underdog, with the poor and repressed. But there's a whole other side to you, Jess, that wants the good life. It's a side that enjoys the limo ride as much as it enjoys standing on the curb and scoffing at it.'

'That's not true.'

'No? Remember last Christmas? At the mission?'

I remembered. We had worked together, side by side, feeding over a thousand homeless. Marcus and Tark had trucked in food, as they had every Christmas for the past four years. Last year it was more of a monumental undertaking, however, because of the recession and all the layoffs. There were moms and dads there who had lived pretty decent lives in the suburbs until one or two paychecks were missed and unemployment ran out. Little kids tugged at their knees, kids who had been raised with piano lessons, nice schools, and summer vacations at the lake. Many were people who had given to charities every year. Some had worked in soup kitchens themselves at one time or another, helping to feed the poor on holidays. Now they were one of them.

In previous years, the city had come up with at least half the funds for Christmas dinners at the Fourth Street Mission, the most overburdened in the city. This time, there simply wasn't enough money in the coffers to handle it. Marcus had taken care of that. He'd made deals with wholesalers he had worked with over the years, people who owed him. Then he'd come up with bucks from his own pocket to underwrite the entire thing. Before the season was through, Marcus had quietly provided food for nearly every mission and homeless center in the city. And not just food for the holiday. I'd heard through Tark that it was still going on. He'd donated enough to keep them fed throughout the year.

'I remember,' I said.

'Well, you can't do that sort of thing as effectively when you're down there with them, Jess. And when people like you, people who have a burning passion to fill empty bellies, get a chance for a life that will give you what you need to do that – Jess, grab it, for God's sake. Don't let guilt hold you back. Or insecurity.'

'It's not insecurity.'

'Sure it is. You've never felt good enough, never up to par. Not in jobs, or relationships. That old tape keeps playing and it just won't quit. The one that says you never do anything right.'

I felt as though I'd been kicked in the gut, hearing Pop's words leave Marcus' mouth: *you never do anything right*. Those words had been coming back too often of late. Translated, they said: better to do nothing than do it all wrong.

'Jess, look at yourself. Look how far you come. You're sober now.'

'I'm sober today. What if I fall apart on you? What if I drink again?'

'Jess . . .'

He sighed, and I looked at him. His palm was upturned, waiting for mine to fill it. I shook my head. Marcus waited. He knew me better than anyone. Better than I know myself.

I sighed, squared my shoulders, and crossed the room. My hand went into his.

'Remember dancing last fall in San Francisco?' he said, pulling me close. 'You looked so beautiful in that black dress with the sequins. Your hair was longer then, but just as shiny.' He touched it.

'It's kinky,' I said.

'It's curly.'

'And I looked like a Barbie doll in that dress.'

'Like an angel.'

I smiled.

'Everyone envied us that night,' he said. 'They knew we belonged together, even if you didn't.'

Marcus put his arms around me. I tried to relax, but I couldn't.

'You're like an old redwood tree, Jess.'

'I'd rather be a mighty oak.'

'Oaks are mighty because they bend with the wind. Redwoods are rigid by nature.'

'Does that mean I can't ever be an oak?'

He smiled. His lips touched my forehead. 'No. It means stick with me, kid, and one day you'll be a willow.'

'Willow. Isn't that the tree that weeps?'

'I prefer to think that it dances . . . and sings.'

'A song-and-dance tree? Like Gene Kelly? Fred Astaire?'

'Like a real human being, Jess.'

A real human being.

I felt Marcus' hands at the small of my back. They were rubbing gently, easing me over the line.

I began to sway.

138

'What are you doing?' He pulled back, his brown eyes curious.
'The hula.'
Marcus laughed softly. 'We're in Florida, not Hawaii.'
'Who cares? Shut up and dance,' I said.

Chapter 20

We did not make love. Not then. Instead, we danced, and then we sat on Marcus' deck, sipping coffee that had been brought to our door by a white-coated waiter. On a folding tray beside us were the remnants of our breakfast: crisp bacon and eggs done to just the right turn . . . fresh homemade biscuits, and fruit. The mid-morning sun was warm on my face. After the blizzard I'd come from, it felt like heaven.

'So, I suppose you own this place,' I said, biting into a biscuit. Marcus lifted a dark brow. 'What makes you think that?'

I wiped butter from my lips with a napkin. 'I know you. You like things nice, and you like a certain amount of security. I wasn't far off in what I sensed, out in the hallway earlier. Those two hotel 'employees' were security people, weren't they? The only reason they didn't stop me was because they had orders to let me pass.'

'Never could fool you, could I?' Marcus said, only slightly irritated.

'Are there actually hotel guests here, then? Or is this a Marcus Andrelli private reserve?' He had several around the world, for himself and Andrelli Enterprises employees only, so the question wasn't that far off base.

'It is private,' he said carefully, 'though I do have guests. I screen them, of course.'

'Of course.'

'And the truth is, if you could screen all the people around you, you'd do it, too. So don't give me that disapproving "you think you're better than us" look. I thought we'd put that behind us earlier.'

'Tell me about that ungodly pink thing,' I said, to change the subject. My glance scanned the manicured lawn with its neat shrubbery and flowers, then the dock.

Marcus smiled. 'I beg your pardon. That "ungodly pink thing" is my boat.'

'You're kidding.'

'No, and I'd thank you not to make fun of it.'

'But how could I not? It sticks out around here like a sore thumb.'

'Mmm. I'm afraid all my rich and famous Star Island neighbors agree with you.'

'Rich and famous?'

'Well, I haven't heard from Gloria Estefan yet, but it's only a matter of time, I fear.'

'Tell me,' I said again.

He rose and leaned against the deck railing, looking out at the boat with a smile of satisfaction on his face. 'She's called *The Flamingo Swan*. And she's my pride and joy.'

I went to stand beside him and he put an arm around my shoulders. 'Do you remember Esther Williams,' he asked, 'and all those musicals in the forties that she played in?'

'Please. You know I'm a nut for old movies, and Esther Williams is still one of my favorites.'

'No kidding.'

'Sure. I loved it the way she could swim under water with a big smile pasted on her face and flowers in her hair. She almost never came up for air. I used to think, if only I could do that. I even practiced. And all I ever got for my trouble was a noseful of Genesee River water.'

Marcus smiled. 'Well . . .' He turned back to the table and picked up a copy of the *Miami Sun* that had come with breakfast, handing it to me. A headline on page one below the fold announced in bold face: BLIGHT ON BISCAYNE BAY.

I flicked a look at Marcus, then scanned the first few grafs. The article was all about *The Flamingo Swan*. Marcus' pride and joy, it seemed, had become a community issue. Half of Miami wanted it moved to some remote shoal off Bora Bora; the other half threatened to blow it to smithereens.

According to the story, *The Flamingo Swan* had been built as part of a set for an Esther Williams splash movie in the forties. In the movie, *Mermaids of the Caribbean*, the *Swan* was a wondrous thing, a Hollywoodian temple of white and gold. It served as a stage for a hundred gorgeous Los Angeles-imported mermaids who splashed around its base with fixed Max Factor smiles, to the tune of 'La Mer'. Meanwhile, Esther rose on a pedestal from the *Swan*'s hollowed-out center, with pastel fountains gushing all around. At the finale, the hundred mermaids arose dripping from the sea to ascend a flight of steps to the *Swan*'s commodious wooden mouth.

I looked at the *Swan*. 'That's really the same boat?'

Marcus nodded, smiling. 'She has an amazing history. When *Mermaids of the Caribbean* finished shooting, a group of well-meaning but probably drunk entrepreneurs purchased the *Swan* from the departing film company, thinking she could be made into a great floating restaurant. Someone had done that with an elephant in Atlantic City early in the century, or perhaps it was Ocean City, I don't quite remember.'

'I don't either, but I think I saw it once, when I was a kid. Sorry. Go on.'

'Well, according to the accounts I've read, the entrepreneurs built their restaurant inside the shell of the *Swan*. They arranged windows as portholes along either wing, and the tail –' he smiled – 'became an ignoble terrace for outside dining. You entered the *Swan* by climbing the steps to her mouth, which, since it was permanently fixed in that open state, gave the poor critter a look of perpetual fright.'

'Maybe she knew they were going to paint her pink,' I said.

Marcus looped an arm over my shoulder. 'As you may imagine, when the upper-crust citizens of Miami saw the finished product, all two stories-high of it, they went wild. The *Swan* was literally run out of town – or in this case, up the river. She ended on a small finger of water near Hialeah. The owners of the race track there welcomed her with open arms. "Gamblers love tawdry," they enthused. "Look at Las Vegas."'

'So the *Swan* became *Splash*,' I said, glancing down again at the newspaper story, 'a restaurant catering to players, bookies, and jockeys.'

'Right. And given the built-in clientele, it wasn't long of course before the New York City mob moved in. They took the *Swan* over, bought her for twice her value and left the Miami entrepreneurs grinning into their beer.'

I looked out at *The Flamingo Swan*. 'You're right. A remarkable history. What happened to her after that?'

'The sixties, it seems, and the real estate boom. Suddenly there were people moving into the area who didn't think much of having the *Swan* and her "questionable elements" in their neighborhood. Retired people who had lived most of their lives in Upper Suburbia foresaw a future riddled with fear if the New York boys didn't pick up their marbles and move on. There were petitions, letters to the editor, complaints from local businesses. And once again the *Swan* was under attack – on the run. This time she ended up deep in the Everglades as a waterside attraction. Her new owner, Indian Joe, sold hot dogs and fake Indian souvenirs through her portholes. Later, he excavated 98 percent of the *Swan*'s cavity and used her to ferry local residents and tourists from one waterway to another. To complete the picture, he hired a strolling guitar player and served guacamole dip.'

'Good God.'

'Precisely,' Marcus said. 'That golden era fortunately ended when Indian Joe went bankrupt and disappeared, leaving the state and county to deal with the *Swan*.'

'Giving them, so to speak, the bird?' I couldn't help saying.

Marcus laughed. His fingers stroked my bare arm. 'I knew there was a reason I've missed you.'

'So how did you end up with the *Swan*?'

I don't think I've ever seen Marcus look so inspired, his face so filled with something I can only describe as delight. Now and then, on rare occasions, I get to see glimpses of the boy he was. This was one of those times.

'I read that she was up for auction here in Miami. She'd been abandoned and sitting in a state boathouse for years. Poor thing, she was showing her age, and no one wanted her. Her steps were rotting and broken, and she'd turned a rusty gray.'

'Sounds about the way I feel some days.'

He turned and kissed me on the temple. 'Not you.'

'But would you still want me if I was rusty gray?'

'Even if your steps were rotten and broken.'

'Wow. So, to save the poor barnacled thing from a desolate old age, you just up and bought her. Is that it?'

'Something like that.'

'A true philanthropist. Selfless. Always giving.'

He laughed. 'Not quite. The truth is, this was something I did for myself. A gift, so to speak.'

'Somehow, I suspected as much.'

He actually blushed. 'I don't think I ever told you, but it just so happens I fell in love with Esther Williams when I was a kid. I used to watch movies on television too, you know. I even remembered the scene the *Swan* was in. So I flew down here a couple of months ago and bought her. I had her towed here to the hotel, and she's been sitting here ever since. My intention was to have her refurbished and set her up as a floating museum for, uh, vintage movies.'

'Really?' I stared at him.

'Well,' he said a bit awkwardly, 'aside from wanting the *Swan* for myself, I thought that maybe . . . maybe I could entice you to come back to me that way.'

'You thought that because I love old movies, you'd just build a little old multi-million dollar museum for me?'

He looked at me warily. 'I suppose that does sound a bit pretentious.'

I grinned. 'Actually, I think it's rather sweet. Astonishing, but sweet.'

He looked relieved, but raised a brow. 'I don't think you've ever referred to me as "sweet" before.'

'Well, shoot, you've never built me a museum before.' I put my arms around his neck. 'I like photography, too, you know. What do you think . . . the George Eastman House, next? A gift for my birthday in the spring?'

He groaned. 'I've created a Frankenstein monster.'

I dropped my arms. 'So what's happening with the *Swan* now? Why is she yet again in the news?'

'Unfortunately, the good citizenry of Star Island have not been happy with me since I found a loophole in the zoning and changed this place into a hotel. So they're even less than pleased with the *Swan*. There was a day, in fact, when they stood twelve abreast in the downstairs lobby and demanded I remove what they called my "flaking, peeling, broken-winged, rusty bird" from their sight.'

'Ridiculous,' I said, seeing *The Flamingo Swan* in a whole new light now. 'She's not that bad. Looks like you've even given her a new coat of paint.'

He grinned. 'I'm afraid that was largely the problem. Would you believe they actually called her "gaudy"?'

'That's terrible! What's wrong with those people?'

'Anyway, that's why I've been in Puerto Rico. I thought I might find her a better home there. Meanwhile, however, there have been all these threats.' He glanced over at the paper, which I'd put back on the table.

'They aren't serious threats, are they? Just grumbles.'

'Hardly that. There's a group calling themselves the Miami

Seven. They've been calling the *Sun* for the past three weeks, saying that one night soon, the *Swan* would be history. The threats range from bombs, to fire, to shooting a ten-foot hole in her hull and applauding while the Seven watch her sink.'

'Good Lord. Who are they? Certainly not neighbors. The rich and famous you talked about?'

'I'd hate to think that. No, it's more likely some Miami group of rabble-rousers who picked up on the dissension over here regarding all this, and decided to get in on it.'

'And this idea to move her to Puerto Rico?'

'I may have to follow through with it, eventually.'

'But for the moment, at least, you can't bring yourself to let them run you out. Is that it?'

He smiled. 'I suppose.'

'And meanwhile?'

'Meanwhile I've put a twenty-four-hour guard on the *Swan*.'

'That's who that white-shirted guy is down there? The one who looks like some sort of groundskeeper, but keeps ambling back and forth in the vicinity of the dock?'

'You noticed that?'

My gaze followed the man in question. 'Just in the last few minutes, actually.'

I sensed Marcus' blithe spirit about the *Swan* was fading; worry was setting in. I turned back to him. 'Hey, remember those shots where Esther and the other swimmers rose up out of the water on pedestals, with lit sparklers in their hands?'

'Yes.' He smiled. 'I always wondered how they did that.'

'Well, I am about to tell you,' I said. 'It was all smoke and mirrors. They ran the film backward.'

'Backward?'

'Sure. The way it was shot, the sparklers were lit and the girls were lowered on their pedestals into the sea. Then, when the film was run backward, it looked like they were actually coming up out of it.'

'No kidding. That's a bit of trivia I missed.'

'You probably haven't been watching TV,' I said. '*Hollywood Presents*.'

'Why watch TV when I've got you?' He leaned down and kissed me on the lips. 'You see, it's just as I said. We complement each other, Jess. We belong together. Think of the worlds we could conquer.'

I turned my head on the pillow and looked at the clock: eleven-forty-five. God. Half a day gone. And I hadn't even left a note for Gramps. I didn't know if I was more concerned that he'd be worried about me, or that he'd have gotten tired of waiting, and gone off half-cocked on his own.

Turning in the other direction, my eyes just about came even with Marcus' chest. My fingers went to the diamond ring on a chain around my neck, the same ring I turned down last spring. 'Never,' I said then. Less than an hour ago I'd changed my tune. 'I'll wear it around my neck for awhile, okay? But give me a little time.'

'Time for what? Jess, you know how you feel. You wouldn't be here, otherwise.'

Turning back to him now, I thought – in that half-awake world where everything still seems a dream – that it felt good to be with someone I loved and trusted, someone I knew would never deliberately hurt me. And I was thinking, too, that despite everything else, despite all the walls I threw up, like differences in lifestyle and income and upbringing, what really mattered was the trust. It was what made love good, made the emotional and the physical end of it good. Trust made everything work.

But would it work if I were the stronger one? If I were the one with the money and the power? Things hadn't changed all that much. Men, even the so-called liberated ones, still need to bring home a check to prove that they're men. Sure, we women learned to 'bring home the bacon, fry it up in a pan'. But the rest of that ditty: 'Never let him forget he's a man'? That's something else again. Because men are so damned stubborn. And proud.

Old issues crop up at the strangest times. I shook that one off, but my fingers left the ring at my neck. A small voice in my head spoke, startling me. What about Mac? it said.

He's still around, I argued. We'll always be friends.

Ha, another part of me said. I'll bet he'd love it if he saw this scene right here, right now, today. He'd be thrilled for you, *friend*.

Marcus stirred. His eyes opened and he looked at me and smiled. 'I knew you'd come back,' he said, running a finger along my cheek.

I stared at him. 'You what?'

'I knew you'd be back.'

'You did,' I said carefully. 'Mind telling me how?'

'Because you belong to me.'

'I . . . belong to you.'

His smile widened. 'You do. And I plan to take very good care of you. Jess, I've been thinking. I can help you with your grandfather and this trouble he's in. Tark told me something about it, and I still have connections here. In fact, I've got it all worked out. One call, one word in the right quarter –'

I swung my legs over the side of the bed and stood, pulling the hotel's terrycloth robe around me. 'Okay. That does it.'

Marcus reached for me, but I slithered away. 'Jess? What's wrong?'

'What's wrong,' I said angrily, my hands shaking as they worked with the belt of the robe, 'is that I don't know why you think you know so damned much about me. Like when you bought that house. What did you think, that I'd become Suzy Homemaker overnight? That I wouldn't want to work anymore?'

He raised up on one elbow. 'Of course not, I've always wanted you to work. I want you to do anything you want to do.'

'No, you don't. You want me to be right where you can find me when you come home from the financial wars. That's why you tried to stick me all the way out there in the country, and don't think I didn't know it.'

He shook his head as if bewildered. 'Jess, this is insane. Why are you bringing this up now? I thought things were all right now.'

'You mean because we had sex? Hell, Marcus, we've had sex before. It never made things all right. You still want to run my life.'

He slid from the bed, his eyes and voice cold as he pulled a pair of sweatpants on, yanking at the drawstring. 'I didn't think of it as having sex. I thought we'd made love. And I thought it meant as much to you as to me.'

'Listen to me, Marcus Andrelli, and listen good. I do not belong to anyone. Get that? Not anyone at all!'

'For God's sake, don't you think I know that by now? All I meant was that it felt good to have you back where you belonged.' He paused, grimacing. 'Dammit, don't look at me like that. Jess, I want you with me. That's all. Just with me.'

'Sure, that's the way it starts out. But it always ends with me doing what you want me to do. I show up here five short hours ago, and already you're telling me you can help me with my problem, that you and Tark had a little talk and you've got it all worked out. *You've* got it worked out. And now here I am in bed with you, your ring around my neck, when I told you quite clearly last spring that I do not want to marry anyone, ever, not you, not Mac –'

I reached up and yanked the chain free, tossing it and the ring down on the dresser. 'Well, get this, and get it straight. I don't need your help with my grandfather. And dammit, I don't need you.'

I pulled on my clothes and left him standing in the middle of the room, the last image in my mind the stricken look on his face. If my eyes teared as I went through the door, I told myself it didn't matter. It wasn't feelings that counted here, but cold, hard logic. And cold, hard logic told me Marcus Andrelli had spent the past five hours closing in on me.

I didn't like that. I didn't like it at all.

Slamming the door behind me, I stood weakly against it, trembling. When my strength came back I took off running, past a new 'maid' in the hall whose eyes followed me, alert and curious. When I got to the rental car I sat hunched over the wheel, my head on my arms.

God, what is wrong with me? What happened just then?

No answer came. The truth was, I didn't know.

Chapter 21

By the time I reached the Lonely Palms I was feeling worse than stupid and contrary: a bitch. The kind who has absolutely no reason to complain about the man in her life, or her life, but just can't help it.

On the other hand, I didn't think I'd change anything, even if I could. Even if Marcus would in fact still talk to me, what would I say? That I didn't mean it? I couldn't be sure that was true.

I stopped in at the front office and checked for messages. There was a different clerk on – Irma, she said – a woman with fried platinum hair and purple eyeshadow. Crystal earrings dangled, their prisms casting rainbows around the tawdry little office like chandeliers.

'Nothing today, honey. You waitin' to hear from a boyfriend, or something?'

'Something.'

'Well, don't feel bad. They never call. Only when they want something . . . then maybe they can pick up a phone and call.'

I smiled.

'But I know how you feel, what with the holidays coming up.'

There was a one-foot tree on the office counter, slightly tilted. Irma stood and bent it from the trunk, as if she did that several times a day, trying to straighten it. The tree flopped right back, its miniature decorations swaying. Irma sighed, rolled her eyes and sat back down. 'My girlfriend, she always has to have a boyfriend at Christmas. But you know what this jerk did to her last year?'

'No, what?'

'He was seeing another woman at the same time, and he gave her and the other woman the exact same thing! He even told her about it. How tacky can you get?'

'Not much worse than that. What was it?'

'An electric blanket.' Irma laughed. 'Of all things.'

'Well, it was a present with a message.'

'Yeah? Like what, you think?'

'Like neither one of them should depend on him to keep them warm.'

Irma tapped on her front teeth with a blood-red fingernail. 'Yeah . . . I never thought of that. Hey, you know, you're real smart. You a psychologist or something?'

'Something.'

She smiled. 'I'll let you know if he calls.'

'Thanks. I'd appreciate that.'

I picked up the little tree and held it high enough to see the plastic base it was centered in. Then I took a business card from the holder on the counter – *Lonely Palms Motel* – and folded it into quarters. I shoved it between the base and the tree.

'How's that?'

Irma looked thoughtful. 'I don't know,' she said finally. 'I've lost my mission. Now what'll I do with my time?'

Taking the card out, I left the tree tilted. 'I know what you mean,' I said.

I drove around the parking lot, which was virtually empty now. The big rigs had moved on early, and so had the usual tourists or businessmen who'd stayed the night. I pulled into the space in front of my room and slid out of the rental car. The minute I was out of the air conditioning, my skin, like an icy glass, began to sweat. By the time I reached my door my mind was close to mush. I remembered that the room key was in my shorts pocket. The shorts were tight, so it took a minute to pry it loose. I looked toward Gramps' room and saw that his curtains were still drawn. The muted sounds of a television show reached my ear. I thought about stopping in to talk. But I was tired, and I needed to get things started against Barney Noonan.

So I was dealing with the heat, with what I had to do, and probably still thinking about the past few hours with Marcus. Which is the only reason I can think of, other than sheer stupidity, that I walked into the trap.

Chapter 22

Opening the door, I stepped into the room. Pain exploded at the stem of my brain. I staggered, fell. A large truck ran me over and stopped to idle on the small of my back. My hair was grabbed, wrenched. My neck was stretched so far I couldn't breathe. I dug my palms into the rug and tried to push up. My forehead was slammed into the floor. And again. I heard something crack. A groan. I was far away by then, in a place filled with brilliant flashes of light and very little sound. I felt hands on my body, flipping me over. I tried to see, but everything was red, then black, then red again. A bloody haze. Pain sheared back and forth across my skull. 'Bitch,' I heard. 'Fucking bitch.'

It was automatic, then, the adrenaline. My knee came up. I screamed: an angry, martial-arts sort of bellow that gave me added strength. A hand clamped down on my mouth, but not before I had the satisfaction of hearing a howl of pain as my knee connected. I got my hands up and scored with my thumbs against eyeballs.

'Fucking bitch!' The hand left my mouth. But the truck was still on me, a half-ton weight. I could see it now. It had a face. A man's face. I saw a raised hand just before it came down and crashed into my cheekbone. Then I didn't see it anymore.

Chapter 23

Barney Noonan wasn't much taller than Gramps. But he was a hell of a lot meaner. His eyes told the story. Barney Noonan was the kid who stole your lunch on the way to school, just swiped it out of your hands, knocked you down, and ran off laughing. He was the neighborhood bully who snapped the head off your Barbie doll, and the one who left you stranded on the skating pond while ice was breaking all around. Barney Noonan was the kid who pointed his finger at you when you wet your pants in school, so that all the other kids looked at you and laughed. And Noonan was the one who, at fifteen, was pinning girls down in the back seat of his Chevy while they pleaded and cried, 'No, Barney, please I don't want to, please.'

You could see all this in his eyes.

The rest of Barney Noonan had evolved to complement the eyes. His hair was iron gray and cut short and stiff, like a marine's. His body was a mean, aggressive little tank, built to haul him through a mean, aggressive little world of its own making. That body was standing over me now, grinning.

I was slumped in the small, straight chair by the room's desk. Noonan had thrown water on me to bring me to. I felt it dripping down my face, my chest, my arms. Looking down, I saw that blood had tinged the water pink.

'Not as tough as you think,' Noonan said. 'No, siree. Not near as tough as you think.' He laughed harshly. 'I just love frisking women. Take 'em by surprise, don't give 'em a chance to run.'

Everything hurt, everywhere. I wet my lips and tasted copper. Blood. 'What do you want, Noonan?'

His smile faded. 'How do you know who I am?'

'I didn't figure you were the Welcome Wagon.'

'Welcome Wagon, huh? So you got a sense of humor.' A meaty hand came up and wrapped itself around my neck. 'Like that grandfather of yours. Real funny. Now where the hell is he, bitch?'

'My grandfather? He's dead. Didn't you hear? He drowned.'

The hand tightened. 'Don't play games. You think I fell for that? Tell me where he is, or this pretty little neck is gonna bend a couple of ways it's not supposed to.'

'Okay, okay, let up,' I gasped. 'I can't talk if I can't breathe.'

'You don't need to breathe. You need to tell me where the old man is. And you make any more noise, any screamin' or anything like that, and, lady, you might get what you're most afraid of.'

I looked into the eyes. They told me he meant it. Noonan wasn't operating on logic, and given any excuse at all, he might blow.

'First,' I said, 'you should know –'

The hand tightened. I spoke quickly.

'You should know I've got your money, dammit! I've got it with me. I want to pay you back.'

Noonan shook his head. 'You stupid bitch. I don't want the fucking money, I want the old man. I want his head, right here in the palm of my hand.'

He held his palm up to show me, just in time. The hand had been tightening, blood gorging in my face, my breath almost gone.

'You want revenge more than five thousand dollars?' I managed. 'Look, I've got it, this could all be over.'

'Five thousand dollars?' Noonan gave a harsh laugh. 'Is that what the old man told you? That this is about five lousy thousand dollars?'

'What do you mean?'

Noonan's eyes narrowed. 'So the old man flim-flammed you, too. I'll bet you ain't even got proof he's your real grandfather. Right?'

Oh, shit. I swallowed and wet my lips. 'Just tell me what the hell is going on.'

'Lady –' He half squatted, shoving his face close to mine. 'Lady, this is what the hell is going on. Your so-called grandfather breezed into this town – my town – and stole my money. And it wasn't just five thousand dollars, either. He took me for seventy thou. Then you know what he did, your goddamned son of a bitchin' grandfather? Your son of a bitchin' grandfather stole my wife. He stole my fucking wife!'

'Huh?' My mind was whirling, my head pounding. I wasn't sure I'd heard right. 'Huh?' I said again.

'You got it, lady. That old bastard stole the only thing that ever mattered to me. He stole my Betty Lou.'

And with that, Barney Noonan did an amazing thing. He staggered back, covered his face with both mean, ugly hands, and began to cry.

Chapter 24

My mom says I used to be a mean kid. Not as mean as Barney Noonan – I didn't pull the wings off butterflies or roast cats in the oven. But I wasn't beyond calling kids names, especially the ones they hated. I used to look for people's weak spots and pounce. More often than not, I'd run off yelling 'Pinhead, Pinhead, nah, nah, nah nah-nah' or some equally dumb-ass thing.

I don't know where that mean streak came from, because Pop wasn't naturally mean . . . only hurtful when he was in his cups. I always figured maybe Aunt Edna. I'll bet that feisty little redhead was a handful at seven.

So anyway, as a result, most of my friends at school were boys. Boys really are made of snakes and snails and puppy dogs' tails. They're thick-skinned, they come housed in an iron-clad shell (which takes most of them a lifetime to shed), and they'll wag their tails at just about anything that comes along.

About that shell: someone said, 'Ask a man what he thinks, he'll tell you. Ask him what he feels, and forget it.' I'm so used to men having protective shells to keep them from knowing what they really feel, it astounds me when I see a grown man cry.

Barney Noonan sat before me, weeping. I couldn't discount

what I knew about him: that he was, in fact, a merciless killer. But his shoulders were hunched, his face was lined, and he was sitting on the edge of my bed, crying like a little kid.

'Uh, look, it's okay,' I said awkwardly. 'It's okay.'

He shook his head, rubbing his eyes with his knuckles. 'You don't know. You just don't know. Betty Lou was everything to me. We were married thirty years. We never had any kids.' His beefy arms fell to hang between his knees. 'I remember when I first met Betty Lou. God, she was beautiful. It was one of those scorcher days, the humidity a hundred and five, and the sun . . . Hell, I was just a rookie, and I was working the beat down by the Fountainebleau Hotel. Took my lunch hour at that hot dog stand used to be on the beach there. I remember I was sittin' out on that old wooden deck, under an umbrella, and along came Betty Lou. Walkin' out of the ocean like that . . . what's her name, Derek? Bo Derek? In that movie, *10*. 'Course, this was long before the movie. Betty Lou . . . her skin so smooth, and her hair all golden and shiny . . . And she looked at me with those eyes . . .'

I never would have believed that the man who had just beaten the crap out of me and left me bleeding from the nose could feel so much for anyone. His hands were working with that kind of frustration that men get when they can't do anything with them: can't win with them, can't change things, can't beat another person into submission – or in this case, I supposed, back into love.

I leaned forward. 'Tell me what happened,' I said quietly.

That quickly, the hands became fists. 'Your goddamned grandfather is what happened! Me and Betty Lou, we were gettin' on great till he came along with his fast talk and his promises. Said he had property down on the Keys, ocean-front, prime. And for seventy thousand bucks total he could put us in it. Said he'd had some reversals and had to sell. Didn't care about the property, just wanted to get free of the taxes. But he had to do it fast.'

'You've lived in Florida a long time, Noonan. I can't believe you haven't seen every real estate scam to come down the pike.'

'Oh, I saw it, all right. At least I suspected. But then Betty Lou, she started pushin' for me to buy. Said she believed the old man. Said he had taken her down there, shown her the property the day before when I was out fishing. It really was prime, she said, an acre and a half along the beach. Shit, she was excited. She wanted to live down there, get out of the city, away from all the crime.'

'What about papers? Did my grandfather show you papers?'

'Oh, he had papers all right. Up the gazoo. I even took 'em to a lawyer, and he checked 'em out. Said they were good. And shit, man, I had Betty Lou on my back every minute of the day. 'Do it, Barney. We'll never get another chance like this, but you've got to move fast. He's got somebody else interested.' And even the lawyer said he didn't see where I could go wrong, said it was a great investment.'

'A lawyer you knew?'

'Yeah, well, somebody Betty Lou knew.'

I could see it working in his eyes . . . the struggle to believe, still, that his Betty Lou had been a victim as well, that she hadn't really been in cahoots with Gramps. Gramps and the lawyer.

'So you went for it. You said, "What the hell, it's for Betty Lou. If it'll make her happy . . ."'

He rubbed his face wearily. 'Yeah. Yeah, that's about the way it happened. And ten minutes later –' His voice rose, a tone of mingled anger and puzzlement. 'Ten minutes after we signed the papers, ten minutes after I handed over the check – seventy thousand bucks, for God's sake, my whole life's savings – they both disappeared.'

'Together?'

He looked at me, his eyes dazed, yet somehow wary. He spoke softly, as if to himself. 'She's gotta be with him now. She's gotta. He's the one she'd run . . .'

He swallowed hard, making an obvious effort to collect himself. 'Motherfucker! When I figured out what they'd done, I went down there, down to see the property. It was swampland, or as good as. Goddamn land had sunk more'n twenty years before, the locals told me. No way you could ever build on it. And Betty Lou – she told me she'd seen it. That it was prime.'

'But my grandfather didn't have anyone with him when he arrived up north to see me. And he never mentioned a woman. What makes you think Betty Lou is with him? Maybe they just split the money and she went off by herself.'

Noonan shook his head. 'Dammit, don't you get it? Either way, he took her from me. Everything was just fine until he showed up. My sweet Betty Lou . . .'

A tear welled in the corner of Barney Noonan's right eye. He seemed embarrassed by it, turning slightly away to wipe at it with a thumb. I felt sorry for the man. Gramps had done a number on him, his wife had left him, and he'd lost his life's savings. Things couldn't get much worse.

So what the hell.

I rose painfully, grabbed my chair, and swung it high in front of me with one swift move. Then I brought it crashing down on Barney Noonan's head.

Chapter 25

Well, I told you I was a mean kid. I was also pretty smart. Still am. And I knew I wouldn't get another crack at Barney Noonan. He was bigger than me and meaner than me. He'd nearly broken me in two already, and I wasn't up to another battle.

So, having been handed Barney Noonan's weak spot, Betty Lou, on a silver platter, so to speak, I pounced. *Carpe diem*, and all that.

He had slumped over on the bed, and I nudged him with a hand. Out cold.

I'd been glancing around the room while Noonan talked. The old fifties-style drapes at the windows had those tie-backs with ball fringes. Perfect. I worked quickly: first the hands, then the feet. Then I rolled him onto his back, ran and got a towel from the bathroom, twirled it into a thin line, and tied it around his mouth. That done, I went to the door connecting my room to Gramps' and twisted the knob. It was locked. I rapped hard a couple of times and called 'Gramps?' but he didn't answer.

All the while Barney Noonan was beating me up, I'd assumed Gramps couldn't hear, because his TV was on so loud. It therefore didn't surprise me that he didn't come running to my rescue. But now, suddenly, a different scenario presented itself. And in that instant, my blood, as they say in the mystery books, ran cold.

Goddamn, goddamn, goddamn, started running through my skull. Noonan got to him first. The old man's dead. I should have been looking after him, I should have known.

I ran and got my key to the connecting door and opened it, not even wanting to look. The terrible things a monster like Barney Noonan might have done to an old man like Johnny James were too painful to even imagine.

My gaze scanned the small room. Empty. I stepped in and threw open the closet door, half expecting a body to fall out. But except for Gramps' clothes, the closet was empty, too. Gramps himself was gone.

Relief came first, then anger. Damn his eyeballs! I knew he wouldn't stay put.

Noonan was stirring. Groaning. I went back and leaned over him. His eyes flickered open.

'Listen, asshole,' I said, 'and listen good. I don't know what the truth is. I don't know what my grandfather did to you, or to Betty Lou, but I intend to find out. Meanwhile, you stay away from me and away from him. Because I'm going after Betty Lou. And when I find her, her life won't be worth shit if you hurt Gramps. Is that clear?'

The eyes were angry. They were mean. They were also something else: worried.

'Is that clear?' I said again, shoving my keys into the soft underbelly of Noonan's chin and pressing hard. He choked a little and looked like he wanted to kill me. But he wasn't in a position to do anything but nod.

Quickly, I washed my swollen face in the bathroom sink, put on a clean shirt, and threw my clothes into my carry-on. Checking Noonan's bonds once more, I left him on the bed, writhing helplessly and making small sounds that managed to convey his rage. I took my bag and went into Gramps' room, closing the connecting door. I packed up his stuff, put both our bags by the door, and sat for a minute on the edge of the bed, considering my options.

Then I swallowed my pride and phoned Marcus.

'I take it you've got your usual coterie of Ivy League thugs with you down here?' I said without preamble.

'I've got back-up staff, if that's what you mean,' he said stiffly. 'Why?'

'I, uh, need a little help, that's all.'

'Help? You need help? And you're asking me for it? My, my.'

'Dammit, Marcus, if I was at home you're the last person I'd call. I've got all kinds of connections there. In fact . . . never mind. Just never mind.' I started to slam the phone down.

'No, don't hang up! Jess, I apologize. You were right to call me for help. I'm glad you did.'

'It's just that I don't know anyone here I can trust, that's all.'

'What is that I heard? Say again? Something about trust?'

'Marcus, don't start. Please, just don't start.'

He laughed softly. 'Sorry. What do you need?'

'I need someone to come to the Lonely Palms in about a half-hour and untie Barney Noonan. He's in my room, Number 12.'

'Noonan?' His laughter turned to concern. 'You found him?'

'More like he found me.'

'Are you all right?' he said sharply.

'A little the worse for wear, but yeah, I'm okay. He's the one who's trussed like a chicken and unhappy as hell.'

A hint of amusement now. 'And you want him untied? Set loose?'

'Right. But then I want him followed. And I need someone else to watch Gramps' room, Number 11. I want him grabbed and removed from here when he comes back. If he does.'

'What do you want us to do with him?'

'Hang onto him. And don't let him fool you. The man is a will-o'-the-wisp. He's got some heavy explaining to do.'

'You sound angry. I wouldn't like to be in your grandfather's shoes.'

'Or his head. Dammit, Marcus, it's gotta be a mess in there.'

'What about you? Where are you going?'

'In search of Bo Derek,' I said.

Chapter 26

It was a little after three. I made a call to Dave Laker on the *Miami Tribune*. Given all the info he'd sent me in Rochester through Marcus' computer, I figured he might be able to set me on the path of Betty Lou. He agreed to meet me for a late lunch at a place called the Crab Shack Too, out on a pier south of the city. We had to fight off gulls and tourists to commandeer a wooden bench and table outside, but, according to Laker, you just had to stare at them long enough. The tourists, that is. The gulls don't care.

'Usually, when people are eating, if you stand and stare at them, they'll finish up pretty quick,' he said.

So that's what we did. We stood balancing crab cocktails with French bread and thick, dark cups of Cuban coffee, and we stared. We didn't relent until a young couple, who were on their last bite of food anyway, got the message. They gathered their cameras and packages and departed, casting us irritable looks.

'That was fun,' I said with satisfaction as I settled onto my seat. 'There's nothing like mentally beating up a couple of innocent tourists to make an insecure person feel good.'

'Works every time,' Dave said, grinning. He had thin, sandy hair, wore glasses, and his eyes darted everywhere, taking in everything, the way a good investigative reporter's eyes will. Khaki shorts and an olive green tee-shirt hung from a rail-thin body.

The sun was moving toward the west, the smells just the way they should be at a place called Crab Shack Too on Biscayne Bay: salt-sea air, a dog nosing around with smelly wet hair, and over all the distinctive odor of fried fish.

We sipped our coffee, and Dave Laker said, 'Nice to see you, Jesse. But if you don't mind my saying so, you look like maybe you've already run into Barney Noonan. Or a tank.' He flicked a look at the rapidly purpling bruises on my forehead and cheek.

'Barney Noonan,' I said. 'But he won't be bragging about it. I left him an unhappy man.'

Surprise showed in Laker's eyes. 'He won't let you forget that.'

'Probably not. But I think I've found Noonan's weak spot – his wife.'

He wrapped a piece of bread around some crab and munched on it. 'Betty Lou . . .' he said thoughtfully between chews. His green eyes became still a moment, and went soft. 'The luscious Betty Lou.'

'Luscious? Still? Barney said they were married thirty years.'

Dave nodded. 'Which puts her in her late fifties. But I don't know a man in this town who wouldn't still go after Betty Lou – provided Barney wasn't around.'

'From what I hear, though, Betty Lou is no longer around.'

'That's the rumor. Of course, Barney isn't talking, not to the press. But gossip has it she just up and left one day last week. Disappeared. Can't say I blame her. Noonan is one ugly customer, and how a woman like her stood it so long . . .'

'You knew her? What's she like?'

'I didn't know her personally. But she was part of the old crowd in Miami, she and Barney both, and they had sort of a high profile because Barney was on the force all those years. Betty Lou stood by him through several rumbles early on, when Internal Affairs would haul him in for questioning. They never could pin anything on him, and I guess as his wife she didn't want to believe it at first.'

'Rumbles. You mean, charges of police brutality?'

'That, and other stuff. Drugs. Pay-offs.'

'Did he ever hurt Betty Lou? Were there rumors of that?'

'Not that I ever heard.' Dave washed his sandwich down with coffee. 'But you know, maybe you're right. About Betty Lou being Noonan's weak spot.'

'So are you saying they seemed happy together?'

'Not at all. Barney's a pretty heavy drinker. He'd get drunk at a party or out in a restaurant, and cause a scene. They'd argue, and either he'd leave her there, or she'd leave him. Other cops, friends of theirs, would drive Betty home. But to hear them tell it, they never got anywhere with her. You'd think she might want a shoulder to lean on, but not Betty Lou Fallon. A good woman. That's why, more'n her looks, probably – which are still real good, don't get me wrong – anyway, that's why the guys all loved her. They knew that despite that miserable son of a bitch she was married to, Betty was true.'

'Hmm.' Until Gramps came along, according to Noonan.

But, jeez, that was hard to believe. This paragon of virtue, this Perfect Ten, is true to her vows for thirty years, and then shimmies off with the likes of Johnny James? Not likely.

'Fallon . . . was that her maiden name?' I asked. 'Did she use it instead of Noonan?'

'Not legally. But her family is well known hereabouts. 'Betty Lou Fallon' was the way people always talked about her.'

'You've been talking about her in the past tense,' I observed thoughtfully. 'As if she's dead.'

Dave looked surprised. 'Have I? Shit, that's not what I've been thinking. I've been thinking that if Betty Lou Fallon is finally free of that nutcase, she's not likely to stick around here. If I was her, I'd head for the Dominican Republic, maybe South America. Enjoy life as far away from Noonan as I could get.'

I watched a sailboat head out to sea. It had a decorated Christmas tree tied to its mast. 'Seventeen shopping days till

Christmas,' I had heard on the car radio earlier, but it was hard to believe, sitting here. The sky was a deep blue, the sun so hot the shade felt welcome when Dave stood to raise our umbrella so it shaded us better. Rochester, and the possibility of a white Christmas, seemed a world away.

Marcus wanted me to spend Christmas with him, he'd said this morning in bed. And New Year's Eve, and every day thereafter. My fingers went to my throat, where the ring had rested against my skin.

'Where are you?' Dave Laker asked. 'You look like you just followed that boat out to sea.'

He was watching me curiously, and I saw that he'd finished his food. Mine was still sitting there, forgotten.

'Tell me more about Betty Lou,' I said. 'I really need to find her.'

Chapter 27

'Start with the family.' That's what Dave Laker had advised.
'When people grow up in a town and live in that town all their
lives, they stay in touch with family when they're in trouble.'

I tended to agree, at least if that family's a good one, and Laker
had said that they were.

It was growing late by the time I reached Coconut Grove, the
sun hanging low in the west. The Fallon house was set back from
the street, in an older, residential area that looked forties or
fifties era. A well-tended lawn and well-established tropical
vegetation had apparently been spared by Hurricane Andrew a
few years before. The style of the house was Spanish, white
stucco with terracotta roof and arched windows. I parked in a
drive lined with a riot of red and yellow flowers, and followed a
path to the front door. Its dark wood was carved and looked
heavy and thick. There was a knocker, but I pushed the simple
bell button beside the door instead.

The woman who answered surprised me. I had expected Betty
Lou's mother, a woman perhaps in her seventies. This woman
was clearly not older than forty. She wore bright yellow shorts, a
yellow shirt, and had a smattering of freckles over her cheeks.
Her hair was long and reddish blonde, the eyes cool and gray.

Maybe they were cool because of my face, which didn't hurt so much now but looked like hell, with bruises that were already turning yellow and purple.

I don't usually go into these things with a fixed plan in mind. I like to see what I'm up against first. Now and then there's an instinctive gut feeling that laying it on the line from the first will net the best results. This was one of those occasions.

'Yes?' the woman said, half closing the door on me.

'I'm Jessica James. I'm sorry to bother you, but I'm looking for Betty Lou. I wondered if she was here.'

The gray eyes became even more wary. 'My sister doesn't live here,' she said stiffly.

'Yes, I know.' I glanced quickly at the ring finger, saw it was bare, and looked back up. 'Ms. . . . Fallon, is it?'

She nodded, but the door didn't widen.

'May I come in? This really isn't about Betty Lou, it's about my grandfather. Apparently, he and your sister are friends. I'd like to talk to her about him.'

The woman looked me up and down, checked my face once more, and said with a heavy sigh, 'Your grandfather. I suppose that would be Johnny James?'

I gave her a rueful smile that said it all, and finally, she stood aside. 'You might as well come in.'

I stepped inside and followed her into a cool, dim living room. The ceiling was arched, the windows shuttered. She crossed to open the shutters, letting in fading rays of sunshine. The room, I saw now, was large and uncluttered, continuing the Spanish style with dark furniture and bright accents. In one corner was a baby grand piano. There were photographs in silver frames on its top. Next to the piano, a wall of glass doors opened out onto a courtyard with a small pool that was lined with rocks and flowers.

'Sit down,' Betty Lou's sister said. She motioned to a long sofa piled high with red and yellow cushions. Sitting in a matching chair across from me, she took a cigarette from a silver case on the coffee table, lighting it with a small silver lighter. She crossed her slender, tanned legs, as if relaxed. But her eyes maintained a watchful guard.

'You might as well know, your grandfather isn't my favorite person at the moment,' she said.

I smiled easily. 'That's okay. He's not exactly mine, either.'

She was silent a moment. 'I . . . I guess I should have asked for some identification.'

'No problem.' I reached into my back jeans pocket, pulled out my wallet, and showed her my Rochester driver's license and several press passes: one from *Newsweek*, another issued by the Rochester PD, and an old one from the *Herald*. She gave them all a thorough going-over.

Looking back at me, she said curiously, 'What happened to your face?'

I figured the truth could only help me more. 'Barney Noonan.'

'Barney did that?'

'Yes.'

She didn't seem surprised. I wondered: was Barney Noonan a wife-beater, too? Had she asked the same question one day of Betty Lou and gotten the same answer?

'I'm Irene,' she said, handing back the IDs. 'Bett's my older sister. She half raised me while both our parents worked to buy this house and give us some sort of solid foundation in life. I don't want anything to happen to her.'

'I understand. All I want, Irene, is to talk to her. My grandfather's gotten himself into a mess of trouble with Barney Noonan, and I'm hoping Betty Lou can tell me something about it.'

Irene tapped her cigarette into a large silver ashtray. She made a sound of scorn and tossed her head. The silky strawberry hair shimmered with gold lights. 'Noonan. Bett's one big mistake in life . . . and wasn't it a beaut?'

I began to relax. She was ready to confide; it would be downhill from here.

'Why did she stay with Barney so long?' I asked.

'Oh, I don't know. I guess she was afraid. Sometimes you

think that if you give something up, there won't be anything to replace it. It wasn't until lately, when Barney got worse . . .'

There was a small silence while she took another drag.

'I just found out about Betty Lou and my grandfather,' I said. 'I don't even know what the true story is. Noonan says they took his money and ran, but she hasn't been with my grandfather. At least, not for the past few days. And he never once mentioned her to me.'

Her tone was caustic. 'Well, if you know your grandfather –'

'That's just it. I don't. I never even knew he existed, in fact, until he showed up on my doorstep the other day.'

Irene looked at me hesitantly. Stubbing out the cigarette, she lit another. 'You do know . . . I mean, you do know what he is.'

I smiled. 'I know I can take everything he says, reverse it, and then – maybe then – come up with the truth.'

Irene smiled fully for the first time. 'Bett loved that about him. She loved the way his mind worked. I think she saw your grandfather as the only person who was smart enough to finally free her of Barney.'

'Are you saying they really did scam on Barney together? They set him up to get that money, so Betty Lou could be free?'

'Well, she never told me that was what they were doing, of course. But I know my sister pretty well. And one thing I know about her is that she'll live with pain for a long time. But when she's done with someone, she's done. I've seen it happen overnight – with friends who let her down, and now with Barney. My guess is he'll never see my sister again.'

'Irene . . . do you know where Betty Lou is?'

She shook her head. 'I haven't heard from Bett since she and your grandfather disappeared from Miami. That was over a week ago.'

'Were they . . .' I didn't know how to put it. 'Were your sister and my grandfather involved?'

She smiled again. 'You mean, in love? I don't really know. They were friends, and she genuinely enjoyed his company. He was different, unlike anyone she'd ever known. Bett liked that.'

'Irene, I hate to put it this way. But how do you know she and my grandfather disappeared together? Could something else have happened to her?'

She narrowed her eyes. 'Such as?'

'Well, my grandfather showed up in New York alone. Is it possible . . . could Barney have caught up with Betty Lou somewhere? I mean, if he lost his temper . . .'

I couldn't finish. Irene's white face told me she hadn't thought of the possibility that her sister might be dead. To her, as to Dave Laker, Betty Lou's disappearance had been a propitious maneuver, nothing more.

'I'm sorry,' I said. 'It's just that as a reporter I've learned to consider all the angles.'

On the other hand, it was hard to believe Barney Noonan's anguish that morning had been a pretense to cover up murder.

'What about your parents? Is it possible they know where Betty Lou is?'

Irene shook her head. 'They've been on a cruise to Hawaii the past three weeks. I haven't even told them what happened. The cruise was a fiftieth anniversary present from us kids . . . and believe me, they deserved it. Their first real vacation in twenty years.'

Dave Laker had told me about the Fallons, that they had both been raised in poverty, growing up in the central Florida Everglades. As newlyweds they had built a successful grocery business from scratch, working together long hours to assure their children a better beginning in life than they'd had.

I wiped perspiration from my forehead. 'I wonder, may I have a glass of water? I'm not used to the heat here yet.'

'Of course. Sorry I didn't think of it.' She stood. 'Would you like something else? Iced tea? Juice?'

'No, water's fine, thanks.'

When she had left the room I stood and crossed to the cluster of photos on the piano. One in particular had caught my eye as we were talking, that of a slightly younger Irene with an arm around a man of similiar age. Her other arm was draped about a slender woman of indeterminate age. She had pale blonde hair that was pulled straight back on one side. On the other, it fell in a thick mane over her shoulder. Next to this woman were an older man and woman, and beside them a younger man. All were dressed in beach clothes and standing with the surf behind them. The background sky was streaked with salmon, the sea aquamarine.

'That's the family,' Irene said from the doorway.

She had come back with a glass of water and ice. Handing it to me, she pointed to the woman with the mane of blonde hair. 'That's Betty Lou. She was fifty-two at the time, and didn't look a day over thirty.' Irene smiled. 'Bett has so much spirit. She loves the unusual, the kinds of surprises life can bring every day. I think that keeps her young.'

'It's probably what my grandfather liked about her.' I took a deep sip of the icy water and felt it hit my stomach. 'Where was this taken?'

'At our beach house near Key Largo. My parents bought the property several years ago, before prices soared. When I was a kid we drove down there on Mom and Dad's days off and built a cottage together.'

'That must have been fun.'

She laughed. 'It was awful! Have you ever spent all your days off for an entire year hammering nails, sawing wood, and lugging buckets of plaster? We thought it'd never be over. But I guess it was worth it. We've got a place to get away to now.'

I studied the photo a moment. 'Maybe that's where Betty Lou went. Is there a phone? Have you tried calling?'

Irene shook her head. 'No phone. But that was my first thought when Barney told me she'd disappeared. I drove down there the next day, when I still hadn't heard from her. The place was closed up tight.'

'When exactly was that?'

'A week ago yesterday.'

'Do you mind if I check it out? Maybe she's been there since then.'

Irene hesitated. Something flickered in her eyes, some emotion, but before I could read it, it was gone. 'You can go down there, I suppose. But somehow I feel certain you won't find her at the cottage.'

'Why not?'

'Because Barney knows where it is.'

Chapter 28

Irene Fallon had given me a key to the cottage. 'All I ask is that if you do find Bett, you'll get her to call me. Now that I know she's not with your grandfather, I'm more worried than ever.'

I tended to agree with her that her sister wouldn't be at the family cottage, or anywhere else that Barney Noonan could easily find her. Irene had also warned that the road to the Fallon cottage was nearly impossible to find at night. 'It's on a spit of sand with only a trail leading to it. Not that difficult once you know where it is, but you could be driving up and down Gray Beach Road forever in the dark.'

I glanced at the Chevy's clock and saw that it was nearly seven. The sky was dark, and the commuter hour was still in full swing. Traffic would be miserable going south to the Keys. Therefore, all things considered, it seemed more productive to find a room somewhere other than the Lonely Palms, and get a safe, uninterrupted night's sleep. I could check out the cottage in the morning.

First things first, however: Gramps. Had he been picked up by Marcus' men? Was he safe? I stopped along the street near a glitzy conglomeration of shops and open-air restaurants called

Coco Walk. There I found a restroom, a cold drink and a phone on the lower level.

The desk clerk at the Tropic Shores told me that Marcus had left word to call him elsewhere. I wrote down the number and punched it in.

'How's it going?' I said when he answered.

'Fine. I've moved over to the *SeaStar*.'

'You brought the yacht down here? Where is it?'

'At a private marina nearby. I thought I might need a place to hide out if the Miami Seven came after me. You know, to string me up.'

'Is that supposed to be funny?'

'Not really. There are times when it's seemed a likelihood.'

'What about Gramps? Any sign of him?'

'He showed up at the motel shortly after you left. Lew brought him here.'

'Is he all right?'

'Seems fine. An interesting fellow, your grandfather. Somewhat of an oddball.'

'You can say that again.'

'An interesting –'

'Okay, stop.'

I could hear his smile through the wires.

'Anyway, he's taking a nap at the moment. What are you up to?'

'Oh, this and that.'

'You can tell me,' he said. 'I won't horn in on your fun.'

'All right. I've been talking to Barney Noonan's sister-in-law.'

'And?'

'And I'm tired now. I need to find a safe place to sleep. Will you do me one more favor and look after Gramps till tomorrow morning?'

'I've a better idea. Why don't you spend the night here?'

'On the yacht?'

He must have heard my note of doubt. 'You can have your

own room, if you wish. I promise I won't touch a hair on that pretty head. Or get near your bed.'

I felt myself blush. 'It's just that I, uh, need plenty of rest,' I explained. 'So I'll be up to whatever I have to do tomorrow.'

'Of course. So come here. You can look in on your grandfather, that way, too.'

I was too tired to argue. 'I suppose that would make sense ...'

He gave me directions to the marina, and I hung up and stood for a moment looking around Coco Walk. A family of four was crossing the courtyard. A weary-looking mom, laden with a diaper bag and two kids, one on each hip, trudged toward the restrooms. Dad, wearing a straw Jamaican hat above a sunburned nose, slumped tiredly onto a bench.

A flicker of fear went through me, one of those things where the stomach tightens and you feel like the bottom is falling out of everything. I didn't know these people, and I didn't precisely know the source of my fear. The only thing I knew for sure was that I never wanted to be like them.

The *SeaStar* was docked away from the other boats, in a private slip. To the east, the land jutted out and was lined with palm trees, providing privacy from the rest of the marina. To the west, there was deserted shoreline and a direct view across the water to the Tropic Shores Hotel and *The Flamingo Swan*. I sat with Marcus on the upper deck of the *SeaStar*, at a table with white linen and candles, wolfing down the best cheeseburger I'd ever tasted. It had been rustled up in the galley by Marcus himself.

'Not bad,' I said between bites as juice ran down my chin.

'It's great, and you know it,' he said, watching me with pleasure. 'You know, I love to watch you eat. You really go at it. It's so frustrating when women just pick at their food.'

'How many women have you been cooking for lately?' I couldn't help asking.

'I simply observe these things,' he said, grinning – clearly pleased that he'd raised a spark of jealousy.

'Yeah, right,' I said. 'You know, I can't believe Gramps is still sleeping. I keep forgetting he's not a spring chicken. Did he say what he was doing when he wasn't at the motel?'

'Not a word. He thanked me for my hospitality, asked if he could take a long hot bath, and came out raving about the towels.'

'Hmmm. Well, don't be fooled. He's not all that innocent. Did he have anything with him when Lew found him? Other than clothes, that is?'

'You mean, the money he owes Barney Noonan? Nothing Lew could see. He didn't search him, of course, or his bags. You didn't want that, did you?'

'No. I suppose not. What about Barney Noonan?'

'I sent one of my men over to release him before your grandfather arrived. He followed Noonan straight to his house on Bonita Street. Noonan was suspicious, of course, at simply being released like that. I'm sure he assumes he's being followed.'

'That's okay, it'll keep him honest. He's still in the house?'

'Hasn't shown his face since this afternoon.'

I finished the cheeseburger and sat back, sipping a cup of espresso. Relaxing, finally, I told Marcus what I'd learned from Irene Fallon. 'I'm driving down to Key Largo in the morning. If Betty Lou Noonan isn't there, I'll talk to neighbors. Maybe someone's seen or heard from her.'

'And if you find her?'

'I'm not sure. But she's Barney Noonan's weak spot. I may be able to use that somehow.'

'Jess, I hate to see you go down there alone. How about if I go with you?'

I gave him a look. 'To protect the little woman, you mean? Dammit, Marcus, since when did you get like this? And why? You used to trust me to take care of myself. It's one of the things I liked most about you, that you didn't treat me like some feminine piece of fluff.'

'I doubt I ever treated you like a piece of fluff. But what's wrong with being feminine?'

'Nothing, till men start treating you like a piece of fluff.'

He sighed. 'And what if I just wanted to go along for company?'

'I don't need company when I'm working. Do you ask me to come over and sit at your desk when you're wheeling and dealing?'

'That's hardly the same thing. Besides, helping your grandfather isn't a journalistic assignment.'

'No, but it's research.'

'For what?'

'For the screenplay I'm writing.'

'You're writing a screenplay?'

I frowned. 'Why does everyone say that, as if it's the last thing in the world I might be expected to do?'

Marcus shook his head as if in wonder. 'Jess . . . I haven't a clue.' He leaned forward in his chair and rested his folded arms on the table. 'But I can see your point. You don't need me tagging along. So why don't you just let me send someone with you? No interference, just back-up.'

'Sure, why don't you do that?' I said sweetly. 'It's just what I need, assorted bodyguards following me around, highlighting my appearance everywhere.' I set my coffee cup down with a thud. 'Really, Marcus, you said you wouldn't interfere.'

'I was thinking about Lew, that's all. You like Lew. And he could help you drive.'

That was too funny – and too obvious – to take offense at. I hooted. '"Help me drive"? And how many shotguns would he load into the trunk before we left town?'

Marcus looked pained. He threw up his hands. 'Never mind.'

I barely noted the luxurious details of the stateroom Marcus put me in. I did note that the bed felt like a cloud. I had to admit, waking up the next morning without the usual kinks or cold, that there are some really great things money can buy.

In the shower with its gold knobs, and afterward, drying off with soft, warmed towels, I thought about Gramps, and the kick he got out of the feel of money. I supposed that was another thing we had in common, aside from our toes: I did like nice things. Much as I might rabble-rouse against the rich and march for the poor, there was this other side of me that wouldn't go away, the side that enjoyed comfort after so many years of growing up without it.

Marcus was right. I liked the 'limo ride'.

Lew had brought my bag along with Gramps'. I found it on a folding stand beside the closet, and opened it up, pulling out a wrinkled pair of shorts and a tee.

Before turning in the night before, I'd checked on Gramps and found him snoring loudly, all tangled up in a silky white sheet. He looked like a little boy, and it was all I could do to remember I was upset with him for leaving the motel when I'd told him not to.

What mission, I wondered, had been that important? What was he doing all that time he was gone?

The obvious answer presented itself: looking for Betty Lou. Or perhaps he didn't need to look for her. What if he knew where she was – and had, all along?

This morning, his stateroom was empty, the bed neatly made. His bags, like mine, were piled onto a folding stand by the closet. I walked over to them, and stood debating with myself: to peek or not to peek? What many secrets might these bags hold? I even touched the zipper of the bag on top.

Then I got a sharp, visual image of someone doing the same with mine, and was forced to stop. Much as I'd like to, I couldn't intrude on the old man's privacy that way.

I left the stateroom and followed my nose to the upper deck, where bacon, eggs, and coffee were apparently being served. There I came upon Gramps, Marcus, and someone I hadn't expected to see: Tark. He was dressed casually, in white shorts and a short-sleeved white shirt, Miami-style. I wasn't sure I'd ever seen him that way. But my heart lifted. Somehow, when Tark is around, things go right. When he's not, it's never the same.

'What are you doing here?' I asked.

He and Marcus exchanged glances. I looked at Gramps. He shrugged.

Then Tark turned to me. 'I have an idea,' he said. 'I wanted to share it with you.'

'An idea?' I slid into the empty chair at the table, next to him. 'About what?'

'About this whole dilemma. The mess your grandfather's in. I think I know a way to move it along.'

'Really,' I said. I poured coffee from a white pot and slowly added cream and sugar to it. While I did that, there was a small silence at the table. I knew precisely what it was about. Marcus had brought in a very big gun: someone he knew I respected and might listen to.

But would I? I could see everyone was wondering that. Uneasy about it. Would I accept help when it came through Tark, in a way that I wouldn't accept it from Marcus – who had an entirely different agenda in offering it?

I looked first at one, then the other. My eyes told them everything I didn't say aloud: *this is bribery, and you damn well know it*.

Marcus met my look with a steady one of his own. I turned away.

'Good morning, Gramps,' I said. 'And how are you this fine morning?'

He grinned. 'Rarin' to go, girl. Rarin' to go.'

'Seems to me you've already *gone*,' I said pointedly. 'I'd like to hear about that. Later.'

'Sure, Jesse, sure. No problem. Later.'

I lifted my coffee cup, took a long, slow, sip, then set it down.

Turning to Tark, I narrowed my eyes. 'It better be a doozy,' I said.

Marcus and Gramps had excused themselves and were standing at a far rail, talking animatedly. Now and then Marcus would point across the water, where the gaudy, two-story-high

Flamingo Swan was docked. I could see why people who'd paid fortunes for their pristine homes on this island might be upset to have this sight foisted upon them. At the same time, I admired Marcus for taking a stand and fighting for the tattered old girl.

I listened to Tark's idea while I ate.

'This guy, Soldando, who's behind Barney Noonan's panic. The one Noonan owes the twenty thousand to.'

'What about him?'

'Well, I wasn't sure when we talked before, but I think maybe we could use him. Remember I told you we had some dealings with him several years ago?'

'Yes, but you didn't mention what kind of dealings. Not drugs?' Marcus claimed never to have been involved in drugs.

'No. Not, at least, with our knowledge. It was supposed to be a clean real estate transaction for some property down here. Or, as clean as anything can get when you're dealing with someone like that. But Soldando threw in a little something extra. He tried to pull off a two-million-dollar shipment of cocaine, under Andrelli Enterprises auspices. Marcus found out what was going on and was livid. He threatened to turn him over to the Feds. Scared the pants off Soldando. The Feds were already out to get him, and this one could have sent him up for twenty years.'

A different steward from the night before had been standing nearby. Noting I was finished with my food, he came over and, without interrupting, took the plate away. The early morning sun was hot on my shoulder; I began to sweat. I took a sip of ice water and asked Tark, 'Did he? Turn Soldando over?'

Tark looked uncomfortable. 'You have to realize, Jesse, this was eight, ten years ago. Things were different then. Marcus had to answer to Jimmy Lucetta.'

'And therefore he did what?'

'Made an arrangement with Soldando, the way Lucetta suggested: the coke deal was out, and Soldando was told never to show his face again up north, and never to have anything to do with the Lucetta family or Andrelli Enterprises again. In return, Marcus kept quiet about it.'

'I'll bet he hated that.'

'Well, it was one of many agreements he had to make with Lucetta that went against the grain. That's largely why he broke off from him when he did.'

'I don't get it, though. Why did Lucetta protect Soldando that way?'

'At the time, he wanted someone in place down here. There was trouble, and no one knew how things would end up between the families up north and the ones here. Soldando – despite the fact that he's a weasel, more likely to attack from the back and in a dark alley – had great connections at the time.'

'And now?'

'I ran a check and it seems he's still connected, but behind the scenes. Largely into gambling.'

'So how do you figure we can use him?'

Tark smiled. 'Well, I'd say he owes us one. There must be a way we can work this problem he's got with Barney Noonan.'

'You have something in mind?'

'Actually, my job was just to pass along this information. The rest is up to you.'

I frowned. 'C'mon, Tark, you always have great ideas.'

He shook his head and sat back, folding his big arms and relaxing. 'Not this time. I've got my orders.' He flicked a look at Marcus.

'Oh, I see. He's getting back at me for saying I didn't want his help.'

Tark grinned. 'Only you, Jesse, would see it as payback, when the man's only giving you what you tell him you want.'

I tapped my fingernails on the table, irritated. 'Look, I know I said that, but I've got to run down to Key Largo today, and that'll probably take hours. Meanwhile, I've got Barney Noonan on ice, and now there's this Soldando business. I can't do *everything*.'

Tark laughed aloud. Marcus and Gramps looked over at us and stopped talking suddenly. I'd have sworn they were plotting against me.

*

'I'm coming with you,' Gramps insisted. 'If you find Betty Lou, I want to be there.'

'You might have told me about her in the first place,' I said crossly. 'And the seventy thousand dollars. Old man, I don't want anyone with me I can't trust. In fact, I should toss you overboard right now. And just where did you go when you left the Lonely Palms yesterday?'

'No place special. I had to see a man about a horse.'

I felt a little jolt. Pop used to say that too: *I had to see a man about a horse*. It was an old expression, meaning anything from: 'I had to take a pee' to 'I had business to take care of, and I don't want to tell you what it was.'

In this case, I wasn't sure if Gramps was being evasive, or he'd actually been to the race track.

I was at the dresser in my stateroom, piling incidentals into a tote bag to take to Key Largo with me. Gramps stood beside me, and in the mirror I could see that his wrinkles had deepened. He was worried.

'Gal, I'm sorry I left you to take on Noonan alone. If I had him here right now, I'd break his sorry neck for layin' a finger on you.'

I met his eyes. 'I'm just glad you were out of there. He might have killed you, you know.'

Gramps shook his head. 'Not till he's got his money. And Betty Lou.'

I hefted the tote onto my shoulder and turned to him. 'Old man, are you telling me the truth? You really don't know where she is?'

'You think I'm hidin' her out, or something?'

'That's precisely what I think. Her, and the money.'

He shook his head. 'I wish you were right. I'd like to know Betty Lou was hidden away somewhere safe. I'm worried about her, gal. And that's the God's honest truth.'

I studied his face. If he was lying, this was the best he'd done since showing up at my door.

'You know, I think I believe you,' I said.

He brightened. 'You'll let me go with you, then?'

I gave a short laugh. 'Not a chance. I believe you about Betty Lou. But I still think you're lying about the money. You've got it, haven't you?'

The pale eyes shifted.

'You do! Where the hell is it? Dammit, Gramps, we could give it back to Noonan and get the hell out of all this.'

'Gal, it's not just the money Noonan wants. You said that yourself. It's Betty Lou. And after what she's done, you think Barney would just forgive and forget? We can't go off like that and let her fend for herself.'

I sighed. 'I know. It's just – Old man, do you love this woman?'

'Betty Lou?'

'No, Madonna. *Yes*, Betty Lou. Are you two in love, or something?'

'No, gal, nothin' like that. We're just good friends. Betty Lou's a fine woman. She deserves better than what she got with Barney Noonan.'

'Then you only want what's best for her?'

'Sure. Absolutely.'

'Then listen up, old man. You are staying here on the yacht today. You will not – *will not* – get in anyone's way. Nor will you leave here even for a second, under penalty of death. Got that?'

He frowned. Briefly, I thought I saw something familiar. Then I knew what it was: my own stubborn, offended reaction, when anyone tried to tell me what to do.

'I got it,' he said sourly. 'But I don't like it.'

'You don't have to like it,' I said more gently. 'But please do it, okay? And I promise I'll do my best to find Betty Lou and keep her safe.'

He must have counted to ten; it took him that long to answer. 'Okay,' he finally muttered. 'Whatever you say.'

I almost believed him.

'I know we're both imposing,' I said to Marcus as I was leaving. 'I apologize for being so stubborn about not needing your help.'

A soft breeze lifted my hair and blew it across my cheek. Automatically, as he'd done many times before, Marcus pushed it gently back behind my ear. 'You are never an imposition, Jess. And I'm sorry I didn't see your point of view. I'm afraid I'm getting worse about wanting to protect you, not better.'

'To be honest, I think I'm beginning to understand that. I feel the same way, now and then, about Gramps.'

Marcus smiled. 'We'll look after him. He won't get away from us again. And Jess . . . remember the *Tancook Whaler*?'

'Of course.' We'd built the wooden boat together, for the most part, working weekends at Marcus' cabin at Irondequoit. Marcus had a love of boats . . . which was why this business with *The Flamingo Swan* hadn't surprised me.

'No, I don't mean do you remember it, as such. Do you remember the night it, and I, almost burned to the ground? And you ran into the barn to save us?'

'Yes.'

'Do you remember how you helped me rebuild it afterward?'

My brow furrowed. 'Of course,' I said, perplexed. 'What are you getting at?'

He shrugged. 'I thought this helping thing worked both ways. That's all.'

Chapter 29

Open heart and open hand,
I wonder when I'll understand.

'Hide and Seek', Katherine Ketner

Marcus has a way of giving me things to chew on just as I'm walking out the door. That way, I have to ponder them while I'm driving wherever I'm driving to. He knows this, and uses it to his advantage. *'I thought this helping thing worked both ways.'* Jeez. He had me there.

More than once, I'd helped Marcus out of a tough spot, and never given it a second thought. But when it came to the other way around, I was one proud lady. Not always, but lately. I knew there were reasons for that, but I didn't especially want to think about it now. So to distract myself, I checked out the scenery.

Key Largo is at the northernmost tip of the Keys; Key West way to the south. Both had been made famous through movies and literature, so I'll admit that, being an old movie freak, there might have been some romantic urge to at least see Key Largo (Humphrey Bogart, Lauren Bacall) while in Florida. I wished I'd brought my old Bertie Higgins *Just Another Day in Paradise* tape along. It would have been perfect for cruising the Keys.

Except for a great sunrise, however, there wasn't much romantic about the drive down to Key Largo. Heading south, as I was, the traffic wasn't too bad. But commuter cars were bumper to bumper on the other side, heading into Miami. Construction had run rampant in the past twenty, thirty years, with gas stations, liquor stores, gun shops and fast food restaurants. WE REPAIR GLASS WHILE YOU WAIT, shouted a red sign over a square, concrete shack decorated with graffiti. I wondered what the odds were of having your car window shot out here while stopped at a light.

The rented wreck's air conditioner wasn't working properly, so I also had a chance to smell the air. It was full of diesel fumes and, occasionally, a slight tang of sewage. Apparently the utility companies hadn't been able to keep up with the burgeoning population. Greed, of course. Florida had begun by enticing people to move here and drop their dollars into the commercial till, but it hadn't given back in terms of accommodation. Not that Florida should be singled out. The message is handed down by the federal government to the states, and from them to the counties: cut library hours, police manpower, food stamps, teachers' salaries, road repairs – but don't forget to raise the taxes that pay for them. Raise the price of postage stamps, too, and take a week to deliver mail that used to cross the country in a couple of days. Oh, and while you're at it, tell people, 'Isn't it great that you don't need to pay a special rate for airmail anymore, because all mail travels by air now?' Then, when they figure out their letters are taking five days to cross the country – the same way they used to do by ground – offer them this wonderful, amazing new service called Express and charge them ten bucks for it.

The attitude of the government seems to be that if you scam on the public gradually enough, they won't see it until it's too late. And except for a handful of watchdogs, they're right. Most people don't know what's happening. Sure, they can look at their paychecks and see that they're not taking home any more than they did ten years ago because their taxes have gone up. And they know Johnny still can't read. But often the scam doesn't hit home until a recession, when layoffs begin. For awhile there's unemployment, but when that runs out, the still unemployed find that after all the years of paying into the coffers, the coffers are now close to bare. Food stamps? They've been cut. Vocational retraining? A farce. They're educating people for jobs that aren't going to be there.

Some days, the only bright light on the horizon is that you can still get a forty-nine-cent hamburger at Burger King.

Just don't ask what's in them at that price.

Talking into a box, I ordered two. I love Burger King. 'Anythin' else?' a heavily accented voice called back through static. 'A small diet Coke,' I answered. 'And French fries.'

The responding question was unintelligible. It could have been 'Would you like a brownie?' or a Haitian voodoo curse. 'Sure,' I said. What the hell. Another surprise.

But even that small joy was denied me by the harried, acne-ridden clerk who glared out his window and repeated what I owed him. 'I tol' you, have it *ready*,' he grouched. Car horns blasted behind me.

Nobody likes their jobs anymore. So maybe a recession's good. Being out of work teaches people gratitude for what they had.

I found a Spanish jazz station on the radio and munched through too many pickles while I drove. The wind was warm on my upstate New York bones, so that was nice, but it looked like I wouldn't get to see the town of Key Largo after all. Gray Beach Road, which led to the Fallon cottage, split off from the Overseas Highway just north of town. By that time, I was so deep into my curmudgeon mode, I was relieved just to get off this No Man's Land Express.

A few straggly cypresses lined the road. There was sand on either side, with row upon row of white cottages, their paint peeling as if, from being squeezed together so closely, they had rubbed each other raw. There was a salt-air breeze, laced with the scent of fish. After a mile or so the Atlantic Ocean came into view. Gray Beach Road ended there, at Spit Key Lane. Following Irene's directions, I turned left. After a few miles I saw the tree Irene had told me about as a marker. Its trunk was twisted into striations that gave it the look of a white and tan barber pole. Just beyond it was a narrow sand trail lined with cypresses, only wide enough to accommodate the Chevy. If you met anyone here, you'd have to back up.

The Chevy took to the trail like silk to glass, slipping and sliding all the way. But then the track widened, and I think even the rented wreck caught its breath. Ahead was a long, empty, white beach and the bluest water I'd ever seen. The sun glinted down on fingers of sea that wound in and out of the surrounding sand. I stopped the car and stepped out. The old Chevy engine went tick, tick, tick, cooling down.

To the left, against a hummock of sand and sea grass, nestled the Fallon cottage. It was just as Irene had described it: small, and painted white with green shutters. It had a screened front porch, and there were a couple of white wooden chairs on it, with dark green cushions.

I looked up and down the stretch of beach and saw no signs of life. 'My parents bought a couple of acres,' Irene had told me, 'for privacy. You could do that back then. The beach doesn't belong to us, but it's private. No one ever bothers us there.'

Leaving my tote in the car, I locked it, pocketed the keys, and went up onto the porch. Looking through the glass of the front door I saw an empty living room lined with bookshelves and furnished in a beach style: woven grass rug and white rattan. There was a black potbellied stove in one corner.

I knocked, just in case, and waited a moment. Then I slid the key Irene had given me into the lock, turned it, and stepped inside.

Chapter 30

There's a thing about vacation cottages. Often, they feel warm and welcoming, perhaps because they're used for vacations, and people are happy when they're in them. Away from the everyday grind, you can swim and laze in the sun all day, dragging your fingers idly through hot sand. You can track that sand into the house while you fix bologna or peanut butter sandwiches and fill Thermoses with iced tea to take back down to the water. And at night, since you don't usually have television, you can gather around a table with coffee and hot chocolate to play board games with the family or tell exciting ghost stories.

This is merely an idea I have, you understand – an idea that stems from watching television and movies. I never had a family, or a vacation, like that.

But I have been in other people's beach or lake cottages, and this is what I've felt. I can attest to the fact that people leave behind certain blithe memories, as well as old sandy shoes, on Labor Day.

The memories in the Fallon cottage were not at all like that. There was the usual musty smell you get when you open up a house that's been closed awhile. But the rest was strangely off.

I walked through, and found a semi-modern kitchen with an

empty fridge and a clean, dry sink. No sign of recent life. Two bedrooms turned up family photos on one wall, a couple of ratty old stuffed animals from someone's childhood, a handmade quilt, and kerosene lamps – apparently for emergencies, since there was working electricity. Closets held worn tennis shoes and old beach clothes. The one bathroom was simply decorated in a fifties-era pink ceramic tile. No clues to Betty Lou's whereabouts there, so far as I could see. No toiletries, no hair in the sink or tub that would indicate someone had stayed here of late.

I returned to the living room and stood in the center of it, looking around. It was then that the vibrations crept in: old arguments, and possibly new ones. Anger. Sometimes if you listen long enough and hard enough, you can almost hear words. It's as if they're retained in the ether, like lingering strains of music when a radio's turned off.

I didn't hear words in the Fallon cottage, but I felt them. They were dark clouds, as palpable as those that were even now drifting across the sun, bringing in an afternoon shower. This cottage hadn't been used, at least not recently, for family fun. Something bad had happened here.

With that in mind, I rechecked everything – closets, drawers, underneath cushions, behind the rattan furniture – and finally under the rug, looking for something hidden, or a trap door. I ran my fingers along curtain valances and the molding above doors. But even rummaging inside the potbellied stove rendered nothing but soot to my elbows. I turned again to the kitchen. Standing in the doorway, I studied the fridge, thinking. Cold air had drifted from it when I opened the door. And the inside light was on. That, in fact, was how I'd known the electricity was working.

Don't people generally, I wondered, unplug a fridge and leave the door ajar when they're closing a place up for any length of time?

I decided to look around outside. Pulling the front door shut behind me, I pocketed the key and stood on the porch, looking at the wooden chairs with their bright green cushions. They struck me now as odd. Why would anyone leave furniture cushions out at this time of year? Given that it was still hurricane season, I'd have expected outdoor furniture to be stored away when no one was here. For that matter, it rains a lot in Florida. Brief rains, usually, but the one that was beginning now was already slanting in and dampening the porch. Before it was over, the cotton sailcloth cushions would be soaked.

Well, Betty Lou's and Irene's parents were away in Hawaii. And Irene had been dealing with her sister's disappearance. Perhaps there hadn't been time or energy for the usual battening down.

Stepping out on the sand, I felt the warm rain on my bare shoulders and face. *Neighbors*, I thought. *Maybe someone had seen Betty Lou down here*. I began to walk.

There were small dunes along this strip of beach that looked temporary, as if they had been created by a recent hurricane tide. Sea grass hadn't yet begun to take hold. Across the beach, waves traveled in spots, forming shallow gullies. Lightning flashed. Suddenly, the rain became a sheer gray curtain blowing from south to north. I strode through it along the surf. For me, there is nothing quite so stimulating as walking in the rain, unless it's swimming in the rain, with lightning all about.

Not much time for a swim today, I thought. *Not much time for any kind of fun, since Gramps entered my life*.

Funny how people you don't even know one week can, in the next, become so important a part of your life that you can't simply turn your back and let them go.

I remembered Gramps the morning before his 'drowning', trudging up the walk to Mrs Binty's porch in the snow, shivering in his thin denim jacket. He'd been scamming on me even then – walking back from the airport after leaving that disguise in a locker, planning to surprise me with his presence on the plane. But I couldn't hold his chicanery against him, somehow. If anything, I admired it.

According to Samved, it's that kind of thinking that lands me into trouble, every time. 'You don't ask enough of people,' he had once said. 'If you asked more in terms of trust, honesty, integrity, they might be inspired to give it.'

'But if I asked, and they still didn't give it, it would be just one more disappointment,' I'd countered.

'How do you feel when you don't ask, and don't get?'

I had frowned. 'Disappointed. But –'

'We teach people how to treat us,' Samved said. 'We give them clues all the time. We say, "Use me, take advantage of me," or "Don't use me, don't take advantage of me. I'm worth more than that."'

'You think I'm a doormat?' I had countered.

'Only in that now and then you lose your grip and slide.'

'Very funny.'

I continued my walk, looking for other cottages or houses close to the shore. When none turned up, I struck out in the direction of a low group of dunes. The brief tropical rain stopped suddenly, and the sun turned hot, scorching my shoulders and arms. My clothes were nearly dry by the time I reached the first dune.

My shoes were another matter. They squished, and the sand they became filled with along the way turned to painful, sodden lumps. I sat and took them off, tying the laces together so I could carry them over a shoulder. As I struck out again, I noted that over the crest of a dune to the right, gulls were wheeling and calling to each other – the universal gull language heralding food. *A house*, I thought. *Must be a house, there. Garbage cans, or an outside deck where people were eating*.

I began climbing, my toes digging in and the backs of my calves and thighs straining. The sand was still wet, and packed down enough so that clearing the top didn't take too long. I stood on the rim of what looked like a mini-volcano, sloping down toward the middle, and saw no house, no sign of human life.

At the 'crater's' lowest point, perhaps fifty feet below me, several gulls picked at the sand. Close up, their cries and pecking seemed more like curiosity than hunger. *Old fish*, I thought. *Old, spoiled fish swept up by the last major storm? No – carried here, most likely, by the gulls. Their own private little diner.*

There were only two ways to go from here: around the rim of the dune, or down into it and then up the opposite side. Walking the rim, as soft as it was, would probably result in time-consuming stumbles and falls. I started down. As I neared the bottom, some of the gulls took flight. A few cast me wary looks but held their places, refusing to be cowed by the stranger in their midst.

I love birds. I've always envied them, in fact, wishing I had wings I could flap to fly away from troubles, not to mention troubling people. There's nothing, however, more aggressive than a hungry gull. Especially if it thinks you've got food. I didn't, but I approached them cautiously anyway.

'Easy does it, guys. I'm just passing by.'

One gull cocked its head and raised its wings as if in greeting. That quickly, another jumped on its back and began pecking at its neck and head. The two birds went at it, jabbing and chasing each other about in circles. Other birds got in on it, running in and just as fast backing away. Sand flew. Topography was rearranged.

I stood a bit off, deciding which direction away would be the safest one to take. They were really into it now, creating a hole a foot deep in the sand.

The hole was so deep, in fact –

Suddenly, I could hardly breathe. I stared at the impression in the sand, growing weak and cold. The gulls' wild ballet had rendered up a terrible sight: a pale, white hand sticking out of the coarse powder, clutching at air as if for its murderer's throat.

I moved in on the birds, chasing them away with loud shouts, waving my arms. They took off. Running to the hole, I cried softly, 'No, dammit, no! Don't let it be Betty Lou.'

I dug around the hand with fingers that shook violently. I saw now that it was connected to a slender arm. Tearing through the sand I uncovered hair, blonde hair. *No, please God, no*. Then a forehead weathered from the sun –

'What the hell are you doing?' a voice yelled from behind me. 'Stop it! Stop it right now or I'll shoot!'

I whirled and looked up into the sun. At the rim of the dune I saw a face in shadow, surrounded by a halo of bright hair. The shadowed form below that stood with feet splayed, holding a rifle. Then I heard the woman's desperate voice again. 'Get away from there! I'm warning you, get away or I'll shoot!'

I stumbled to my feet. I stared at the woman. Then, slowly, I began to climb. When I was no more than five feet below her I stopped, and with my voice no more than a whisper, I said, 'Betty Lou. Thank God. I thought that terrible thing was you.'

Chapter 31

The woman stepped back. Her mouth was a tight line, and her voice shook, but she didn't lower the rifle. 'Who are you? What are you doing here? How do you know me?'

I wiped a hand across my mouth. 'Johnny James. He's my grandfather.'

The rifle began to lower. Betty Lou's voice was less hostile now. 'Your grandfather? Are you Jesse?'

I nodded. Betty Lou stepped down beside me. She was shorter than I'd thought, and her touch was gentle. She took my hand. 'I'm sorry I frightened you.'

I looked into the face of Barney Noonan's Perfect Ten. It was young for the fifty-six or -seven I understood her to be. There were worry lines around the eyes, but the mouth hadn't given up and turned down permanently, the way some do. Blue eyes were dark with concern.

'It wasn't you who frightened me,' I said. 'It was that – that thing, down there in the sand. Who is it?'

'Paul,' she said, her mouth trembling.

'Paul?'

Tears filled her eyes. 'Come. I'll show you.'

I followed her back to the body. Gently, as if unwrapping a

shroud, she uncovered the face of a man: angular and long, with delicate cheekbones and nose. The features looked as if they'd been arranged lovingly after death, rather than left in agony.

Betty Lou touched the stiffened cheek. A strong scent of decay was evident now. There were ants. But she didn't stop. She pushed sand away from the rest of the body, below the waist. My stomach turned over and I began to wretch.

There were no legs.

'For God's sake,' I said hoarsely, pushing sand back onto the exposed torso. 'Don't look at this, Betty Lou. Cover it up!'

Her hands shook. 'But it's all I have left of him now. This is all Barney left me with.'

She began weeping, and I pulled her back away from the corpse, holding her until her sobs had stopped.

'Who is he?' I said then. 'Who is Paul?'

'Paul Tracey.' She wiped her eyes. 'My friend. He . . . he lived up the road.'

'And Barney did this?'

The blue eyes looked at me, filled with the recollection of horror. 'Last week. I think it was last week . . . maybe longer. I don't know, I seem to be losing track of time. Living with this everyday . . .' She gave a shudder. 'Anyway, Barney found us together, just walking on the beach. He shot him. And then he . . . how could any human being do a thing like this? And I keep thinking, was Paul still alive when Barney did that . . . when he did that to his legs? Did Barney wound him, then torture . . .'

Her voice broke. She couldn't finish.

'But he didn't hurt you?' I said.

'No. When it first started to happen, Paul and I both ran, and I thought he was right there behind me. I could hear Barney shooting, but I thought he'd missed. I heard Paul yell, 'Keep going, Betty, don't stop!' Finally, when I couldn't run any longer, I fell onto the sand and looked around for Paul. He wasn't there. I . . . I didn't find him here till the next day. The gulls uncovered . . .' She started to cry again.

'I know. I know.' I patted her back, feeling inept. What does one say in the face of such depravity? There are no adequate words.

Betty Lou straightened, wiping her face and pulling herself together. 'I've been hiding at Paul's place. Barney didn't know him. He'd never even met him, so I didn't think he'd find me there. But I've been so afraid.'

Looking back at the still-exposed parts of Paul Tracey's body, she shivered. 'I didn't want to just leave him here for predators to feed on. But I hadn't the strength to drag him to the ocean. And, I couldn't stand to think of him ending up that way. I've always been afraid of water, myself. I'm the only one in the family who can't swim, and I didn't want Paul . . .' Her hand fluttered to her chest.

'Betty Lou, why didn't you just call the police and have Barney arrested? You'd have been free of him that way.'

'You don't understand. I don't know who I can trust anymore in the department. Not in Miami, and not even here. I couldn't be sure he'd be arrested.'

'Were you afraid that he might hurt you, if you talked?'

'Probably. But not as afraid as I used to be. Since Barney did this, I just haven't cared much what happens to me.'

'So you haven't seen or even talked to Barney since it happened?'

She shook her head. 'No, I've just been at Paul's house, hiding, waiting for Johnny –'

She seemed to mentally bite her tongue.

'For my grandfather? You're waiting for him?'

'He said he'd come.' Her mouth trembled. 'He has my money, nearly seventy thousand dollars, and he said he'd bring it to me so I can go away. I've just been waiting. Do you know where he is?'

'You mean you don't?'

'No. I did reach him a few days ago at the number he gave me in New York.'

'New York. You mean, my number? In Rochester?'

'I think so. When he left here, he said he'd be staying up north with you until things cooled down a bit.'

Damn the man. I'd never even met him at the time.

'So let me get this straight. You told Johnny James a few days ago that you were hiding out in Paul Tracey's house. And he said he'd come back to Florida, get the money from wherever he'd stashed it, and bring it to you.'

'Yes . . . Why are you looking at me like that?'

I couldn't tell her. I couldn't say to this woman who'd just lost one good friend in a horrifying manner that another 'good friend', Johnny James, had been conning her all along. But I was certain now that when he left the motel yesterday to pick up the money from wherever he'd hidden it, good old Gramps had been planning to fly the coop.

And without Betty Lou.

Together, we covered Paul Tracey's body with so much sand, it would take major winds to reveal it again. Then Betty Lou took me to Paul's house, which was tucked into a cove a couple of miles south of the Fallon cottage. It was up on stilts, with floor to ceiling windows. Inside, the walls and furniture were white with soft blue accents. Huge windows opened up to the sand.

'I've been afraid here at night,' Betty Lou confided. 'Even though Barney didn't know who Paul was, or where he lived, I couldn't be sure he wouldn't find me here. Then, one night, I heard him outside. He was yelling my name over and over, like he'd gone crazy. I heard gears clashing and saw the outline of a jeep across the dunes. It had spotlights, and they kept sweeping back and forth, back and forth. I felt sure he'd be able to see right through the curtains, so I hid in a closet. I got on my knees, and just prayed and prayed. When I came out, sometime around dawn, Barney was gone.' She gave a shaky laugh. 'I remembered Paul saying he chose this spot because it was hard to find, and he liked the privacy. Neither of us ever thought . . .'

We were at a dining-room table with a glass top. At its center was a bunch of white daisies. I drank iced tea while Betty smoked. 'Do you mind?' she had said. 'I quit, but I still need one when I'm really tense.' The sun touched her blonde hair, bringing out highlights of red. She looked like Irene in some ways: the pale face, white skin, slender body and legs.

I could see why Betty Lou Fallon had always been loved. And not only by men, I guessed, but by anyone who knew her. It wasn't necessarily that she was attractive, although she was: slender and shapely in blue cotton slacks and a white shirt. It was more that she was still an innocent. Despite what must have been an abhorrent marriage to Barney Noonan, Betty Lou still believed in the ultimate good of the universe. It hadn't occurred to her yet that Gramps might have taken off with her money, leaving her to fend for herself.

'Barney was always violent,' she said softly, 'but he never hurt me until after he left the force. He changed, then. He'd sit around the house all morning, blame me for his troubles, and then go out somewhere. When he came home he was usually drunk, and he started hitting me. I began coming down here to the cottage to get away, but then one night about six months ago, Barney figured out where I was and he came down after me. We had a terrible fight. I think he would have killed me that night if I hadn't managed to get away. I ran that night, too. I didn't know where I was going, but then all of a sudden I looked up and there was a light on in here. I'd heard that someone new had moved in months ago, a retired teacher, but I'd never met him. That night, I ran to his door and asked him if I could come in. I pretended to just be passing by, a friendly neighborhood visit . . .'

She paused, looking out over the water, her eyes haunted. 'After that, I started coming down here just to see him.'

She fell silent.

'I'm not sure,' I said gently, 'how my grandfather fits into all this.'

She looked at me and smiled. 'I met Johnny by chance one day, at an outdoor table at the Coco Walk. Do you know it?'

'Slightly.' I raised a skeptical brow. 'All this was by chance?'

'Well,' she said, laughing, 'it seemed that way. With Johnny James one can never really know.'

'You don't have to explain that to me.'

She took another drag, and studied her cigarette. 'This was a few months ago, about the time I'd decided I had to break free of Barney. I suspected from the first that Johnny was a con. But he's not essentially bad, you know.'

'Huh,' was about all I could think to say.

'Anyway, I got a kick out of him. We became friends. And it was Johnny who came up with the idea. He said, "You've worked too hard just putting up with Noonan all these years to leave everything behind. Let's get you a piece of that bank account, and then fix it so you can disappear."'

I shook my head, wonderingly. 'Betty Lou . . . look, I'm sorry, but you never once thought he might be working things out so he could get his hands on the money and run?'

Her eyes met mine, bewildered. 'I trusted Johnny. I still do.'

'And if you're wrong about him? Then what?'

'I . . . Jesse, I *need* to trust him. I need to trust *someone*. I can't go on like this much longer, afraid every minute that Barney will find me.'

I reached over and touched her hand. It was small, but not as fragile as it looked. 'I can't speak for my grandfather. But I'll help you . . . if you want me to.'

She wasn't as stubborn as I. The word 'help' only filled her with hope. It was in those candid blue eyes.

'All right, then,' I said. 'If you're up to it, here's what we'll do.'

Chapter 32

I arrived back at the *SeasStar* after dark, with Betty Lou. One of the deck hands helped me up, after assisting Betty Lou, who was dressed in rolled-up black pants and a black shirt from Paul's closet. The clothes helped her to blend into the dark – a last-minute disguise.

Tark had met us in the parking lot at the entrance to the marina, and he waited there still, making sure we hadn't been followed. Betty Lou and I slipped silently across the deck and through the door Marcus held open, into the main cabin. Dark blue curtains had been pulled around all the windows for privacy. Cushy white sofas and chairs nestled closely together for comfortable conversation, and brass lamps were lit, but dim.

Not so dim, however, that Gramps didn't recognize my companion immediately. He looked as if he'd been pacing. When we came into view he whirled around, spotted Betty Lou, and his old face lit up.

'Now, ain't you a sight for sore eyes,' he said with a big grin.

'Johnny James. You don't look so bad yourself.'

Gramps came over and hugged her a bit awkwardly. She hugged back. Then her shoulders slumped tiredly. It had been a long, exhausting week for Betty Lou. Some of it she had told me about in the car.

'Here, sit down,' Gramps said quickly, giving her his arm as he led her to an easy chair. Though they were about the same size and height, with Gramps not an inch taller or a gram heavier, Betty Lou leaned against him gratefully. He puffed out his chest, patted her back manfully, and seemed to grow before my eyes. Betty Lou smiled.

'Thank you, Johnny. Always the gentleman.'

'And who wouldn't be, with the likes of you?'

He was laying it on pretty thick. Either he really did care for Betty Lou Noonan, or he was softening her up for another con. I intended to see he didn't get to her this time.

'Everything all right?' Marcus asked.

I nodded. 'I've got some fast work to do, though. Barney Noonan is crazier, and sicker, than I ever imagined.' I looked over at Betty Lou. 'She's a nice person. I promised her that I'd help her. Marcus?'

'Yes?'

'I can't do this alone. I promised her you'd help her, too.'

We sat around a big mahogany table in a conference room on the yacht: me, Gramps, Betty Lou, Marcus, and Tark. I'd had my doubts about letting Gramps in on this, but he wouldn't be put off. I agreed, finally, because if I had him by my side, I might at least know what he was up to.

There was a carafe of good, hot coffee on the table, and I poured my third cup, having laid out only part of my plan. 'I've been thinking about this all the way back from Key Largo,' I said, 'and I think it'll work. The timing will be the most difficult thing, but if we all pull together . . .'

I hesitated.

'You've caught *my* interest,' Tark said. 'But why do I feel I'm waiting for the other shoe to drop?'

'I was about to say the same thing,' Marcus said with a frown. 'Why would you want to bring Mac Devlin down here? I'll admit he was a big help in Arizona last spring. But I thought we'd seen the last of him.'

I gave him a look that said, *You wish*.

'For one thing,' I said, 'Mac has a seaplane. He can fly her from here to a safe place, where Barney will never find her. And we can trust Mac. He'll never tell a soul.'

'That's it? That's the plan, girl?' Gramps said. 'Heck, it don't feel like much to me. Why not just take her wherever she wants to go by boat? Or hire somebody down here to fly her?'

Marcus leaned forward. 'He's right. And so is Tark. Drop that other shoe, Jess. What are you holding back?'

I toyed with my coffee. Taking my time, I stirred in cream and sugar. 'I, uh . . . there is something else. It's a bit of a favor.'

'I'm listening,' he said.

'Okay. I'd like to use *The Flamingo Swan*.'

He sat back, an expression of surprise crossing his face.

'The *Swan*? For what?'

'A little diversionary tactic, that's all.'

'Uh-oh,' Tark said, groaning. 'I feel a headache coming on.'

I flashed him an irritated look. 'It can work,' I said. 'I know it can work. It's just a bit tricky.'

'Tricky,' Marcus said mildly. 'Jess . . . what do you want with my *Swan*?'

'I want to blow her up,' I said.

Go for the shock value, I figured. That way, when I tell him what I really have in mind for the *Swan*, he might be half relieved.

But I couldn't have predicted this reaction, not in a million years.

Marcus threw back his head and laughed. He laughed so much, in fact, tears ran down his cheeks. He had to wipe them away.

Tark was watching him, a small smile playing around his lips. Then he looked at me. His expression said: *He's glad to have you back*.

'Jess,' Marcus said finally, 'life has been so dull without you.'

My mouth had dropped open, so it was a little difficult to talk, but I managed. 'I guess I didn't really think you'd take it this way. I mean, your pride and joy, and all that? Your Esther Williams boat? You'd let me blow her up?'

He laughed again, but softly this time. 'Jess, I said life had been dull. I didn't say I'd let you do it.'

'Oh.'

I must have looked crestfallen. He leaned forward and rested his chin on tented fingers. 'But do tell me what you had in mind.'

I stood at a presentation board next to the conference table, drawing a diagram. 'So if we place the explosives just right,' I continued, 'there should be no damage.'

'None at all?' Tark asked.

'Well, maybe a little smoke.' I flicked a look at Marcus.

'A *little smoke*,' he said dryly.

'You know I'd help you clean it up, afterward,' I said quickly. 'We could work together on it. Like the *Tancook Whaler*.'

His eyes met mine, and for a moment they stilled. I wouldn't make a commitment like this, he knew, unless I planned to stick around.

But there was a question in those dark eyes, as well. What did my sticking around mean? How far did it go?

Betty Lou spoke up. 'I don't know anything at all about these fake explosives, as you call them, but it sounds dangerous to me.'

'Not if they're handled right,' I reassured her. 'And Mac knows all about that. He sets them up at the Davies School for Executive Bodyguards.'

I told her about the training course there, and the fact that I'd met Mac the day he rigged a 'bank building' to blow up while I, and other trainees, were inside it. 'There's a lot of noise and smoke, but if you know how to react, you're okay.'

Marcus' tone was doubtful. 'And you want to do this to the *Swan* - pretend to blow her up - as a distraction while we're getting Betty Lou out to sea? Doesn't that seem a bit of an overkill?'

'I agree,' Tark said, looking thoughtful. 'You must have a three-legged man on you, Jess.'

'A three-legged man?'

'Yet one more shoe to drop?'

'Oh, yeah. Well . . . there is one more thing.'

Gramps cackled. 'I knew it. I knew you'd come up with somethin' real bright, gal. What is it?'

'That seventy thousand dollars you brought on board with you, Gramps. I want it. *Now*.'

His face grew red. 'Lookee here, you wait just a minute, gal –'

'Oh, and, *kerplop*,' I said.

'Kerplop?'

'My final shoe. Betty Lou's got to die. It's the only way.'

Gramps was on his feet. 'You're not getting that money! It belongs to Betty Lou. And you're not puttin' her in danger with this hare brained scheme of yours!'

'Harebrained? A minute ago you said it was brilliant.'

'Not if it involves hurtin' Betty Lou, it ain't.'

'Hush,' Betty Lou said firmly, taking matches and a pack of cigarettes from her shirt pocket. 'Let her talk.'

Gramps looked at her, then me, and opened his mouth again.

'I said hush,' Betty Lou repeated, tapping out a cigarette and lighting up. 'Please, Johnny, sit down.'

Gramps threw up his hands and sat. 'I'll let her talk. I ain't sayin' I like it, though.'

'Thank you,' I said. I addressed Betty Lou. 'You remember we were talking in the car on the way here from Key Largo, and you said you didn't think Barney would ever let you go? That he's so obsessed, he'd find you no matter how far you ran?'

'Yes. I'm afraid that's probably true.'

'Betty, after what I saw down there today, I have to agree. Barney isn't just mad. He's evil. So I got to thinking, why not make it seem the *Swan* blew up, and you with her? It's not that far-fetched, after all.' I pointed to a copy of the latest *Miami Sun* on the conference table. 'According to that piece on the front page, the Miami Seven are at it again – calling the paper, renewing threats to blow up the *Swan* if Marcus doesn't have her towed away. No one in Miami would be surprised if she blew up now – or at least, seemed to.'

Betty Lou picked up the paper and scanned it. She had changed into denim shorts and a white blouse, and her hair was pulled back into a ponytail. Except for the cigarette, she looked about twelve. But a smart twelve.

'I think I see what you mean. How would you want to do it? What would I have to do?'

'Just play Esther Williams,' I said.

Gramps and Betty Lou had excused themselves and gone to Gramps' stateroom to talk this out. I still hadn't seen the seventy thousand dollars, but my bet was that Betty Lou would talk him into turning it over, to help the cause.

Marcus, Tark, and I sat alone at the conference table, munching on turkey sandwiches.

'I must admit,' Marcus said, 'I'm impressed at the way you've worked everything out.'

I downed the remainder of an ice-cold glass of milk. 'Not quite everything. There's one small detail. Will you let me use the *Swan*?'

His smile was pained. 'Why do I feel you're doing this as a test? Surely you could have figured out any number of ways to "kill off" Betty Lou.'

'Ah, but nothing quite so dramatic. And nothing that will be confirmed in all the morning papers, *after* Barney Noonan's seen it with his own eyes. How could he doubt it for a minute?'

'May I point out that you're missing one thing?'

'What?'

'A body.'

'Mmm, well, that would be nice. On the other hand, lots of people are lost at sea. Shoot, there may be a whole passel of them at the bottom of the Miami River, courtesy of Barney Noonan himself.'

'Jess... everything else aside, have you thought that this *could* be dangerous for Betty Lou? Fake explosives or no, something might go wrong?'

'I've thought about it, yes. But the odds are slim. And you heard her, just now. She said she wants to do it. Hell, she's even excited about it. She wants Barney to see her "die" so she'll be free of him once and for all.' I leaned forward on the table, talking softly. 'Marcus, I'm not taking this as lightly as it sounds. That's just me, getting high on the scam. You know how I am. But I've worked with this stuff, and so has Mac. Between us, we can set it up so it works. Aside from Betty Lou, you don't honestly think I'd put the *Swan* at risk, do you? I know how much she means to you.'

He held my eyes a moment. 'And you know how much you mean to me. You don't honestly think I'd say no?'

I smiled, relieved. 'I wasn't sure you'd trust me.'

'After all this time? I'd trust you with my life.'

I hadn't a clue, at the moment, how prophetic a statement that would turn out to be.

Marcus and I went up on deck, while Tark excused himself to make business calls to Rochester. Candles had been lit, casting a soft glow. The sky, I was startled to see after so many hours below, was an inky black. Stars sizzled like cold diamonds on a hot cast-iron pan. I settled into a lounge chair with Marcus' absolutely unscannable, state-of-the-art phone, and a cup of coffee. Marcus sat across from me, pretending not to listen.

'Hey, Mac,' I said when he answered sleepily. 'Sorry to call so late.'

'Jesse?' There was a brief note of caution, something I've come to expect when talking with Mac since last spring. It passed, however. 'What's up?' he said. 'Where are you?' It sounded as if he was shaking sleep from his head. 'Hell, where am I?'

I laughed. 'You're safe in bed in Rochester, New York. I'm in Miami with my grandfather, and we're both in trouble. I wondered if you might help us.'

This time a cautious silence. But then, finally, 'Shoot, gal. Tell me what you need. If I can help, I will.'

I told him what was going on with Gramps and Barney Noonan, as briefly as possible. When I was finished he said, 'Sounds like an adventure to me.'

Since Mac was generally up for adventures, I took this to mean he was in.

'I'll have to do some shifting around with my schedule,' he added, 'but hell, it can't be any worse than ramming a water tower in a Beech 18.'

I gave a shudder. 'Don't remind me. And you're sure you can lay your hands on enough explosives?'

'I'd say we could make a pretty loud noise.'

'But you agree we can set it up so no one gets hurt?'

'Shoot, gal, I do this all the time. Isn't that why you called me?'

'Of course.'

'I mean, it couldn't be anything personal, could it? Like you wanted to see me?'

I hesitated, and looked at Marcus, who was tapping his fingers impatiently on the arm of his lounge chair. 'Mac, we can talk when you get here, okay?'

'Anything you say, gal. You're running the show.'

I ignored the *double entendre*.

'And we can do all this by midnight tomorrow, right?'

'I don't see why not. I'll leave early in the morning, get there by mid-afternoon at the latest, depending. That'll give us several hours.'

We arranged it that when he got to town he'd take a room in a hotel close to the MacArthur Causeway, and call me here. I gave him Marcus' private number.

'Where is that?' he asked.

'It's, uh . . . on Star Island.'

'Pretty ritzy. A hotel?'

'Actually, a boat.'

'Okay . . . You wanta tell me the name of this boat, and just where it might be docked?'

His voice had tensed up, so I figured he'd already guessed.

'The *SeaStar*,' I admitted. 'Gramps and I are staying on Marcus' yacht.'

A silence at the other end.

'Mac?'

'Yeah?'

'I know this is asking a lot. I won't forget it.'

'I'm countin' on that,' he said.

I held the phone out to Marcus. 'Your turn.'

He took it, but before he pressed the TALK button he said, 'And how is our pilot friend?'

I gave a casual shrug. 'About the same.'

Marcus studied me a moment. Then he removed a slip of paper from his shirt pocket. On it, he'd written Luis Soldando's private telephone number, which Tark had unearthed from old files.

He punched in the number. While he waited for Soldando to answer, his entire demeanor changed. Personal issues were forgotten. His back straightened; tension moved in. He was all business now.

'Luis?' he said in a clipped tone when Soldando answered. 'Marcus Andrelli here.'

There was a brief silence at this end.

'I thought you might remember,' Marcus said pointedly.

He listened, then held the phone away from his ear a bit. I could hear the voice at the other end: worried, tremulous.

'I didn't call to harass you, Luis. On the contrary. I understand you're having a bit of trouble with an ex-police officer from the Miami PD. One Barney Noonan.'

A flurry of words from that end. Marcus looked at me, rolled his eyes, and said, 'Yes, yes, I know. Things are tough all around these days, Luis. You can't trust anyone. That's why I called. I may be able to help you with this.'

More words.

'That's what I'm saying, Luis. I think I can get your money back for you. Precisely. Now, this is what I'm prepared to do.'

Speaking softly but firmly, Marcus outlined the plan: Barney Noonan would arrive at Soldando's door the next day by noon, with the twenty thousand dollars he owed Luis.

'Never mind how I know that,' Marcus said. 'Yes, I'm reasonably certain I can promise it. Now, Luis, in return, I want something from you. For old time's sake, you might say.'

It took only a few more minutes of conversation to tie up details.

'Are you sure we can trust him?' I asked when Marcus had hung up and handed me back the phone. 'What if he betrays you?'

He quirked an eyebrow. 'Surely you jest,' he said.

We sat for awhile in comfortable silence, relaxing for the first time that night. The *SeaStar*'s hull made soft slapping sounds as she rocked gently with the tide. Across the water, *The Flamingo Swan* stood high and proud, illuminated by spotlights. At night, she stuck out more than ever like a very sore thumb.

'You do like to rub their noses in it, don't you?' I said.

'Meaning what?'

'The *Swan*. All that light.'

'It's for security,' Marcus protested innocently.

'Uh-huh.'

He chuckled.

'You know, all this fuss over the *Swan* must have been on the wire services. I wonder why I never heard about it.'

He shrugged. 'Knowing you? Easily. What have you been doing the past month or so?'

I cast back in memory. 'Working on my screenplay, I guess.'

'Mm-hmm. You hide out when you're deep into a project. You don't eat, don't talk, don't turn on the television . . .'

'... don't dress, don't wash,' I finished for him. 'Well, not until noon half the time.'

'You yell at your dog and cuss at the newsboy ...'

'... I forget to clean, and I run out of toilet paper. Sometimes I wonder why you'd ever even want me around.'

'Well, I already know your foibles. It'd be real work, getting used to someone else's.'

He was teasing. There was humor in his voice. But something about what he had said struck home; the kind of truth you don't often think of but that is no less true.

'We have known each other quite awhile,' I said quietly.

I looked again at *The Flamingo Swan*. Who else but Marcus would have done such an oddball thing? To set it up in full view of Miami's most upscale residents, not to mention Miami itself ...

It was the kind of bizarre, outlandish thing that excited me, that turned me on. And maybe that's not much to base a life together on. But it made me smile, and it made me think. The *Swan* had a history. Marcus and I had a history. And he was offering us both a shot at the future. A chance to see how far we could go together, how rich and rewarding our lives together might become.

Only someone without a spirit of adventure, I thought, would fear the journey ahead. Only someone who had given up – not only on love but on life. And none of us knows how much of life is left.

'Marcus?' I turned to him and met the look of expectation in his eyes.

'I think ...'

But at that moment we were interrupted, as the door from the main cabin swung open. Betty Lou stepped out, dressed in her long blue cotton pants and a simple white shirt with stand-up collar. I had thought she might be in bed for the night by now, and wondered why she had changed from the shorts she'd worn earlier. She stood half in shadow from the surrounding candles, and didn't speak.

'Betty Lou?' I said. 'What's up? Everything all right?'

She smiled, and hesitated. Her hand went to her chest, in the feminine gesture that seemed to be a habit with her. Then she shoved her hands into her pockets and came toward me, her hips swaying just a bit. It was a very subtle, sensual style that I'd noticed right off when we met. Probably the same one all the men in Miami had noticed, according to Dave Laker. Her blonde hair swung softly, one side brushing her cheek. As she drew closer my own smile faded. I felt a small shock.

'Well, I'll be damned,' I said.

'Probably. But not for a few more years yet.'

It was Gramps.

Gramps perched on a locker that held life jackets, and grinned.

'Gotcha good, didn't I?'

'I must admit you got me, too,' Marcus said wonderingly. 'You're a dead ringer.'

Gramps winced. 'Don't say dead.'

Betty Lou slipped onto the deck to join us. Her hair was covered now by a dark kerchief, and she wore a navy blue sweater over her white blouse.

'Isn't he great?' she said, like a little girl admiring a magician. 'Johnny is so talented at these things.'

'I'm not certain I'd use the word great,' I said, 'but he certainly is amazing. Gramps, don't you have anything better to do than play dress-up? And where'd you get that wig?'

'Gal, I didn't do this to pass the time. Don't you get it? I'm gonna be Betty Lou!'

'What are you talking about?'

'I'm taking her place on the *Swan* tomorrow night. That way she can't possibly get hurt.'

'Forget it,' I said. 'All I need is you mixing in . . .'

But then I fell silent and just looked at him, thinking. Was it possible? Would it work?

'I don't know . . .' I said doubtfully. 'What if you had to talk?

You couldn't possibly fool Noonan. He'd know his own wife's voice.'

'I don't see how that could happen, the way you got it worked out,' he countered. 'Not with everything happening so fast.'

I shook my head. 'It's risky.'

'Hell, gal, *life* is risky. But this sort of thing's a piece of cake for me, you know that. Now, Betty Lou, here, it'd be tougher for her. She's got an emotional stake, and that gets in the way every time.'

Behind Betty Lou, Tark had appeared. He crossed over to me, handed me a long white envelope, and took a chair.

I put the envelope on the table, said 'Thanks', and asked him how it came out.

He smiled. 'I think I outdid myself.'

'Impossible.'

I looked over at Gramps and Betty Lou. 'So, what do you think about this idea of Gramps'?' I asked Tark. 'Were you listening?'

'I was. And I think your grandfather has a point.'

Betty Lou frowned. 'The only thing I don't like is that this is my problem, not his. It's not any of yours, really, and I hate to drag you all into it.'

'Nonsense,' Gramps said valiantly. 'Barney's after me, too. For that matter, if it wasn't for me and my schemin', you wouldn't even be in this fix.'

'No . . . the truth is, I might very well be dead.' Betty Lou looked at each of us in turn. 'I can't tell you how much this means to me, that you're willing to do all this.'

'All right, then, it's settled,' Gramps said. 'So this is what we're going to do –'

'No,' I interrupted. '*This* is what we're going to do.'

I talked to them both for a good ten minutes, working out a better way. When I had finished, Gramps was reasonably happy about his part in the affair.

I gave him a stern look. 'But remember – loose lips sink ships.'

He tossed back his head and cackled. 'I can't believe you said that.'

I sighed. 'Me neither.'

'Just one thing . . .

'Now what, Esther?'

'I ain't wearin' gardenias in my hair, and I ain't smilin' under water, you hear?'

After everyone went to bed, I could see that Marcus wanted to talk. He wanted to know what I'd been about to say before the whole crew showed up.

'You know, I'm really tired,' I said, yawning. Standing, I picked up the envelope Tark had given me. 'And I've still got to take this to a messenger service in Miami.'

'I can have someone do that for you, Jess. For that matter, I'm sure Tark would gladly –'

'No, I think I should do it myself. I'd feel better about it that way.'

He stood facing me. 'Why don't I go with you, then? We can talk in the car.'

I shook my head. 'I'm sorry. I just think I'm all talked out. I really am tired, Marcus. Can it wait?'

'Of course,' he said thinly. 'Doesn't it always?'

Chapter 33

I woke early the next morning to sunlight drifting through the windows of my stateroom, which had a view toward Miami Beach. *I could live like this forever*, was my first thought, the kind of gut feeling one has sometimes before logic creeps in. My next thought was: *Get going, girl. Who do you think you are, the idle rich? There's work to do.*

Words from my mother's lips, for most of my childhood years. No wonder I was all messed up and couldn't relax in the lap of luxury.

At the same moment I got a picture of her, Pops, and me, at about eight, on a Sunday outing. We had driven to some lake or other, probably Cayuga, and it was all supposed to be happy, happy, happy. But Mom had ended up doing all the work while Pop drank. I remembered her looking weary and frazzled by the end of the day. It took both of us to pile Pop into the passenger seat, after fighting with him for the key.

I knew, then, that it wasn't the tourist family at Coco Walk that I was afraid of becoming like: it was my own family. Somehow the two had become jumbled together in my mind.

I reached for the phone beside my bed and called the Lonely Palms for messages. 'You've got a few,' Irma said. 'But you wanta be careful the next few days. The planets are all screwy. Confusion reigns.'

'Are you an astrologer?' I asked.

'Nah. I just read this stuff. But you'd be surprised how often they're right.'

I'd had six messages, she said, throughout the night – all of them from a Barney Noonan. 'The last one was less than an hour ago, and they're all pretty much the same: 'Call me right away. Urgent.' That's all it says. That, and a number.' She read it off to me. Then she said, 'Look, are you coming back here at all? Not that I need the room, or anything, but I wondered.'

I wanted Noonan to think I was still staying there, so I told her that yes, I wanted to keep the room.

I sat on the edge of the bed and punched in Barney Noonan's number.

'Yeah?' It was his voice, but it sounded different – hesitant, as if afraid to hear who the caller was.

'It's me, Jessica James. What do you want, Noonan?'

He started out okay. Placating, reasonable. 'Look, I'm ready to forget what happened between us.'

I fingered my still sore forehead. 'I can't tell you how much that means to me. You wanta do lunch? Take in a show?'

I could hear his lungs working, the strain in the voice, the effort to control the temper. 'I just need to know if you found Betty Lou.'

'If I did, I wouldn't tell you, asshole.'

'Dammit! Fucking dammit, James, this is important!'

I held the receiver away and let a small silence take place.

'James. Are you there? Fuck it all –'

'Come to think of it, I wouldn't be caught dead lunching with you, Noonan. You've got the foulest mouth I've ever heard on a man.'

'Look, will you shut up and just listen?' His tone became desperate. 'I got this note. It says they've got Betty Lou.'

'Who's got Betty Lou?'

'Never mind who, I just need to know if it's possible. Did you find her? Is she okay?'

I let another silence take place.

'James?' A harsh, urgent whisper.

'Okay,' I said. 'You tell me who you think has her, and I'll tell you what I know.'

'You know something? Look, if you know something you've got to tell me.'

'You first,' I said, yawning.

His rage was almost palpable. I wouldn't have been surprised to feel a meaty hand snake through the receiver and wind itself around my throat.

'Not on the phone,' he said finally.

'Okay, I'll meet you.'

'My house. It's on Bonita –'

'No way. In public or not at all.'

'All right, all right! Meet me at the Last Ditch. It's on the river, just east of the Orange Bowl.'

'The Last Ditch, huh? Sounds lovely.'

'It's a coffee shop, and it's public. What're you afraid of, anyway? You afraid I'll wring your pretty little neck over a cup of coffee?' His tone said that if he didn't need me to find Betty Lou, he would do just that, in one hot second.

'It's not that I'm afraid, Noonan. I just don't want to ruin my rep by being seen with you. Not anywhere important, anyway.'

'*Be* there,' he said, the bullying tone coming back. 'I'll give you thirty minutes to show your face, then I'm comin' after you.'

'Make it forty-five,' I said, just to be difficult.

I found Noonan on the outside deck of the Last Ditch, at a table beneath a tattered Cinzano umbrella. Freighters passed by on the Miami River, along with luxury yachts, smaller craft, and a large tour catamaran with a gaggle of boy scouts on its decks. A harbor patrol boat screamed by, its sirens blasting. There was a hotel across the river, several restaurants that were more upscale than the Last Ditch, and what looked to be luxury apartments.

Sandwiched between the money temples were forties and fifties holdouts like the one we were at. Judging by the crowd here today, it seemed to be frequented by merchant marines, bank robbers, and South American terrorists.

Still, it was public. As long as I kept my hands above the table and didn't make any too-fast moves, I probably wouldn't get shot.

Noonan didn't waste time on small talk. The moment I sat down, he handed me a note. 'I got this last night,' he said. The note was hand-printed in block letters, and read:

I'VE GOT YOUR WIFE. BRING THE MONEY BY NOON TOMORROW, OR SHE DIES

It was signed with a lurid red 'S', which I couldn't help admiring. Tark had indeed outdone himself.

I looked across the white plastic table at Barney Noonan. He wore a rumpled, pale green jacket made of some sort of shiny material, like in the old *Miami Vice*. His eyes were worried, and sweat poured down his forehead.

'So who's the note from?' I said. 'Who's got Betty Lou?'

'A guy named Soldando. Luis Soldando. That's what the "S" is.' He tapped the note with a large, blunt finger. 'That's his mark.'

'Who is he?'

'A local businessman. He runs things around here.'

'Mob? Drugs?'

He made an impatient gesture. 'Shit like that.'

'So what's he want from you? Why would he take Betty Lou?'

'He, uh . . . he thinks I owe him some money.'

'Do you?'

'Maybe.'

'How much money?'

He hesitated. 'Twenty thou.'

I gave a low whistle. 'For what?'

'He thinks I took something that belonged to him. He wants to be paid.'

'You were in a drug deal with Soldando?'

'No, it wasn't like that. I arrested one of his boys a couple of years ago for dealing, and when the case finally came to trial a month ago, there wasn't as much in the evidence locker as the perp had been holding when he was caught. Soldando thinks I took a little something after the arrest.'

'And did you?'

'Fuck, anybody could have taken those drugs out of the evidence locker. It happens all the time.'

'Yeah, but *did* you?'

His big hands wrapped tightly around his coffee mug. 'It doesn't matter, dammit! The only thing that matters is that Soldando thinks I did and he wants me to pay, and he claims he's got Betty Lou. That's why I need to know – is he bluffing? Did you find her?'

I shook my head. 'I talked to her sister, and I checked out the Fallon cottage in Key Largo. I didn't find your wife.'

He searched my face. 'What about Irene? Are you sure she was telling the truth?'

'Irene is genuinely worried. She thinks you did something to her sister. For that matter, I'm not so sure she's wrong. Maybe this whole thing, this note –' I tapped it with a fingernail – 'is a scam to make people think Soldando did something to your wife. Maybe you hit her once too often and once too hard.'

I gave the note a contemptuous shove. It landed in a small puddle of coffee that had spilled because Noonan's hands were shaking.

He stared at the note, passed a palm over his eyes, and blinked. 'I don't know whether to believe you. But if you don't know . . .' He looked away, clenching a fist. 'They've got her, then. It's true.'

'And who the hell is to blame? You, Noonan, you jerk. If Soldando's known about this for a month, why the hell haven't you paid him off by now?'

Noonan looked at me with something close to hate. 'You stupid broad. I was about to, when your goddamned son-of-a-bitch grandfather took me for every cent I had. What the hell am I supposed to pay Soldando with now? And why the fuck do you think I've been breaking my ass looking for that old bastard?'

'I thought you were after him because he stole your wife from you. You mean, all this time, it's been because of the money?'

'Both, dammit. I want the cash, and I want Betty Lou.'

'How do you know she doesn't have the money, instead of my grandfather? And come to think of it, if Soldando even suspects Betty Lou's got it, what might he do to pry it out of her?'

'Jesus H. Have you got any brains at all? That's why I've got to find her. Soldando will kill her if he doesn't need her.'

'Maybe he has already.'

He paled. 'No. No, if he already had the money, he wouldn't have sent the note.'

But Noonan didn't look too sure. And I didn't argue with him this time. Better to just let the possibilities sink in.

'So what do you want from me, Noonan? You could have asked me over the phone if I'd found Betty Lou.'

'I want your fucking grandfather,' he said hoarsely. 'And you're gonna tell me where he is.'

I laughed. 'What makes you think so? Why would I help an asshole like you?'

His face came close to mine. In the hard eyes I caught a glimpse of pure evil. 'Because, James, I've got your landlady. Binty, I think the name is?'

I felt my mouth start to move into scorn at the audacity of the lie. But then, looking into his eyes, I knew it was true. My heart missed a beat.

'What the hell have you done?'

He gave a casual shrug. 'She's okay for now. I've got somebody with her.'

I had to restrain myself from reaching across the table and strangling him. 'Who?'

'You met him. He's been up there awhile.'

Suntan.

'Where is Mrs Binty?'

'Not to worry, she's in her house, safe and sound – so long as you and Johnny James give me what I want.'

What about Joey Martino? I thought. *Joey and Denny.* Wouldn't they sense something was wrong? Had Mrs Binty been able to get a message to them?

Noonan must have read my thoughts. 'Not a chance, James. She sent the contractors away. Told them, at my boy Lonnie's insistence, of course, that she'd decided to hold off on any more work until the weather improved. So your sweet little old landlady and my boy Lonnie have the place all to themselves. Isn't that cosy?'

My hands were shaking so much, I knocked over my water glass. I half rose to my feet. 'If he hurts her –'

And Toni. What if Toni went over there and got mixed up in it?

'Easy does it,' Noonan said coldly. He leaned over the table and grabbed my wrist, twisting the skin until it burned. 'Isn't that what they teach you ex-drunks? Easy does it? Now sit down, bitch, and pretend everything's all right.'

I looked right to left, wondering if anyone was watching. I expected things about me to have changed, the way my world had changed in the past few moments. But life was going on as usual. No one seemed to care that I was sitting in a dive along the Miami River and hearing that a woman I loved like a grandmother, a best friend, was in danger a thousand miles away.

I could imagine her, tiny and frail, standing up to her captor in spirited anger – and all the while quaking underneath. Angry tears filled my eyes.

I sat. 'What do you want me to do?'

'It's simple. I want your grandfather. And I want my money. I've got a real good feeling you know where both of them are.'

I made a call to the yacht from a grimy phone booth at the Last Ditch. Noonan stood close by, listening to my end of the conversation. 'Gramps?' I said, when one of the stewards answered. 'It's Jesse.'

The steward began to answer, 'This isn't your grandfather...' but I cut him short, saying, 'Gramps, turn that TV down, dammit! This is important.'

Fortunately, the man had worked for Marcus long enough to understand what was going on. In no more time than it would have taken to actually turn a television down, he had Marcus on the line.

'Jess? What's wrong?'

'That's better. Now, listen up, Gramps. I'm here with Barney Noonan, and things have changed. His man has Mrs Binty.'

There was a heavy silence on the other end of the line. Marcus loved Mrs Binty as much as I did. 'What does Noonan want?' he said tersely.

'He wants the money. And he wants you.'

'Can you stall? A half-hour, say?'

'Listen, old man, I'm tired of protecting your worthless hide, and I don't give a shit about the money. All that matters is Mrs B, and if you and the money are not at the Palms when we get there, I'll track you down and kill you myself.'

'Jess, you're taking Noonan to the Lonely Palms? Do you think that's a good –'

'You heard me. Just be there.'

'All right, I understand. I don't like it, but I'll have your grandfather there waiting. It's not precisely what we planned, but we can work it this way.'

'*With* the money. Don't forget. And don't play around with me on this, old man.'

'Be careful, Jess.'

I slammed down the phone.

At the Lonely Palms, I pulled the rental car into a space at the back. Noonan walked close behind me to Room 12.

Gramps must have been watching through the window; he opened the door almost immediately. Noonan pushed past me, crossing quickly to the bathroom and looking in. Then he slammed the door. He did the same with the closet. Satisfied that no one else was here, he turned his mean gaze on me, then Gramps. From beneath the silk jacket came a service revolver.

'Get the money,' he said, flexing the fist of his free hand. '*Get the goddamned money*!'

Gramps hesitated. He flicked a look at me. 'I tried to tell you on the phone, gal. I . . . I just don't have it.'

Barney Noonan crossed the room in three angry strides and yanked Gramps nearly off his feet.

'Let him go!' I yelled. 'If he says he hasn't got it, he hasn't got it.'

'*Get the money*,' Noonan ordered again. '*Get it now*!'

Gramps shook his head. 'I don't have it, I swear I don't –'

'Shit. The fuck with that.' Noonan kept the revolver on us as he pulled dresser drawers out, then scanned quickly beneath the bed. 'For cryin' out loud, is that the best you can do? Get under there, you dumb old bastard. Pull that briefcase out.'

Gramps looked nervously at me. I said angrily, 'Do it. Do what he says, dammit. Do you realize how much danger you've put Mrs Binty in? I warned you not to scam on me again.'

His old gray eyes looked hurt, but he scampered. 'I was gonna give you half, a whole half,' he said as he inched under the bed and then out again with the briefcase. 'I wasn't gonna keep it all.'

Noonan yanked the briefcase from his hand. He set it on the bed, while holding the gun straight out toward us. 'Now just stay back, nice and easy, both of you.'

With his free hand he snapped open the catches. Inside were hundreds of bills, packaged in several denominations. He flipped through the packets, examining them closely and counting. Finally he nodded with satisfaction, locked the briefcase again, and picked it up, glancing at his watch.

'All right, now, you two just lucked out. I haven't got enough time to deep-six you both and get to Luis Soldando with this. So I'll tell you what we're gonna do. You two are gonna stay out of my way the next few hours, while I get to Soldando and buy back my Betty Lou. Meanwhile, Lonnie's gonna keep the old lady company, just to be sure you don't try nothin' funny. Once I know the money's in Soldando's hands so he won't be trackin' me around the whole damned world, and once I get my Betty Lou back, we're headin' for a place where there's no extradition. After we're there, I call my boy and tell him to release the old lady. And after that I don't give a shit what you do. Because you know what? You won't be able to do a goddamned fucking thing.'

'Look, why not let Betty Lou go?' Gramps said anxiously. 'Can't you just let her be?'

Barney turned on him. 'You actually think I'd leave Betty Lou behind so everybody I know can laugh behind my back about her running off with some old geezer who can't keep his pecker out of somebody else's wife?'

'If you hurt her –'

'Shut up, you old fool. You expect me to believe you'd do anything about it? You're weak, old man. Weak and spineless. You've never been any good to anybody. You think I don't know about you? I saw your kind all the time when I worked Fraud. You've spent your whole life running away from everybody and everything. Shit – I thought I wanted to kill you, but you know what? You're not worth the bullet. You're nothin', old man. Worse than nothin'. Look at you, standin' there shakin' like your shit's about to hit the ground.'

I looked at Gramps. He was indeed trembling violently. And I was startled at the feelings of protection that rose in me.

'Get out of here,' I said roughly to Noonan. 'Just get the hell out.'

He crossed to the door with the briefcase and made a gesture like the tip of a hat. He holstered his service revolver. 'See you in the post office, old man.'

I took a step toward Noonan, but that quickly he was gone.

For several moments Gramps and I stood motionless, silent, staring at the hotel-room door. I counted to twenty or so, and then I turned and faced Gramps. He still looked pale, but he'd stopped shaking.

'Well. That's that,' he said.

I nodded. 'It, uh . . . went rather well, don't you think?'

'Rather *well*?' Gramps began grinning. 'Rather *well*? It was perfect! Gimme a high-five, girl!'

He held up his palm and I slapped it.

'We did get the cash to him . . .' I said thoughtfully. 'If not exactly the way we planned it. That monkey wrench he threw in about Mrs Binty changed things.'

Gramps sobered. 'You don't think Suntan would really hurt her, do you? He seemed sorta harmless.'

'Yeah, well, sometimes that's the worst kind. And remember how persistent he was about following orders. I don't know . . . I'm really worried. I've got to get back to the yacht, make some phone calls to people up there.'

'Andrelli was already doin' that when I left,' he said. 'He told me he'd make sure she didn't get hurt.'

'Who was he talking to?'

'I don't rightly know. I had to hustle to get over here fast.'

'Let's get out of here,' I said. I want to find out for myself if she's all right.'

Marcus had sent Gramps in a car, so he rode back with me. Along the way he said, 'Well, one thing, the scam'll work better this way. Noonan thinks he forced me to hand over the cash, which makes him feel in control. There's no way he can suspect we're in on it.'

'So he'll take Soldando his twenty thou,' I said, 'and Soldando will tell him he can't have Betty Lou until tonight, after he's made sure the money's clean. He'll tell him he can pick her up at midnight, at the dock of the Tropic Shores hotel.'

I paused, and shook my head. 'That's the one part that puzzles me. Old man, that act you put on for Barney Noonan, saying you didn't have the money, making him hunt for it. For a minute, I almost believed you. What was that about?'

'Shoot, gal. It's more real that way. You gotta play hard to get, make the other guy think you're not givin' up that easy.'

'Right. I get that. What I don't get is that you still don't seem too downhearted about giving up that seventy thousand. Not after fighting so hard to hang onto it.'

The pale eyes shifted away. 'Well, now, I couldn't let that nice Mrs Binty be hurt.'

'So you just decided to do the right thing? That's it?'

'Sure, gal. That's it.'

I somehow didn't believe it. I wanted to. But I'd developed an instinct for Gramps' ambling around the truth.

'You're up to something. What is it?' I demanded.

'Nothin', gal, nothin'. Honest.'

He was up to something.

'Old man, I will tell you one thing. No one had better get hurt.'

'Nobody's gettin' hurt, Jesse girl. Nobody's gettin' hurt at all.'

Chapter 34

We arrived at the *SeaStar*, and Gramps, who I was still pondering over, went below decks to find Betty Lou. I discovered Mac and Marcus in the conference room, squaring off like two dogs pissing on a fire hydrant: each fighting for his own territory and each trying to out-piss the other.

'I just feel we can handle this alone now,' Marcus was saying stiffly. 'Tark knows a few things about explosives.'

'Not these explosives,' Mac answered stubbornly, his chin up. He wore the usual pilot's cap, but a white shirt rolled up at the sleeves replaced the leather jacket – a nod, I supposed, to the warm Miami weather. Other than that, he looked about as comfortable on this luxury yacht as a fish who'd been tossed up on deck by a wave.

'It's much more difficult,' Mac said caustically, 'to not blow things up than it is to blow them up. I suppose you and Tark would have more experience with the latter.'

Marcus' face darkened.

I stepped into the fray. 'Hey, guys, nice to see the two of you are sitting here worrying about Gramps and me. We did fine, thanks. Went off without a hitch.'

Marcus swung around in his chair to face me. 'Sorry, Jess. I have been worried about you, in fact. Quite worried. It went all right?'

'He bought the note, and he's on his way to Soldando with the money. Right now, however, I'm more concerned about Mrs Binty. What's going on?'

'I got on the phone the minute we hung up. Bobby Dell was at the penthouse. You remember him, from Arizona?'

'Yes.' I slung my tote down and sat in a chair opposite them both. Gramps sat beside me. 'Bobby's in Rochester now?'

'Temporarily. He got a message to your contractors, Joey and Denny. They're supposed to show up and pretend they left needed equipment behind. Bobby told them not to try anything foolish on their own, but to see if they can get a look inside and make sure Mrs Binty is all right. I also called Grady North.'

I lifted a brow. 'You called Grady? How did *that* go?'

'Let's just say we decided to table our differences for Mrs Binty's sake. He's rounding up an expert in hostage situations. He said to tell you not to worry, he'll make sure nothing happens to her.'

Gramps frowned. 'I don't know . . . I don't like trusting a stranger with Mrs B's safety.'

'Grady's known her as long as I have. He's no stranger.'

'Mebbe not, but this other guy . . .'

'Actually, I agree,' Marcus said. 'That's why I called Abe, as well. He's promised the Three will be around in case they're needed.'

I shook my head. 'Grady North, a couple of contractors, and the Genesee Three? I'm not sure that's a mixture I'd have thought of.' I looked at Marcus and Mac and said dryly, 'I don't suppose anyone considered the FBI?'

'Hell, no,' Mac said. 'They'd only get in the way.'

'That's what I decided,' Marcus added. 'They'd ask too many questions, and they don't have a personal interest. It would have taken too long to even get them on the scene.'

I knew he was right.

'Jess –' Marcus leaned forward. 'We don't know for certain, yet, what Denny and Joey will find. It could be . . .'

I frowned. 'That it's all too late? I know. But let's not think that way right now, okay?'

Gramps put a consoling hand on mine. 'It'll be all right, Jesse girl,' he said gruffly. 'Don't you worry none, you hear?'

Mac came over and gave me a hug, then stood behind me, laying a proprietary hand on my shoulder. From across the way, Marcus watched silently. A tic began beneath his left eye.

'Thanks for coming down here,' I said, turning to Mac. 'We all appreciate your help. Don't we, Marcus?' I sent him a look.

His tone was grudging. 'Of course. We couldn't have done this without your help. But as I was saying earlier, now that we have the explosives –'

'Now that we have the explosives,' I said, 'Mac and I should get over to *The Flamingo Swan* and start setting things up. Right, Mac?'

He grinned and pushed back his cap. 'I'm ready if you are.'

'Okay.' I turned back to Marcus, who looked like he'd just as soon toss Mac overboard. 'Where's Tark?'

'He's at the Tropic Shores, meeting with Security. We're to go over there now in the tender. That way it will be there later, for Betty Lou's escape.'

'And Betty Lou?'

'I talked her into taking a nap, so she'll be rested for tonight.'

'Good. And you briefed Mac on what to do after the explosion?'

Mac grinned. 'Is that what it was, a briefing?' he drawled. 'Seemed more like the old heave-ho, to me.'

Marcus frowned and looked away.

'You know, I don't really need this,' I snapped. 'Not from either of you.'

They both looked uncomfortable, and I felt like a mother reprimanding her two small boys. 'Are we together on this, now? If not, Gramps, Betty Lou and I can damned well do it by ourselves.'

'We're together,' Marcus said grudgingly.

'Like peas in a pod,' Mac added with a drawl.

'Then, let's go. Gramps? This'll take a few hours. You'll stay here and look after Betty Lou?'

'It'll be my pleasure, gal.'

We all went above and began loading up the tender with everything we'd need on the *Swan* that night, including the fake explosives. Then we climbed in ourselves, and as we pulled away, Gramps stood at the rail looking down and giving us the old V for victory sign with two fingers. I couldn't help smiling.

But there was still that business about him and the money, nagging away in my head. What was there about that deal that didn't feel right?

I thought of mentioning it to Marcus and Mac, but decided against it. We all needed a positive attitude to pull this off tonight. It wouldn't do to let doubts creep in.

We pulled up to the dock of the Tropic Shores, unloaded the tender quickly, and had one of Marcus' nearby 'gardeners' take it around and tie it to the far side of the *Swan*, out of sight from the shore. Marcus then went up to the hotel to meet with Tark, reluctantly leaving Mac and me alone on the broad, curving steps that led up to the mouth of the *Swan*.

It was my first time aboard, more for lack of time than curiosity. I felt a bit of a tingle, and my arms broke out in goosebumps. Whether it was from fear or excitement, I wasn't sure.

'Whew,' Mac said, scanning the *Swan*'s garish pink exterior. 'What the heck *is* this thing?'

'I told you on the phone. It's a boat.'

He hefted the backpack of explosives and other equipment he'd brought on board. 'I know what you told me. But this is like no boat I ever did see. You say Andrelli actually bought it?'

'It's his dream.'

'More like a nightmare, if you ask me.'

'He wants to make it into a floating museum for old movies,' I said.

Mac let out a hoot. 'Sounds like he's got too much money and doesn't know what to do with it.'

'Actually, he was doing it for me.'

The gray eyes swung my way. 'For you?'

'Because I'm an old-movie buff.'

He lifted a brow, and frowned. 'I didn't know that.'

I switched hands with the heavy bag I was carrying, and we proceeded on up the stairs. Mac inspected their condition along the way. 'These are pretty rickety. You didn't tell me that.'

'Well, I haven't actually been on the *Swan* before. Marcus did warn me about the steps, but I figured we wouldn't have to use them at all. If everything takes place inside the belly, and at the top of the steps by the door –' I broke off. 'You're not saying we can't do it because of this?' I said anxiously.

'No. But you'll want to make sure you do stay at the top. Provided, that is, things are in better shape up there.'

'They are. Marcus had nearly everything redone. He just hasn't gotten to the stairs yet. Mac – I meant it when I said nothing can happen to the *Swan*. We've got to make sure of that.'

'Well, to be honest,' he said, shaking his head, 'now that I see it, I'm not sure I understand why you're so damned worried. Andrelli could build a dozen of these, with all the dough he's got.'

'But it wouldn't be the same. This is an original. It's historic, and it means a lot to him.'

He reached the top and paused, looking back to study me. 'Therefore, it means a lot to you. Is that right?'

I couldn't meet his eyes. 'Something like that.'

We stood on a five-by-eight platform at the mouth of the *Swan*, where Esther Williams had once stood in a gold lamé bathing suit, and where Betty Lou and I would stand at midnight. Mac knelt to search for flaws in the construction. I looked down at the flight of steps before me, and imagined what it would be like here tonight. Not much like the movie: no hundred gorgeous bathing beauties with spiny sparklers in their hands.

A breeze came up, lifting my hair and cooling the back of my neck. Standing, Mac lifted the backpack. 'Let's go inside,' he said. He sounded grumpy now.

I checked out the route from the *Swan*'s belly to the small tender, which was tied up on the far side, out of sight of anyone on shore or the dock. After I'd made sure nothing was in the way that we might trip over in the dark, I returned to the main cavity, which Marcus hadn't yet finished remodeling. The belly had been gutted, the sides and floor paneled with new, smooth wood, and unobstructed.

'Mac?'

'Up here, Jess.'

He was working at the top of the wide inner staircase that Marcus had built for museum guests to take up to the mouth of the *Swan*. His plan was to have an observation deck there; a place to sit and relax over coffee, catch a breath of fresh air between viewing old films that would run continuously in several small rooms.

'How's it going?'

'I can use your help now,' Mac said.

I jogged up the stairs and took the end of wire he handed me, following his instructions about threading it down the stairs. 'You're finished outside?' I asked as he followed me down, keeping the wire taut so it wouldn't tangle.

'Yeah. Just so you won't be surprised, there should be plenty of smoke.'

'That's good.'

'And I brought this new stuff with me that simulates flames. Works on the same principle as special effects in the movies.'

'Appropriate,' I said.

'It lends a lot more believability.' He half smiled. 'One guy at the school the other day came running out of a "blazing building" thinking he was really burned. Took him a few minutes to realize it was all in his mind.' Sobering, he added, 'One thing, it doesn't mix well with certain chemicals. No problem here, though. The place is whistle clean.'

'I don't know . . .' I said doubtfully. 'Maybe we should pass on that.'

His chin went up. 'You saying you don't trust me, gal?'

He smiled, but there seemed an edge to it.

'Of course I trust you,' I said. 'So, okay. Do it.' I rubbed my arms, though, feeling a chill.

I was kneeling on the floor, double-wrapping the bare ends of wires to make sure they didn't short, when Mac came from the tail end of the *Swan*, wiping his hands on a rag. Sunlight from outside glanced over his handsome, world-weary face. 'All done. There should be a damned good-looking blaze now. We're sure goin' to a lot of trouble, though, for a lady you don't hardly know.'

'I know her well enough,' I said, standing. 'She's a good person.'

'You really think this Noonan guy would harm her if he got her back?'

'Absolutely. He's still obsessed with Betty Lou, even though he suspects she's been with another man. His thinking is all screwed up where she's concerned.'

He began to put tools back into the canvas pack. 'I guess I can relate to that.'

I didn't answer, and he continued to work, cleaning up carefully so there would be nothing at all to get in our way tonight.

'You're with him again, aren't you?' he said suddenly, not meeting my eyes.

'Marcus?' I hesitated. 'I'm not sure.'

He nodded. 'You're with him. I just wonder if it'll be permanent this time.'

Permanent.

That image came up again, the one of the family worn out, no longer communicating, all the joy seemingly gone out of their marriage. To me that seemed a living death. But was it just old stuff, old fears, that made me think I'd end like that, if I married? I wasn't Mom. And neither Marcus nor Mac was Pop.

I thought about Marcus' house in the country, the one he'd bought in Rochester the previous spring: a beautiful old Victorian with a porch, a porch swing, a vegetable garden, and tons of lilacs, my favorite flower. Marcus had the house remodeled, putting sunken tubs in the bathrooms. One bathroom is done in aquamarine . . . my favorite color.

The house in the country stands vacant now. It's been a sore point between Marcus and me.

'The ever-changeable Jesse James,' Mac said tightly. 'I seem to remember a pair of Nikes under my bed, once.'

Zap.

'Mac, look, I know I haven't been fair. Not with either of you. But before we leave here I just want to say you've been great. I didn't know if you could forgive me enough to come down here and help. I didn't know if you'd have it in you.'

He stepped close. 'To lie? To fake? To cover up?' His lips came down on mine in a quick, hard kiss. 'I've been doing that since last summer. Every time I pretend not to love you.'

It was at that moment that Marcus walked in.

'I thought I'd just see how things were coming along,' he said.

Chapter 35

I stood on Marcus' balcony at the Tropic Shores hotel, leaning against the rail. *The Flamingo Swan* bobbed gently; it was near dusk now. The sky was a deeper blue, the air as soft as a baby's breath. Windows in the tall hotels along the Miami Beach shore became pillars of fire from the last red rays of sun. Distant boats at their docks had Christmas bulbs strung on their masts and around their rails. A few twinkled on, another jarring reminder that the holidays were right around the bend. I wondered what kind of Christmas Betty Lou Noonan would have this year. I hoped it would be happier for our efforts. I hoped our little plan would go off without a hitch.

'What are you thinking?' Marcus asked quietly, coming to stand beside me.

I glanced uneasily at *The Flamingo Swan*, its florid presence only a bit muted by the coming of twilight. 'Some of the scams the Genesee Three and I have pulled, and how easily things can go wrong.'

'Are you worried?'

'No more than usual. Except . . . I can't get over how readily Gramps turned over that money. You were here. How did he seem when you told him he had to bring it to the Lonely Palms and give it to Barney Noonan? Was he still protesting all the way?'

'As a matter of fact, no. He was upset about Mrs Binty, as we all were.'

'No more arguments about how it was Betty Lou's money, and he wasn't handing it over?'

'None at all. But Betty Lou was right here, too. I think she would have argued with him if he'd tried to hang onto it under those circumstances.'

'Also, he wouldn't have looked much like that shining knight he likes her to think he is. It's funny about the two of them. They seem so happy around each other.'

'Speaking of which,' he said a bit tersely, 'you seemed happy to see Mac today. And the two of you work well together, I've noticed.'

I didn't know what to say. For a few seconds, I just watched the *Swan*. One moment it was ablaze with the final kiss of a setting sun, and the next it was in the dark. No searchlights this night.

'What do you think of Betty Lou?' I said at last.

'I think she's a brave lady who deserves a fresh start. We had a talk today while you were gone. Noonan did terrible things to her emotionally, even before the physical abuse began.'

'She told you about that?'

'And the fact that she really wants to do this tonight. To be honest, I tried to dissuade her. She's not very strong, physically. And did you know she's terrified of water?'

'Dammit! As a matter of fact, I did. I'd forgotten.'

'She didn't want you to remember. She just wants to get on with this, and get it over with.'

I rubbed my face wearily. 'I'll be glad when it's over with, too. I'll be glad when Betty Lou and Gramps are both safe.'

'What about us, Jess?' he said softly. 'Will we be safe?'

I couldn't answer. There was a wall between us, now, with Mac here. I didn't know how to breach it.

I turned to him. 'Maybe after tonight. Maybe when this is all over, we can talk.'

'Talk. That sounds ominous.'

'Does it? Maybe it's just that I am rather worried about tonight. I don't like to think that way, but there it is.'

'Anything specific?'

'It feels like there's something we've overlooked. I keep racking my brain over it, but nothing comes.'

'Opening-night jitters?'

'Possibly.'

Betty Lou stuck her head out the sliding glass doors. 'Coast clear? Can I come out?'

'Sure,' I said. 'Sit down, though. Don't stand at the rail.' I pulled two chairs to a position behind a pillar that blocked the view from the lawn and shore. She sat in one, and I took the other.

Marcus looked at her, then me. 'I think I'll order coffee, then make some phone calls. Would either of you like anything?'

'Coffee,' we both said in unison.

'Hot and black,' I added. 'Thanks.'

I knew that he, as well as I, had noted the tension in Betty Lou's face. He was giving us time to talk alone.

I sat silently with Betty Lou for several moments, watching the sky grow dark. Finally I said, 'What is it? You look worried. Are you having second thoughts?'

She shook her head. 'Not about tonight. I am worried, though. About Irene.'

'Are you thinking Barney might go after your sister?'

'I suppose it depends on whether he believes I'm dead. If he does, he'll probably leave her alone. But if Barney suspects we've pulled something over on him, there's no telling what he'll do. Jesse . . . the thing I really hate is letting Irene think I'm dead.'

'Well, we talked about this, earlier. If we let her in on it, and Barney shows up at her door, she might not be able to convince him she's grieving. Without meaning to, she could give him reason to suspect what we've done. Then everything would go down the drain. He'd be after you again.'

'I know.' She sighed. 'I guess I just feel I'm leaving so many loose ends. Things I should take care of. I wanted to close up Paul's house and notify the authorities of his death . . . and I wanted to see that he got buried properly.'

'What about his family?'

'He told me he didn't have any.'

'Betty Lou,' I said gently, 'if the police are informed, there will be an investigation into the way he died. If Paul ever mentioned you – to a friend, say – your name could come up.'

'I know.' She looked more tired than ever.

'Look . . . tell you what. I'll see what I can do. Even if it means going to the State Attorney General's Office, I'll get out the story you told me about that day. And if I have to testify in court, I will. Maybe we can get Barney locked up. It'll take some time, though.'

I didn't tell her, but I'd been thinking along these lines anyway. I just wanted her safely out of Noonan's range before I started anything up.

'Jesse, no!' she said. 'Barney would only come after you.'

I grimaced. 'Shit, I'd welcome the opportunity to beat that bastard to a pulp.'

She looked at me, shocked. Then she laughed out loud. It was a wonderful sound, and I grinned.

'Just think,' I said, 'once this is all over and Barney's up the proverbial river, you can come home. You and Irene can throw a party, and I'll come down and help you celebrate. How would that be?'

Tears filled her eyes. 'I can't tell you how I feel about the way you've helped me.'

I gave an awkward shrug. 'You deserve all the help you can get, lady. You've got a lot of guts.'

'Have I?' She wiped at the moisture on her cheek. 'That's funny. I've been thinking just the opposite. To have stayed with Barney so long . . . to have put up with the abuse . . .'

'Well, my mom did that, too,' I said, 'until my father died. He wasn't physically abusive, but verbally and emotionally. Sometimes I think that's worse. But she stayed for some thirty years. And now she has a new life, with someone she loves. Someone who's good to her.'

I might never completely trust Charlie Browne, but I had to admit he was good to my mom.

'It must have been hard for you, growing up with an abusive father,' Betty Lou said. 'I'm glad Barney and I never had children.'

'It was tough,' I agreed. 'And for a long time I blamed my mom. I couldn't understand why she stayed. It was only later that I realized she'd done the best she could. She didn't have the kinds of support systems we've got now, and aside from Aunt Edna, she didn't know where to turn. So she worked two jobs to feed and clothe me while Pop was spending all his paychecks on booze. And that took guts.'

I touched her hand, giving it a squeeze. 'Betty, it's too easy to lay blame on people for things they did in another time, another age. You have to look at where they are today. And where *you* are today, my friend, it that you are one fine lady.'

She gripped my hand firmly. 'Thank you, Jesse. Thank you for everything. I'll never forget you,' she said.

Nor would I forget her. Somehow, I felt I'd come a long way since meeting Betty Lou.

Chapter 36

I stood at an open porthole on *The Flamingo Swan*, my feet braced against the sway as a brightly lit motor launch passed a few hundred yards away. I hoped that was the last we'd see of other craft; it was something I hadn't thought of, that the bay would be alive at this hour. One of those small details that can throw timing and outcome off. I realized that even though the air was warm, I was shivering.

Eleven-thirty-two, and the night sky was black now at its lower rim. Reflected lights from Miami Beach shimmered over the rest of it, softening shadows and illuminating objects along the shore. A moon shuttled in and out between clouds. Buoys clanged, their red lights bobbing. Tall hotels glittered. A mild salty breeze touched my cheek.

From this vantage point, I could see the entire length of the shoreline either way, though not well because of the dark. The usual *Swan* spotlights were off, and only one utility light on a pole illuminated the dock. The hotel had been closed; every one of the thirteen guests Marcus had expected for the night had been driven by limo, complete with champagne and hors-d'oeuvres, to a five-star hotel on Miami Beach. They would be wined and dined luxuriously there for their trouble, courtesy of Andrelli Enterprises.

Here at the Tropic Shores a female security person stood at the entrance to the drive, dressed as a parking valet, and with orders to diplomatically prevent anyone but Barney Noonan from getting through. Inside, security personnel played the part of bellhops and desk clerks.

My guess, however, was that Noonan wouldn't come through the front door. While Marcus owned several acres here, setting the hotel at a distance from surrounding neighbors, the shoreline wasn't so easily controlled. There was often the occasional reporter and/or photographer hoping to find the Miami Seven here, causing a ruckus over the *Swan*. While these intrusions didn't normally occur at night, Marcus had stationed a security person at either end of the property along the shore. If Barney Noonan appeared, he wouldn't spot them because of the dense shrubbery and trees that rimmed the edges of the property there. Anyone else would be stopped.

I clicked on the two-way radio attached to my belt. 'Tark?'

'Right here.'

I couldn't see him, but I knew he was somewhere in the shadows of the hotel.

'Nothing yet?'

'A false alarm.' He sounded tense. 'Billy reported a dog in the bushes along the front drive. Not the Barney kind, though.'

'Anything from Mac?'

'All quiet on the water front.'

Mac waited in the tender, the *StarGazer*, for the moment when Betty Lou would make her escape. No other boats were docked or anchored nearby. *The Flamingo Swan* stood outcast and alone, as she had since Marcus had had her towed here a couple of months before. Water lapped softly against her hull.

As I waited, a strange whuffing noise sounded from just beyond the dock. I strained anxiously to see in the dark. A dog – a large shepherd mix. Probably the one Security had spotted in front earlier. Damn. He could be trouble.

Someone whistled softly. The dog froze. He raised his head and pricked his ears. I heard Marcus say in a low voice, 'Here, boy.'

I leaned to see far to the right, and saw him, dressed all in black and hunkered down beside a large hibiscus near the path up to the hotel. What the hell? Marcus was supposed to be in a limo in the hotel parking lot, waiting for his part in this. What was he doing here?

The dog hesitated. Marcus whistled again. The dog began to edge away from the dock, ears still high and alert. 'C'mon, boy,' Marcus said softly. 'Here.' The shepherd crept closer and paused at his feet. Marcus patted his head, reached into a pocket and pulled something out: a collar and leash. He slipped the collar over the dog's neck and stood, leading him quietly up a path in the direction of the hotel. Within seconds they were out of sight.

I let out a long-held breath, relieving tension, and glanced at my watch again: eleven-forty-six. The past few minutes had been an eternity long. When I'm planning these things, it's all great fun. In my mind I see them being played out as if on a stage. Then reality sets in and, with it, any number of potential problems. In this case, it was the special effects that had me worried.

'What if something goes wrong?' I said to Mac earlier, pacing the *Swan*'s timbered cavity. 'What if we haven't done it right? Is there any possibility –'

It was the *Tancook Whaler* I was thinking of: Marcus' other labor of love, and the disaster that had struck her because of me. What if something happened to the *Swan*? And why did I keep drawing Marcus into these things? Why did I keep telling him I knew what I was doing, when the truth was, I was never sure. Was he right – was it a test? *Look at me – I do things the hard way, always. I need the kick, the feeling of being on the edge.*

How long can you accept me this way?

The radio crackled softly. I yanked it from my belt. 'Jess?' Tark said in a husky whisper. 'He just passed the guard to the east. We should see him here in about five.'

'Right,' I murmured back.

Clicking out, I began to sweat.

A dark, lumbering figure became visible to the east, still several hundred yards away and moving cautiously along the walk that followed the shore. As I watched, the figure stopped and seemed to turn toward a cluster of palm trees there, as if listening.

I flicked my flashlight on and went quickly back into the tail, where Betty Lou sat waiting in the dark, on an upturned wooden box. Even in the dim glow, her blonde hair was like a halo.

'Ready for your entrance?' I asked.

She nodded. 'Ready as I'll ever be.'

'Are you having second thoughts?'

'No.'

'It'll be okay,' I said with more confidence than I felt.

'Sure it will.' She smiled and looked me up and down. 'Johnny did a great job with you. You look almost like me.'

'Well, I wouldn't pass in a good light. But Barney won't have a chance to see me that way.' I felt the blond wig. 'Is it straight?'

She stood and touched it lightly, rearranging a lock. 'Perfect. It's too bad we couldn't find a pants and shirt that were exactly the same. The blue is a little too dark . . .'

'Hell, Betty Lou, men don't notice those things.'

She laughed softly.

'One more quick run-through,' I said, feeling the pressure of time rush like adrenaline through my veins. 'The most important thing is that you get back inside the *Swan* the minute that first smoke bomb envelopes the platform.'

'Right. And while you take my place, I make my way back down the stairs and out that side exit to the tender. Mac will be waiting there to take me to the seaplane.'

'And remember, you've got to hurry, because the first smoke won't last. I've got to trip the second explosion precisely two minutes later. You want to be taking off in the seaplane when that happens. You especially don't want to be caught inside the *Swan* when all hell breaks loose.'

She squeezed my hand reassuringly. 'Don't worry, Jesse. I've done five practice runs. They all came out just right.'

'I know, but you didn't have smoke this afternoon. I'm just worried you'll lose your position when you can't see, and get too near the edge of the platform.'

She shook her head, smiling. 'I won't. I've counted every step. I know exactly what to do.'

I hesitated only a moment more, then nodded and turned. 'Okay. Let's go.'

But then I thought I detected a familiar scent, now that Betty Lou was standing close. 'Have you been smoking?' I said worriedly. My gaze fell on the small red box and surrounding wiring Mac had set up in here earlier for the flame effect. It was tucked into a natural alcove created by the tail of the *Swan*.

'I . . . yes, I did have one cigarette,' she said shamefaced. 'I tried not to, but I was so nervous –'

I sighed. So many things to think of, and I stupidly hadn't thought to warn her not to smoke around all this stuff. Still, cigarettes weren't the same as chemicals, which was the only thing Mac had warned me about. And looking around, everything seemed all right. 'What did you do with the butt?'

'I tossed it into the water.' She nodded toward a porthole low on the tail of the *Swan*.

'Good.' I swept another glance around. 'All right, then. Let's do it.'

I led the way and Betty Lou followed me through the *Swan*'s gutted belly. Stopping at a porthole a moment, I scanned the shore for Barney. Damn. We'd wasted too much time back there; he was closer now than I'd expected him to be. In the dim light from the reflecting sky, I could now see the pale green jacket.

'Time,' I whispered to Betty Lou.

We went silently up the inside stairs that led to the mouth of the *Swan*. Opening the double doors a crack, I glanced out at the five-by-eight platform, two stories above the water. Barney Noonan was now at the edge of the dock. His head swung from right to left and back again, as he searched for signs of life. Then he glanced up at the *Swan*.

'Luis?' he called out. 'Soldando, where the fuck are you? I want my wife!'

'Now?' I said.

'Now,' Betty Lou answered firmly.

She went through the doors, while I stood back, watching through a narrow opening from inside. Betty Lou took a step forward and paused on the platform, a hand on the ornate flamingo railing. The one light on the dock illuminated the platform enough for Barney Noonan to see up here, but not well. He would catch the blonde hair, the figure, the familiar blue pants and white shirt. He would recognize the voice. But there wouldn't be time for details when things started coming down.

'Barney?' Betty Lou called softly.

His head swiveled in her direction.

'Betty Lou?' He came closer. 'Is that you?'

He paused and squinted up. At that moment, from behind him, Tark appeared with two security men. They were dressed in white jackets with the Tropic Shores logo on each upper left-hand pocket. Tark wore an expensive tailored suit, and a badge.

'Sorry, sir,' he said firmly. 'The dock is closed for tonight. I'll have to ask you to leave.'

'Closed?' Barney said irritably. 'What do you mean, closed?'

'We had some trouble here earlier tonight. A bomb threat. The area's been closed to the public, sir.'

Noonan shook his head. Then he looked at the *Swan* again, apparently realizing for the first time that the boat before him was the infamous *Flamingo Swan*. 'Oh, yeah. The Miami Seven.' He laughed shortly. 'We had Miami Tens and Twelves when I was on the PD. They don't scare me.'

He raised his voice. 'Betty Lou! Get your ass on down from there. I don't know what the fuck Luis is up to, but –'

'Sir,' Tark said, this time firmly taking his arm. 'I repeat, you've got to leave.' He looked sharply at Betty Lou. 'Who is that woman? What's she doing up there?'

'Fuck if I know,' Barney said angrily. He shook Tark off and moved toward the stairway leading up to the platform.

Tark grabbed him again. 'Stay right here.' He turned to the two security men. 'Billy . . . Ron. Go up there and get her down.'

'You keep your hands off her,' Barney snapped. 'She's my wife. And you, you turd – get your hands off me.'

Billy and Ron hesitated as Barney made a quick, angry effort to pull away from Tark. He gained only a few inches, but it was enough to get his hand inside his jacket and come up with a revolver. He jammed it into Tark's solar plexus. 'Just stay goddamned fucking back,' he said in a soft, malignant tone that chilled me. Then he swiveled back to the *Swan*, and in the same tone called out, 'Betty Lou? Little girl . . . you want to live?'

'Barney, I . . .'

'It's all right,' he said softly, persuasively. 'I forgive you. We're goin' away together. All you have to do is come down here. Come down here to Papa, where you belong, baby.'

I looked at Barney Noonan's face and heard his voice, and in my heart I knew that if he got her he would kill her.

'Right now!' he ordered when she didn't move.

Betty Lou shook her head frantically and pressed up against the door. 'I can't, Barney. I don't want to go with you.'

Noonan shoved Tark away and moved toward the stairs, keeping the gun straight out and moving it slowly back and forth between Tark and the two security men. 'Nobody moves. Got that? And you, Betty Lou . . . when I get my hands on you . . .'

She began to shake. I could feel it through the wooden panel of the door. 'It's okay,' I whispered. 'Just hang tight.' I put my foot next to the hot button Mac and I had rigged to set off the first explosion.

Barney had reached the bottom stair when Tark said loudly, anxiously, 'Billy, what was that?'

His head swung in the direction of the belly of the *Swan*. 'Who else is on the boat?'

'Nobody, far as I know,' Billy said. 'We checked it out –'

'I don't give a damn, I saw someone,' Tark insisted. 'There's somebody there.'

Billy and Ron both looked up at the *Swan*. 'What the *hell*?' they said almost in unison.

I jammed my foot down on the hot button. A loud rumble sounded throughout the boat, followed by a thunderous *boom*. A cloud of smoke billowed up from beneath the staircase. It rose higher and higher, obscuring the platform and doors.

Tark yelled, 'Shit, they're blowing it up! Ron, Billy, get back!'

I reached out, grabbed Betty Lou's arm, dragging her inside.

'Run!' I said, giving her a slight push toward the belly of the *Swan*. Stepping out onto the platform, I caught a glimpse of Noonan through a pinhole opening in the smoke. He was backing away, his eyes wide and horrified. I began to count off fifty seconds, as planned, the amount of time it would take for Betty Lou to safely make it to the tender before I triggered the second explosion. *One-one thousand, two-one thousand . . .*

But I was barely to five when a terrible roar swept through the *Swan*. A second later there was a fierce *woosh* – a sickening *boom* – then another and another. The *Swan* lit up from inside, her portholes blazing. Hot, red smoke engulfed me, stinging my eyes with bitter, acid-like fumes.

This wasn't the way it was supposed to be. What the hell had we done?

'Betty Lou!' Barney yelled. 'Betty Lou!'

Another thunderous roar, a frightening din. The last thing I heard before the *Swan* lit up like a Roman candle was Noonan, nearby on the steps – crying out wildly in agony and rage.

The *Swan* began rocking, swaying back and forth, violently. I fell, my legs sliding under the ornate rail. The boat tilted seaward. My forehead struck something hard. I grabbed for the rail as a pendulum moon hurtled side to side. My arm muscles screamed. Pain flashed. The boat pitched again and I lost my hold. The sea rose up.

'Jesse! Jesse, grab hold!' Incredibly, Betty Lou was there on the platform, stretching out a hand. I reached for it. We touched, and our fingers grabbed. For a moment Betty's blonde hair was framed against a clear patch of red sky. Then the boat gave another mighty heave. Betty Lou fell against the rail. Within seconds she was gone.

'*Oh, God,*' I screamed. Panic gave me strength. I fought the rocky boat and struggled to my feet. *She can't swim. Oh, God, she can't swim.* I slid under the rail to dive in. But the *Swan* pitched the other way and slammed me up against the opposite side. One savage boom followed another, and in that instant the smoke cleared. Looking down I saw Barney standing midway up the staircase, the rotting steps crumbling beneath him. One moment he was there, and the next a strange, horrified look crossed his face as he fell through a gaping hole to the sea below.

The *Swan* shuddered. It settled back. The explosions stopped, though the flames kept on. I was flat on my belly but still on the platform, shaking. I scrabbled across the wet platform like a crab.

'Betty Lou!' I screamed. The water was black with a dull red glow over its surface. I couldn't see her anywhere.

I raised my arms and dove in. Striking the water, I felt lumber from the rotting steps all about me, a sea of floating two-by-fours. I opened my eyes and strained to see through the murky depths. It was almost impossible; there was no real light, only a dismal, bloody-red glow.

Kicking hard, I broke through to the surface for air. Opening my mouth, I started to shout again for Betty Lou. But then I saw her. She was twenty feet away, clinging to a jumble of flotsam from the broken stairs. I struck out toward her, and in ten long strokes had reached her.

She was pale, shivering, frightened to death. I put my arm around her waist and with my opposite hand clung to the makeshift raft. At first, she didn't know I was there. Her eyes were shut, her fingers so tight on the floating debris, they looked like nothing but skin and bones.

'Betty Lou,' I said softly, treading water, 'it's me, Jesse. I've got you. It's okay now.'

I had to repeat it a few times, but she finally opened her eyes and saw me. 'Jesse . . . are you okay?' she said, screwing up her face and beginning to cry.

'Yes, I'm fine. I'm fine. Don't cry.'

'I'm so sorry. Please forgive me, it was all my fault.'

I thought she was out of her head, in shock. 'Don't talk now.' Scanning the shore quickly, I saw that we'd drifted west of the hotel and dock. We were now a hundred feet or more from the *Swan*.

I swung my head around, looking for Mac. Where was he? The *StarGazer* had been tied up to the *Swan*. If Mac had been hurt – No. He knew how to take care of himself.

But then, why wasn't he here? Was he still back there, waiting for Betty Lou?

I didn't have time to work it out. We were perhaps a hundred yards away from shore, and drifting steadily out to sea. Back at the *Swan*, the flames had died down, and everything was dark and quiet. Where the staircase had been there was nothing left but a dark, jagged wound. But she hadn't gone down. For that, at least, I was grateful.

My attention was caught by a small light at the edge of the water. A flashlight, I realized – scanning the surface of the water.

It had to be Tark. I lifted an arm to wave, then saw that the beam of light didn't reach this far. I started to call out, but for some reason thought better of it.

I turned to Betty Lou. 'Can you trust me enough to let go of that timber? I can get us both to shore, if you're not too afraid.'

She hesitated. Her grip tightened on the buoyant, more promising, raft. 'I . . . I thought Mac might come with the boat.'

'I know. But he doesn't seem to be here, and we've got to hurry. Someone on the island, or maybe even Miami Beach, will have reported the explosion. We don't want to be around, still, when the authorities arrive.'

She looked back at the *Swan*, frightened. 'But what about Barney? Is he still there?'

'I'm not sure. We may not have to worry about him anymore.'

Her eyes widened. But all I wanted on her mind right now was getting to safety. 'Are you ready? Will you trust me?' I said.

She nodded gamely.

'Relax, then. Let go of that lumber. Just pretend you really are Esther.'

I carried her in a life-saving position, on her back, and with one of my hands cupped under her chin while the other arm stroked. The water was filled with debris, now, from the steps of the *Swan*. It took all my remaining strength to keep Betty Lou's head up, and keep her from swallowing water. A couple of times, she panicked and almost pulled us both under. I seriously considered knocking her out, the way the lifeguards used to do in old movies. But I wasn't sure that really worked, and at any rate she kept coming back up, sputtering, and insisting, 'I'll be okay. Keep going.' She even tried to help by kicking her feet and paddling with her arms, to keep herself afloat.

As we neared the shore I saw that I was right: it was Tark there, holding the two-way radio to his ear. In another few moments he spotted us. Dropping the radio and flashlight, he tore off his jacket and shoes and strode into the water, striking out in our direction. Knowing he was coming gave me the last burst of strength I needed. Just as I was fading for the final time, he reached us and grabbed hold of Betty Lou. Between us we got her onto the small patch of beach, then into a thick clump of shrubbery and trees. Betty Lou and I fell exhausted onto the ground, gasping for air, while Tark ran to retrieve his clothes and gear.

When I could breathe normally, I fussed over Betty Lou, wiping her wet face with the tail of my shirt. She started to cry again. 'You shouldn't have done so much for me, I don't deserve it.'

'Hush. You don't know what you're saying.'

'You don't understand. I did it. It was all my fault . . . that beautiful boat.'

'What are you talking about?'

'I dropped my lighter somewhere in the *Swan*.'

'Your lighter?' For a moment, I didn't see the connection. Then it came clear: *lighter fluid. A chemical reaction that might not have mixed with Mac's new special effects.*

'I realized it the minute things blew sky-high,' Betty Lou said, trembling. 'And when I reached for my pocket to check, it wasn't there.'

'But you can't be sure –' I began.

'Hold it,' Tark said. 'Quiet.' He was standing a few feet away, looking east along the shoreline. There, soaking wet and stumbling like some horrible monster from the deep, was Barney Noonan. He shuffled along in our direction, aimlessly, as if in shock. As he reached the *Swan* he turned toward it, stood swaying, and cried out in a baffled voice, 'Betty Lou? Betty Lou . . . where are you?'

In the next moment another flash erupted from the *Swan*. A bright spear of flame shot straight up into the sky, illuminating everything around, including the broken stairs, the empty platform, the desolate floating timbers.

'Betty Louuuuuuu!' Noonan bellowed. The sound was primitive, a wounded-animal wail.

It was then that a man stepped out of the trees, onto the dock, and shot Barney Noonan in the chest. The blast threw him into the air, arms flailing above his head. Noonan landed with a sickening thud, gathering about him a pool of blood.

Tark and I stood gaping.

'Holy shit,' I said.

This part wasn't in my plan.

Chapter 37

The man who had shot Barney Noonan disappeared in the dark as quickly as he'd come, but not before spray-painting a lurid red S on Barney's chest, right over the green silk jacket, and yelling out dramatically, 'No one cheats Soldando!'

Only in Miami.

As for us, we escaped the grounds in Marcus' limo only seconds before the entire Greater Miami Fire Department – or so it seemed – arrived. We passed them, their sirens blasting, as they raced along East Star Island Drive. There were six of us in the back of the limo: me, Gramps, Betty Lou, Mac, Marcus, and Marcus' new friend – the dog from the hotel. Tark stayed behind to deal with the authorities, to report the 'threats and subsequent attack by the Miami Seven'.

As for Barney Noonan, there was nothing to tie him to us. We left him there, and the only one who gave him a backward glance was Betty Lou. Thirty years of marriage, I guess, will do that to you.

'That guy with the gun,' Gramps said, shuddering. 'Came right out of nowhere!'

Marcus scratched the dog's head, which rested on his knee. 'That "guy", as you call him, was Soldando himself. He's not really a killer. In fact, it puzzles me that he went after Noonan like that. Whatever Barney did, it must have been bad.'

Gramps' crafty eyes shifted away. 'Well, he *was* bad. Can't say I'd've wished that kind of ending on him, though . . . not if I'd thought it through.'

Marcus' gaze met mine. He arched a brow.

'Gramps?' I said. 'Thought what through?'

He shrugged his thin shoulders and looked only mildly guilty. 'The money, gal. See, it wasn't exactly real.'

Betty Lou and I both gasped at once. 'The money you turned over to Barney Noonan? What do you mean, it wasn't real?'

'I mean, gal, I have a connection here. You know that day I left the Lonely Palms and you got all shook up about it? I was pickin' up the counterfeit dough. Shoot, I couldn't take any chances Barney might get his fingers on the real stuff.'

'And just where exactly is the *real stuff*?' I demanded.

'It's in a safe place, gal . . . just waitin' for Betty Lou.'

He linked his arm through hers. 'I always thought it'd be kinda nice to marry into money. How'd you like to get hitched, Betty Lou?'

She smiled and kissed him on the cheek. 'Now, what would I be doing, marrying a will-o'-the-wisp like you?'

Then she sobered. 'I think I suspected Johnny had done something like that, when he stopped being worried about giving Barney the money. So it's my fault, really, what happened to Barney. I could have spoken up . . . but I didn't.' She looked at Marcus. 'Just like I didn't think when I took cigarettes and a lighter on board the *Swan*. I'm so sorry. I destroyed your wonderful boat. And I almost cost Mac his life.'

Marcus shook his head. 'Don't worry about the *Swan*. The steps needed fixing anyway. As for the rest . . . well, she's still standing. I'm thinking a good clean-up and a little paint and nails, and she'll be brand new.'

'And don't worry about me,' Mac said. His fingers reached up to touch a gash on his forehead. 'It was my own damned fault, falling into the drink that way. "Always be prepared for the unexpected," they say. Guess I had my mind on other things.'

He flicked a meaningful glance my way. 'You want to catch a ride home with me, gal? I'll be flyin' out of here in an hour or two.'

I could feel Marcus' eyes on me.

'I'll think about it,' I heard myself say.

When we arrived at the yacht there was a message that Grady North had called. He'd left Mrs Binty's phone number for me to call him back.

I punched the number in, my fingers shaking. Was he there as a friend? Or as Homicide? For the past few hours I hadn't had time to dwell on it, and that had been a blessing.

When Mrs Binty herself answered I was so relieved, my knees turned to jelly.

'Oh, Jesse, I'm so glad you called. It was so exciting! You know I've always envied you your daring life, all those scrapes you get into and the stories you write. And now I know what it's really like!'

'You enjoyed being a hostage, Mrs B?' *Good God*.

'Well, it was frightening at first, of course. But you know, Jesse, when you get to be my age, even being a little frightened now and then is better than boredom. At least you know you're alive.'

I smiled. The thing I'd always loved most about Mrs Binty was her spirit. For awhile, it seemed she'd lost some of it, along with her memory. Now, thanks to Barney Noonan, oddly enough, she'd gotten it back.

Something good comes of everything, Samved would say.

Or was that *The Sound of Music* again? God knew.

'I'm just glad you're all right, Mrs B. I'll be home soon.'

'That's good. I miss you. But, Jesse, I want you to know I'm all right about your going to Los Angeles now. If it's what you want to do, you should do it. You're a wonderful person. You deserve to be happy.'

'Uh, thanks, Mrs B.' I swallowed a lump in my throat. To get the subject off me, I said, 'Is Grady North still there?'

'No, Joey and Abe are here with me now. Lieutenant North said he would talk to you when you got home.'

I'll just bet, I thought.

I hung up, and then placed another call to Rochester: to Becky Anderson. 'You wanted an exclusive?' I said when she answered. 'Well, grab a pencil, kiddo. I'm about to give you one hell of a lolla-paloo.'

Epilogue

Open canyons in my mind,
Reaching in is not so kind.
Hide and seek is always best.
It gives my heart a chance to rest.

'Hide and Seek', Katherine Ketner

I didn't go home with Mac. I stayed at the hotel to help Marcus
repair the *Swan*, as promised. Once my mind cleared, I realized
there hadn't been a need to think about it. I was learning to do
what *felt* right – what my instincts, not logic, were telling me to
do.

I'd been back in Rochester only a few days when I knew that
Gramps was holding out on me. That morning, a telegram had
arrived. He had ripped it open, read it, and shoved it into his
back pocket. He didn't think I saw. But I did.

All day, I watched him . . . waiting for him to take it out and lay
it down somewhere. He never did. Finally, I couldn't stand it. I
was in the living room on my sleeping bag, working on my
script, when it came to me that I had to know. I marched into my
room and found him in his pajamas on my bed, which we'd
dragged up after I got home.

'What's in that telegram?' I demanded, shaking his arm.

'Huh? What?' He struggled up sleepily. 'What telegram?'

'Don't play innocent with me. The telegram that came this morning, the one you kept in your pocket all day so I wouldn't be able to read it.' I pointed with my script pages to the rolled-up heap of jeans on the floor.

'Oh, that telegram.'

'Gramps!'

'Okay, okay, I'll tell ya. But maybe you don't really wanta know.'

'I do want to know. Tell me.'

'Well, see, now, don't get the wrong idea, I didn't ask for this, didn't go lookin' for it . . . but, well, it's from this fella out west . . .'

'What fella out west?'

His old eyes shifted away. 'It's kind of complicated, girl.'

'Aha! Another scam! I knew it!'

'No, this is on the up and up . . . well, at least as well as these things can be on the up and up. See, it's from this fella named Bosco –'

'Bosco. You mean, like that old drink? That chocolate mix?'

'Yeah, that's it, I guess. Anyway –' He hesitated again, looking at me nervously.

'Spit it out, old man. It can't be any worse than anything else you've done.'

'Well, he, uh, he read about me in the papers.'

'What papers?'

'The *LA Times*, he said. And he wants me to, uh, write this screenplay –'

'*What*?'

He backed up against the pillows.

'What the hell are you talking about? *What* screenplay?'

'He wants the story of my life,' Gramps said. 'And he wants me to, uh, you know, write the, uh, screenplay . . . or whatever it is they call it on television.'

'Your life? You can't write the story of your life! *I'm* writing it!'

261

'You *are?*' His eyes widened. 'Well, now, how was I supposed to know that? You keep everything so secret.'

'Well, I am, I'm writing it. It's called *The Fox and the Damned Old Lazy Dog*, and you can't steal my idea and sell it to some idiot named –' I stopped as a horrible thought entered my head.

It couldn't be. It *couldn't*.

'You crazy old man . . . who did you say this guy was?'

'What guy?'

'The one who wants the screenplay, dammit, what was his name?'

'Bosco. I told ya, Bosco. Somethin' like that.'

'What do you know about him? What else has he done? Has he done anything good?'

'Girl, I don't watch television, how would I know? He mentioned somethin' about having a show, once, with cops. *Hill Street* somethin' or other. And some lawyer show. But you know how they are in Hollywood, it's all talk. Can't say as I ever heard of the damned thing.'

Holy shit.

'I don't suppose you ever heard of *LA Law*, either!' I advanced on Johnny James, shoving my screenplay at his nose.

He cringed. Over his wizened face passed a look that I could only believe was genuine bewilderment.

'*Bochco*,' I said. 'Steven *Bochco*. And you haven't a clue, have you? I've been working my ass off for months on this thing –' I waved the screenplay at him – 'and you waltz off with my story, *and* with one of the best producers and directors ever to hit the scene!'

He raised his palms to ward me off. 'I . . . I didn't know. Honest, girl, I didn't know.' I could see it working behind his eyes – the new scam. 'But lookee, now, maybe we could collaborate.'

'Collaborate? With you? Never! Never in a million years.'

'It'd be fun,' he wheedled. 'We could go out there together. I could introduce you to this fella, this Bosco, Bochco, whatever his name is, and we could get a real nice house together with a pool and a view. Girl, we could get a limo of our very own and start mixin' with all the stars! You'd never have to drive that old Dodge again, never have to see snow again, never have to work for anybody else, never have to do a darned thing you didn't want . . .'

I left him talking to a blank wall.

I drove out to Pittsford and the Center for Natural Healing. Along the way the snowplows had rumbled through and the streets were scraped raw. The town of Pittsford, however, was an ice-encrusted fairytale scene.

I found Samved in his ascetic little cubicle, reading *The Practice of the Presence of God*. He does this for my benefit, so I won't think he's been watching the twenty-inch television set he keeps in a nook behind a curtain. He prefers me to believe that he prepares himself spiritually for our talks.

I sat on the prayer rug across from him. 'I missed that white robe when you turned Fundamentalist and were being Henry Dreeb. Is Henry Dreeb really your given name?'

'The term "really" implies there is a basis for reality,' Samved said mildly.

'There isn't?'

'Nor is life a fountain.' His scraggly white beard looked as if it had recently been combed and sprayed.

'Never mind. I'm just glad you've come back to the Center.' When Samved had his late-life crisis and went Fundamentalist, I followed him to his office in the city with the Bible on the outer desk and the banks of telephones for donations. Somehow, it was never the same.

'I need to talk to you about Marcus,' I said.

Samved gave me his patient here-we-go-again look. 'Is there some new problem, or are we merely rerunning the old?'

'Okay, okay, so you've heard it before. But nothing is static, it keeps changing.' I rubbed my face and sought for the right words. 'When I sent him away last spring, it was awful. I felt my insides growing hard, like I'd swallowed a stone and it had lodged in my chest. And I knew that I'd been incredibly stupid to have swallowed that stone. I kept wanting to cry.'

Samved smiled. 'What you describe is the closest we mortals generally come to love. And you consider this a problem?'

'Well, forget logic – we still have to be sensible in life, don't we? We have to think things through.'

'And what has your thinking gained you? Has it brought you joy?'

'Sometimes it holds back the pain.'

'So, then, what you are feeling is neither joy nor pain.' Samved peered at me wisely. 'Numb, would you say?'

Heat rose to my face. 'I'm happy. I've got my work, my friends.'

'I detest the word "happy". It means nothing. If what you feel is neither agony nor ecstasy, then you are spiritually numb, child. There is no other word for it. Do you honestly prefer this?'

I folded my arms and fixed him with a green-eyed glare. 'I prefer not to talk on these esoteric levels. I came here to ask what you think about Marcus and me together. If we could ever make it, given all our differences.'

My guru-shrink sighed. 'I try so hard to bring you along . . .'

'Samved!'

He placed his palms together, prayer-like, at his chest. 'What precisely is the problem now?'

I frowned. 'I'm confused. When he was gone, I thought I wanted him back. Then when I found him again, I got scared.'

'While Marcus, I would imagine, was as sure of himself – and you – as ever.'

I crossed to the window and stared out at the snow crystallizing trees along the Erie Canal. The water was moving, but sluggishly, burdened by flecks of gray ice. With my fingertip I traced frost on the window, an idle gesture, then touched the tip of my tongue. The cold was like a laser cut. It healed a few slumbering wounds.

I turned to Samved, grateful for his presence. I would like to think I'm strong enough not to need teachers anymore, yet things happen in my life at regular intervals to show me that I do.

'That's what it's all about, then. Fear. And getting over it. Knowing it's all right to be afraid, people are afraid all the time. But they don't let it stop them. Hell, it doesn't usually stop me. But this love thing, you know, it's a big one. I've just got to get a grip on it, right?'

Samved smiled through those wise old eyes and waved a dismissing hand. 'Will that be all? It's just about time for *Jeopardy*,' he said.

'You know, Jesse girl,' Gramps said last night, 'what Barney Noonan accused me of in the hotel room that day was true. I hate to admit it, but it's true.'

We were sitting side by side on my couch, which Joey and Denny had brought up for the Christmas holidays, and we were soaking our feet in hot water after a trip to Midtown Mall. Toni had gotten a young friend of hers to go with us so we'd be allowed on the monorail. It was a sight to behold – Gramps waving his skinny arms gleefully, like a silly kid, cackling and laughing as the little train chugged its way around Magic Mountain. He made me go on with him. I tried to hunker over and stay out of sight, hoping no one I knew was there.

Then, last night, we talked. Bach played softly on my small tape recorder. 'I don't remember,' I said in a warm, lazy glow. 'What did Barney Noonan say?'

'That I've never been any good to anybody in my life. That I've spent my whole life running away.'

'Weak knees run in the family, Gramps. There's not much you can do about it now.'

There was a long silence.

Gramps lifted a foot above the water and inspected it. 'So you believe I'm your grandfather now?'

'I could never doubt it.' I yawned. 'Our toes are too much alike.'

'I'll tell you, girl, I care about you. You're the one person I've never wanted to run from, not since the first day I stood on your doorstep, there.'

'That was only a couple of weeks ago, Gramps. Give yourself time.'

'I mean it, Jesse. I think we could be a great team. I want you to come to LA with me.'

'And watch you sell your life story to Bochco?'

He shot me a sly glance. 'You don't really want me to pass up a chance like this, do you?'

No . . . I did not want him to pass up this chance. What the hell, it was only a couple of days to Christmas. I couldn't begrudge Gramps his success. I've had some of my own, after all.

This year, for instance, I drink less than last.

And this year – by the grace of whatever saints are still with me – I may love more.

I'd had a talk with Mac the day before. 'I love him,' I said. 'I love Marcus. It may not be smart, and it may not make sense to anyone but us, but you can't deny feelings. You can't go through your life that way. I think this is what I'm supposed to learn.'

Marcus is coming for Christmas. We're having it at Mrs Binty's, by her tree. There will be turkey and trimmings, and the scent of nutmeg and cinnamon. A fire will be built and candles lit. Carols will play.

Marcus and I will hold hands. I'll accept his ring. Promises will be made at last. I know this, because I know it's time. But it still scares me half to death. I don't know if this marriage thing will work. For that matter, in my heart of hearts, I wonder if it will ever come off. I need time to think. I always need time to think.

So, after the New Year I'll go with Gramps for a month-long stay in LA. Gramps may think he needs me, but I need him more. He's a prickly, lying, scheming, crazy old man. And I need him more than I can say. Gramps, like the sorry cliché, has become my sunshine on a cloudy day.

Perhaps this is what being 'happy' comes down to, then . . . a flicker of sun in the winter. Or love, a flicker of warmth in the cold.

And thus we learn to get our needs met in small, flawed ways. A bit this decade, a bit the next. Maybe one fine morning, by the grace of whatever saints are with me then, I'll wake and find that I am whole.

The Women's Press is Britain's leading women's publishing house. Established in 1978, we publish high-quality fiction and non-fiction from outstanding women writers worldwide. Our exciting and diverse list includes literary fiction, detective novels, biography and autobiography, health, women's studies, handbooks, literary criticism, psychology and self help, the arts, our popular Livewire Books series for young women and the bestselling annual *Women Artists Diary* featuring beautiful colour and black-and-white illustrations from the best in contemporary women's art.

If you would like more information about our books or about our mail order book club, please send an A5 sae for our latest catalogue and complete list to:

The Sales Department
The Women's Press Ltd
34 Great Sutton Street
London EC1V 0DX
Tel: 0171 251 3007
Fax: 0171 608 1938

Also of interest:

Meg O'Brien
The Daphne Decisions
A Jesse James mystery

Murder doesn't get much colder than on the icy shores of Lake Ontario where Jessica James is on the trail of a property fraud that has led to a string of costly accidents. But it's no accident that lands Jesse in hospital bandaged from head to toe, with everyone insisting she's really Daphne Malcross, a bright young socialite with more connections and cash than common sense.

However, Jesse decides it's to her advantage to keep everyone in the dark while she pursues her investigation, and the opportunity to take on the trappings of such an affluent lifestyle are more than she can resist – until it's too late . . .

'Five stars! Here is a mystery with verve, style, wit and a gutsy new heroine who is always good-hearted if often wrong-headed. This new heroine will quickly become an old favourite.' Carolyn G Hart

'Irresistible.' *Publishers Weekly*

Crime Fiction £5.99
ISBN 0 7043 4360 6

Sarah Dreher
Bad Company
A Stoner McTavish mystery

When Stoner McTavish is called in to investigate a series of minor accidents at an exclusive hotel, it seems the perfect opportunity for an expenses-paid break with her partner Gwen. But neither Stoner nor Gwen are prepared for the hostilities that greet them on their arrival at The Cottage. And, as a vicious game of sabotage begins to unfold, McTavish faces a killer with a desperate grudge . . .

'**What makes Dreher's novels so special beyond their intriguing plots and engaging characters is Dreher's infectious sense of humour, her vivid descriptions and emotional integrity.**' Elynor Vine

'**A unique private eye with mystery adventures that are sure to please any devotee of the genre.**'
Midwest Book Review

Crime Fiction £5.99
ISBN 0 7043 4469 6

Marcia Muller
A Wild and Lonely Place
A Sharon McCone mystery

Sharon McCone. Private Investigator. Determined. Decisive.
Daring. Now drawn into a world of international crime . . .

A series of diplomats have been the targets of a vicious bombing
campaign. Reluctantly, Sharon McCone agrees to help a security
firm protect their client and, behind a wall of diplomatic immunity,
uncovers a sinister web of intrigue, corruption and murder. Now
a child's life is in peril and, as McCone's trail leads back to those
she's been hired to defend, she finds herself in the sights of a
ruthless and cold-blooded killer . . .

'**Marcia Muller and her private investigator, Sharon
McCone, hold hands and jump off the deep end . . . The
professional risks pay off all round.**' *New York Times*

'**Muller produces the sort of thrillers that enthusiasts
always hope for but rarely get.**' *The Sunday Times*

'**Excitement amplified.**' *Literary Review*

Crime Fiction £5.99
ISBN 0 7043 4454 8

Meg O'Brien
Salmon in the Soup
A Jesse James mystery

When beautiful and sophisticated lawyer, Barbara Sloan, is shot dead on Marcus Andrelli's yacht, Andrelli is immediately taken into custody. His bodyguard has fled – even from his long-time friend, Jessica James – and Andrelli won't talk, not even to save himself.

Determined to discover the truth, with or without help, and convinced that murder is not Andrelli's style, Jesse sets out to investigate. But before she knows it she has found herself in the midst of a malevolent Mafia maelstrom . . .

'A verve and naturalness unmatched since Sue Grafton teamed up with a Gatling gun.' *Clues*

'Meg O'Brien is a real find. Credible characters, wonderful dialogue. A bestseller.' Ted Allbeury

Crime Fiction £6.99
ISBN 0 7043 4361 4

Meg O'Brien
Hare Today, Gone Tomorrow
A Jesse James mystery

Jessica James has a nose for a good story, but she isn't sure how much she likes what she's hearing from her mother's charming new boyfriend with the improbable name of Charlie Browne. Especially since it all seems mixed up with the *Hare* – a stolen painting that is now hidden under Jesse's own bed.

Jesse's investigation into Charlie's background turns up a hole big enough to smuggle the *Mona Lisa* through – and before she knows it Jesse has uncovered a ring of art criminals and two murders she has to solve before the killer strikes again . . .

'**Jessica James is back! . . . Fans of Sara Paretsky and Sue Grafton will love her.'** *Mystery News*

'**A bright female narrator who joins the growing ranks of heroines to dispute male dominance of the crime genre.'** *Publishers Weekly*

Crime Fiction £5.99
ISBN 0 7043 4366 5

Meg O'Brien
Eagles Die Too
A Jesse James mystery

It's springtime in upstate New York, where the lilacs are in
bloom and love is all around — even for Jessica James, full-time
investigative reporter and part-time fool. Ah well, everyone else
is in love: her mother, still honeymooning with the charming
Charlie Browne; and Jesse's sometime lover, mobster Marcus
Andrelli, now involved with another woman.

Then Jesse realises that her new love interest, Mac Devlin, is
being shadowed by a mysterious man. What does this stranger
want? And how does it involve her mother's elusive new husband
who disappears as quickly as he appears, always with Jesse's mum
in tow? Reluctantly, Jesse finds herself drawn into a perilous and
deadly game of blackmail and past secrets, where the high-flying
stakes mean life or death . . .

'A fast-moving, street-smart heroine in the V I
Warshawski mould . . . Fast-moving, feisty and fun.'
The Sunday Times

'Cinematic effects and irresistible emotional appeal.'
Publishers Weekly

Crime Fiction £5.99
ISBN 0 7043 4381 9

Anne Wilson
Truth or Dare
A Sara Kingsley mystery

Caroline Blythe has always seemed the epitome of success. A journalist, wife and mother, she is confident, assured, sophisticated and self-contained. So why should she suddenly turn to Sara Kingsley – an overworked, underpaid, community counsellor – for help? And what's behind her concern for a 'friend' who's involved in a dangerous affair with a married man?

Unconvinced by Caroline's story, Sara insists there is nothing she can do. Then Caroline is found dead of a drug overdose – and questions start to surface. Who was the 'friend' Caroline had been so anxious to protect? Was her death suicide or murder? And is Sara herself partly to blame? Despite the pressures of work and single motherhood, Sara feels impelled to undertake a perilous investigation that, if she dares, may bring her closer to the truth . .

Crime Fiction £5.99
ISBN 0 7043 4461 0

Sharon Gwyn Short
Past Pretense
A Patricia Delaney mystery

Gigi Lafferty is haunted by ominous dreams and memories of a
hidden past. Terrified that the secrets of her youth will be
betrayed, she turns to the one person she believes she can trust.
If investigator Patricia Delaney can't uncover the truth about her
former life, perhaps her future is secure.

At first sight, Delaney fails to recognise Gigi. After all, it's been
years since she worked as a bouncer in the downtown night club
where her client once danced. By the time she makes the
connection, Gigi Lafferty has vanished and police are questioning
Delaney about a body found floating face-down in a pool . . .

'A fine addition to the ranks of professional sleuths.'
Sue Grafton

'Fast and furious.' *Time Out*

Sharon Gwyn Short is also the author of *Angel's Bidding,* the first
Patricia Delaney mystery (The Women's Press, 1995).

Crime Fiction £5.99
ISBN 0 7043 4464 5

Hannah Wakefield
Cruel April
A Dee Street crime thriller

Dee Street doesn't want to fall out with her old friend, Janey
Riordan. After all, Janey has just found her a key defence witness
for an upcoming murder trial. But Janey still owes Dee's law firm
a lot of money and no amount of favours can replace the cash.
Now Janey's refusing to pay and, even worse, is risking their
friendship with a nasty, and very public, argument.

Then Janey is found murdered – and all the evidence points to
Dee . . .

'Excellent and original.' *Daily Telegraph*

'An engaging first-person heroine with real depth and a
distinctive voice.' *Time Out*

'Lively, entertaining and legally accurate.' *Guardian*

'Riveting.' Patricia Craig, *London Review of Books*

Crime Fiction £5.99
ISBN 0 7043 4475 0

Ellen Hart
A Small Sacrifice
A Jane Lawless mystery

It's been twenty years since Jane Lawless' best friend, Cordelia,
has seen her five closest friends from college. So a sudden
invitation to a three-day reunion is far from unwelcome. But as
Jane and Cordelia quickly discover, reminiscing is not on the
agenda.

Instead they discover a tense and secretive circle in which veiled
animosities are slowly beginning to surface. Then a member of
the group suddenly dies, and long-simmering jealousies and
resentments explode with a vengeance . . .

'**An intricate yarn from a storyteller who more than
keeps you guessing.**' **Katherine V Forrest**

'**Murder most fab . . . Drama that will keep even the
most jaded mystery readers amongst us turning the
pages.**' *The Crack*

'**A wonderful creation . . . Christie crossed with early P D
James and a sense of humour . . . Very enjoyable.**'
Gay Times

'**The psychological maze of a Barbara Vine mystery and
the feel of Agatha Christie.**' *Publishers Weekly*

Crime Fiction £6.99
ISBN 0 7043 4479 3

Sarah Dreher
Stoner McTavish

Stoner McTavish is reluctant to leave her fledgling travel business and turn detective. But Eleanor Burton is convinced her granddaughter's new husband is a dangerous fortune hunter and that Gwen's life is in jeopardy. Against her better judgement, McTavish bows to the pressure of old family ties and agrees to investigate. Only to discover that Eleanor's fears are far from unfounded and that she's about to fall in love with the newly wedded bride . . .

'Full of humor, spiced with suspense . . . *Stoner McTavish* is a real treat.' *Washington Blade*

'Sarah Dreher's endearing creation, Stoner McTavish, is on every list of beloved lesbian detectives.' *Bay Windows*

Crime Fiction £5.99
ISBN 0 7043 4470 X